REMOTELY LOVE

LORI THORN

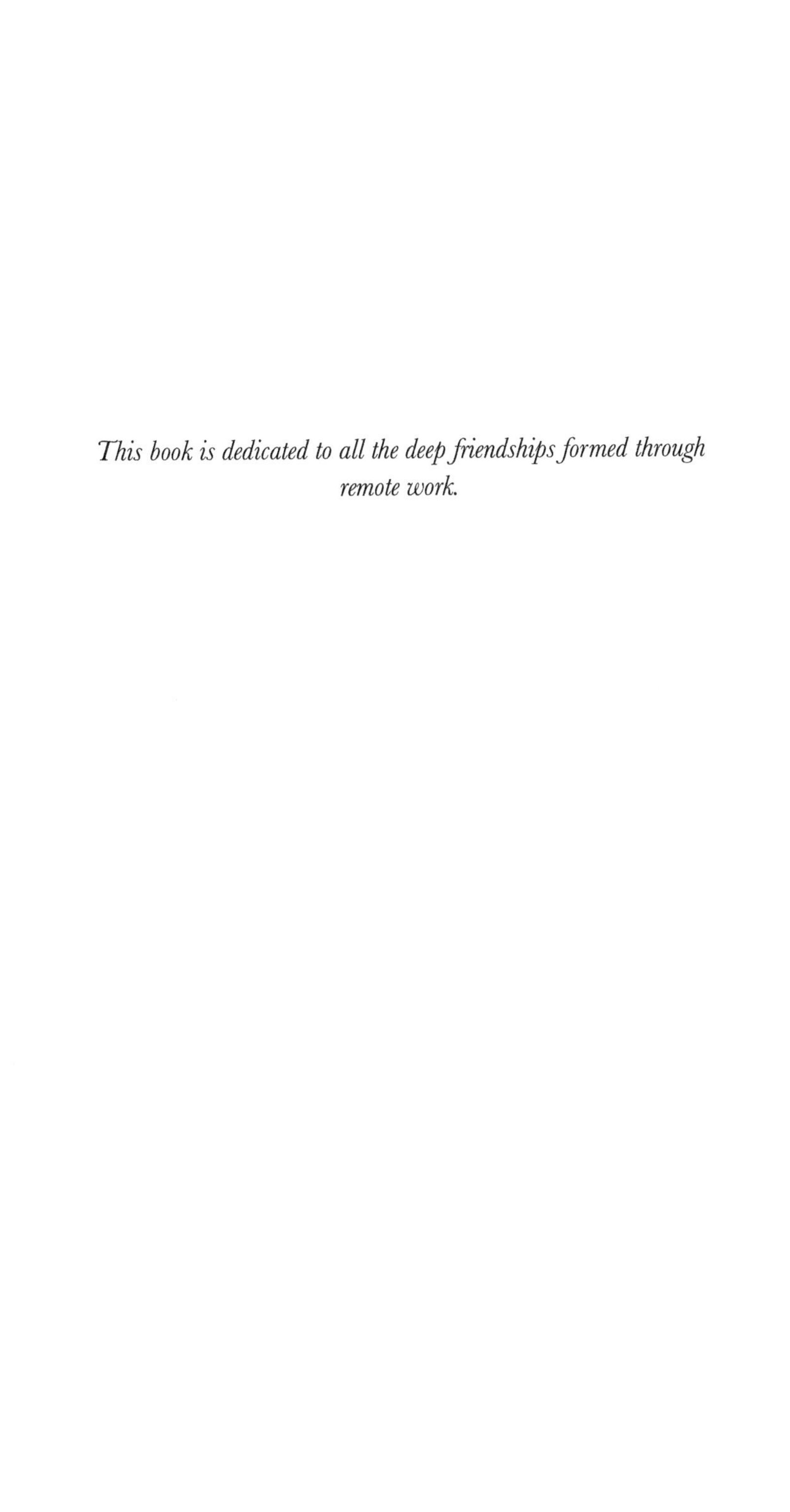

This book is dedicated to all the deep friendships formed through remote work.

CHAPTER 1

ASK FOR FEEDBACK

"Asking for feedback is a great practice in any work environment but can be easy to overlook, especially in a remote workplace."

ONE YEAR EARLIER...

THE ROOM WAS GROWING DARK, and the glare from the computer screen washed over Hazel's face. Her cursor was hovering over an email that had announced its arrival with a swooshing sound. It was late, and she was ready to leave for the day but was stymied by that sound, her heart immediately catching in her throat. This email, whatever it said, would impact her career at FutureApp.

She clicked it.

The white of the email shifted the screen's brightness to a higher intensity causing her to squint her eyes. "We're sorry to inform you that, at this time, we've decided to move forward with other candidates. We encourage you to keep applying with the Training Team when future opportunities are posted."

Fuck.

She felt angry and ashamed for crying over a job rejection, but she couldn't stop the tears from flowing. All her energy was suddenly raw and displaced. Not knowing exactly what to do with herself, she re-opened Chatter, the chat client FutureApp employees used, and scrolled through her list of conversations until finding the one with Sam. He was offline, but she messaged him anyway, "I didn't get it." She waited a few minutes to see if, by chance, he might see it and reply, but no such luck.

Sam had been her mentor since she started at FutureApp, nearly 6 years ago, so she could imagine what he would say. It would feel so much better hearing it from him instead of inside her head in his voice. Ugh. She'd have to tell Tamra, her new boss, tomorrow too. She wondered how that conversation would go, but soon the let-down became too much to think about.

The darkness in the room enveloped her as she closed the laptop. She sat there for a few more minutes, numb, not really thinking. Then stood up and walked out of the office.

She awoke the next morning feeling slightly better. Recalling her Mom's old words of wisdom, "Sleep on it, Hazel. If it's a big decision you're making or if things feel rough, remember to sleep on it." She had zombied herself through the rest of the evening, even wholly ignoring a text Rosie had sent inviting her out for Sangria. Mom's advice had held true; she could at least think a little clearer after she slept. She made a note to reply to Rosie later and explain.

She caught her eyes in the mirror as she pulled a comb

through her hair. She smiled at herself and then stuck her tongue out, which made her smirk. Despite this setback, she knew she was slowly healing from the hardness of the past couple of years. She could see it in the mirror looking back at her. Her skin was healthier, her eyes brighter than they had been. She could now put things in perspective instead of circling into the abyss.

She reminded herself that despite not getting the Training position she had tried so hard to attain, she still had a good job.

It was going to suck today, though.

The thought brought a weak smile to her lips.

She delayed logging in for as long as possible, first, by way of making her coffee as complicated as she could, even frothing the creamer. Then, when she found she still wasn't ready to face talking to anyone just yet, by going on her daily walk early.

9am still came, though, and it brought enough pressure that she logged in to face the day. She settled into her chair, opened the laptop lid, and signed into the VPN. Hazel usually had a routine to keep her day structured, beginning with checking her Calendar and replying to emails. However, she had also never logged in to find she had 12 Chatter notifications. Every one of them from Sam.

Hazel Rogers

I didn't get it. 8:13pm

Sam Pierce

They are really going to miss out on the best person for the role. 7:55am

Sam Pierce

I'm so sorry Hazel, I know how much time you put in preparing to interview. 7:55am

Sam Pierce

How can I help? 7:58am

Sam Pierce

Don't let this get you down. You're one of the most talented people I've worked with, we'll keep trying. 7:59am

Sam Pierce

I'm going to schedule us a meeting later so it's on your Cal 8:00am

Sam Pierce

4pm, be there or else. 8:00am

Sam Pierce

That was a threat Rogers... 8:00am

Sam Pierce

"The meetings will continue until morale improves!" 8:01am

Sam Pierce

> Get it? Meetings instead of beatings? XD
> 8:01am

Sam Pierce

> Hey where are you? You're usually green by
> now. 8:10am

Sam Pierce

> Hazelberry? 8:15am

Sam Pierce

> Okay, well hit me up as soon as you're in
> 8:17am

IT WASN'T LIKE him to send so many messages without getting a response, but she couldn't help but feel lighter reading through them. She typed back, "Oh, we're doing threats now? Or else what, SPierce?" He replied, "Little do you know that I've had all this time to prepare your best next steps. We'll discuss at 4." She rolled her eyes at his transition back into mentor mode.

She shot back replies to her mail and checked the calendar. It was thankfully a slow sort of day, only a smattering of meetings.

Her first meeting was with Tamra, who had only joined the Communications team a few weeks ago. She joined the SyncUp App used for video conferencing a little early to check that her hair was not an embarrassment. There was a small tinkling sound when Tamra entered the room; she shot Hazel a reserved smile. "Hi Hazel, how are you today?"

Hazel hesitated, not knowing exactly how to answer. "Umm, I'm… hanging in there, I guess. Remember I told you I was interviewing for the Training position? I learned late yesterday that I didn't get it."

The slight smile flattened on Tamra's face. "I'm sorry to hear that. I remember you said you made it to the final round of interviews, right?"

"Yeah, that's right."

"Did they say why they went with someone else?"

"Ah, no, it was like a form email. Definitely not personal sounding."

"Okay, well, have you asked for feedback yet?"

Hazel frowned slightly. She had not made that request yet. The rejection still stung and hearing about how she failed sounded depressing. "No, I haven't yet. I know I should. It's just so soon, you know?"

Tamra seemed to think. In fact, she took so long to reply, making several starts but then stopping that she said, "I'm sorry, I'm thinking how to say it… I know I'm new, and I don't know you nearly as well as I want to, as we will know each other in the future. I do think it's important to request your feedback soon. Even if it hurts. Look at it this way, they will have your interviews much fresher in their minds to give high-quality feedback."

Hazel chewed the inside of her cheek and looked down. "You're right. And I appreciate the advice."

Tamra seemed more empowered by the acceptance and perked up. "You know, I never asked before, why do you want to move to Training anyway?"

Without hesitation, Hazel replied, "I love telling stories. I'll be honest, I got into Communication because I thought I'd be telling stories." She wobbled her head a little. "I mean, sometimes I get to spin a tale here, but it's rare.

More often, our job is attending meetings, waiting for a series of approvals that take so long, and hemming and hawing about word choice that may or may not even make a difference. In Training, they develop scenarios, use storytelling to teach effectively, they onboard our new hires, and get to explain the legend of our culture. It feels like what I intended to do in the first place."

Tamra held Hazel's gaze, digesting what she had explained. It made Hazel worry she had shared too much. She inserted, "Not that I dislike it here, please don't think that, just that I think I could capitalize on my love of storytelling better in Training."

"I didn't take it that way," she shook her head, "I get where you're coming from, actually. It makes sense to me." She paused. "Let me know what they say when you get your feedback. I'd really like to help you get there however I can."

The rest of the meeting was regarding the usual: project statuses, roadblocks and bottlenecks, reviewing communication plans, and the like. Hazel left feeling more endeared to Tamra. Her offer to help was genuine, and even the fact she asked about what made her interested in moving to Training. Not many people had inquired about that, and it struck Hazel as an authentic curiosity. Maybe Tamra would be a good fit for this team.

DURING HER LUNCH BREAK, Hazel sent Rosie an apology. Rosie was her best friend. She would understand. "Hey, sorry for not replying last night. You know I love a fruit salad. As I was logging out, I got the rejection from Training, and it was… a lot." There wouldn't be a reply for a few hours because their lunch breaks weren't usually aligned, but Hazel felt a little more relieved to have gotten the response out. She'd talked with Tamra, and now she had replied to Rosie. The only other discussion about this would be with Sam in a few hours, which would be the easiest of the conversations. He had the most knowledge about her career desires and had helped her prepare for applying and interviewing.

HAZEL JOINED Sam's SyncUp room at 3:58pm. He was already there and sporting a shit-eating grin. He offered, "Beat you!" as his greeting.

Even though she knew they would discuss the position, she immediately felt at ease. Their comfortable banter was something like home.

"Of course you did." She rolled her eyes. "You know, your being able to be at our meetings early so perpetually makes me wonder how much you're actually working over there. Some of us have responsibilities."

Sam laughed, exposing his perfect white teeth. Hazel sometimes thought he must have paid big money to get a smile like his. "You caught me. It's good to see you still have your sense of humor."

The conversation paused as if they were both delaying the moments of lightheartedness before broaching the heavier subject.

"Mmm," Sam began with a deep rumble, "I've been thinking about what I'd recommend from here. First, I really am relieved to see you doing so well, considering." Sam looked down at his desk. "You've done so much healing, and I was worried…"

"That this would knock me back on my ass completely?" Hazel interrupted.

He returned his stare to Hazel, studying her face. "That's one way to put it, yes."

"Honestly, I was kind of scared of that too. Last night

was rough, but when I got up this morning, I don't know. Things didn't seem as bleak."

Sam unclenched his jaw. His eyes twinkled at her with what might have been pride. Voice a little deeper, he said, "Good job, Hazelberry." He observed her a few seconds longer before shaking his head back and forth as if emerging from a daze and continuing, "Well, you know what you have to do next, then?"

Hazel said in unison with Sam, "Ask for feedback." Only Hazel had said it with sarcasm.

"Oh good, so you do know?"

She sighed. "I do, of course, and just in case I didn't, now both you and Tamra have reminded me. I'm going to do it. I'll send them the request before leaving today."

"I had a good feeling about that Tamra; glad to hear she's toeing the line with quality advice."

Hazel pursed her lips and raised her eyebrows. "As it's the same as your advice, I can see how you might think it *high quality*. Anyway, I'll let you know what they say. Despite not getting it, I'm still grateful for all your help getting ready for the interviews."

"It's my pleasure. You know I live to serve." Sam gave a wink.

"Moving on!" Announced Hazel, "What weekend plans do you have?"

The conversation moved into personal territory. Sam shared about the Apple Festival 10k he was running Sunday. Hazel shared the latest novel her book club had started in on.

The conversation had run past their allotted meeting window, and they both needed to attend to other things. As they were wrapping up, Hazel added, "Oh, and Rosie fixed me up on a date. It's not a big deal, though. Meeting him at a coffee shop Saturday afternoon."

Sam made an indistinguishable face but turned it into a

smile. "Wait, what?! You're just going to drop this news on me and run? I thought you weren't ready yet?"

She shrugged her shoulders. "I'm not, but will I ever feel ready? Rosie begged me until I gave in. You have no idea what she's like when she gets an idea in her head, and she keeps reminding me it's been six months now. I'm… It's going to be casual, and no pressure. It has to be."

"Well, good luck then."

"And to you, on your 10k."

Before logging off for the night, Hazel penned an email to Ariel Gooding and Jasmond Merrill, the two Training Program Managers she had interviewed with last. She reread it before hitting send.

Hello Ariel and Jasmond,

Though I'm disappointed I won't be moving forward on the interview path, I still had a great time meeting with you both, and it is still a goal of mine to find my way to Training one day. I would love to get some feedback from you on my interview and ask for your advice on how I can prepare to be an asset to Training.

Thanks,

Hazel Rogers

SHE HIT send and closed her laptop.

Hazel reached for her phone and realized Rosie had replied, "Gah, I'm sorry, that sucks! I'll accept a raincheck, and we'll talk about how stupid your Training team is. Honestly, maybe you shouldn't even want to join them."

· · ·

Although she started work the following day at her usual early hour, she already had a response from Ariel and Jasmond in the form of a Calendar invitation with a note, "Absolutely! So glad you reached out to ask."

She felt nervous logging into their SyncUp later that day. She arrived first, but Jasmond entered immediately after her and greeted her with a warm baritone, "Hello! I think Ariel is running a couple minutes behind, but I want to go ahead and tell you that you were the only person we interviewed who asked for feedback. It says a lot about you, and I'm impressed you requested it."

"Oh, well, thank you! I would have figured everyone would ask." She shook her head in confusion.

"Everyone *should* ask, but it's rare."

At this, Ariel joined the room, looking slightly frantic, and said, "I'm so sorry I'm late. I got hung up in my last meeting for a few minutes."

Hazel chuckled and said, "As one does, please don't worry. Thank you both for meeting with me."

Ariel addressed Jasmond, "Did you tell her she was the only one to ask?!" He nodded in confirmation, and Ariel spoke to Hazel, "We were really impressed by you already, but when we got your email requesting feedback, it was a wow moment."

Jasmond kept nodding in agreement and then indicated he would pull up their notes from the interview. "Listen, we want to give you actionable feedback, and I'm worried this will seem lacking. The thing is, we loved your interview." It was Ariel's turn to nod her head now. "You clearly understand our mission, your ideas about where we might head in the future were exciting, and even your personality… You'd fit in on the team seamlessly." He swallowed.

Ariel continued, "It was between you and one other

person. They had experience working with Training, and it was the thing that gave them the slightest edge."

Hazel tried to digest this. She had done well, which was good, but it wasn't enough. She breathed, "Well, I'm glad to hear it wasn't a disaster anyway."

Jasmond exclaimed, "Far from it!"

"What can I do to fill in that gap of experience? Working directly with Training is something I'd love to do even if I'm not in the department officially."

Ariel and Jasmond smiled, but Ariel answered, "If an obvious opportunity arises, we will reach out, but the real challenge is for you to accomplish that on your own. Find a way to influence or incorporate Training even in your current role. That's your action."

CHAPTER 2

CREATE A ROUTINE

"It takes self-discipline to work from home. Nobody else sets your schedule or even sees it! Creating a daily rhythm or routine will elevate your productivity."

PRESENT DAY...

HAZEL CRACKED her eyes open only the slightest bit to assess the light out of her bedroom window. She was hoping it might still be dark; early enough she could drift back to sleep for a few minutes. However, what she beheld was the soft grey sky of the morning. She relented and opened her eyes fully to check the time. It was two minutes until her alarm would sound. Fair enough.

She stood up from the bed, stretched her arms towards the ceiling, and leaned from side to side. She moved into a shoulder stretch as she walked into the bathroom, pulling one arm across her chest to the other side, swinging her hands out wide, then alternating arms.

Hazel had a morning routine, and she was in it. It wasn't something she even had to think about, like a list of tasks; these steps were ingrained. She would use the bathroom and catch up with the news on her phone, get dressed, brush her teeth, splash her face with water, comb her hair, take a vitamin, and roll on some aluminum-free deodorant, all in just a few minutes.

Feeling clean, she padded out to the kitchen to begin her usual tasks there. Coffee was her favorite morning treat, so she started it as soon as she reached the kitchen, filling the electric kettle with water, grinding the beans, and emptying them into the French Press. She settled on cereal for the breakfast of the day and ate while the coffee steeped. She cleaned the kitchen, then poured herself a steaming mug of the good stuff. This ritual was the part that made her feel present. She poured half and half into the dark potion and watched as it feathered through the drink like a dance. She dropped a spoon into the cup and stirred, listening as it clanked against the porcelain.

Grabbing her cup and phone, she slid open the door to her small back porch. A dainty table and chair were facing out toward the yard. The rest of the area was covered with an assortment of potted plants, most of which she had cultivated from clipping plants she found on her walks around the neighborhood. The view of the yard felt cut short as it was met with dense trees that were part of a preserved park, but that didn't bother Hazel. She settled into the chair, savored her first sip of coffee, and started reading the ebook on her phone. The book club she was in was reading a modern-day retelling of Beauty and the Beast this month, and she needed to read through chapter 10 before Thursday evening.

It was difficult to lift herself out of the story, but her alarm had sounded angrily, announcing the need for her to relocate to her office and get the workday started. Here begins the work routine. However, this one does require thoughtful engagement. Hazel had learned the lesson early in her work-from-home career. After six months of staying late, struggling to keep up with things, and becoming so frustrated she nearly quit, she found that making a "rough schedule" was the solution. Her routine needed to be flexible enough to change her schedule quickly but stable enough to provide a usual structure. At this point, she proudly considered herself an expert at being efficient and productive while working remotely. She sometimes even got to help other FutureApp employees who were struggling to adjust to an at-home environment.

The computer booted up, and Hazel logged into the VPN. Dings, chimes, and whistles sounded from various applications announcing their alerts. She verified her meetings in Calendar, volleyed email responses, caught up in Chatter, and started building a retrospective presentation of her latest project within 8 minutes. Her plan would be to finish the first draft of the presentation by the end of the day. She could easily work on it while handling one-off items between meetings, and getting it done early would make Tamra happy.

She had finished the first few slides when her Cal alerted her that the All Comms meeting was starting soon. This was a monthly meeting where the entire Communication team met to discuss the state of the business and anything on the horizon. She minimized her presentation, fetched her water bottle, then logged into the event.

Chatter started chiming frantically. Hazel already knew why. She clicked onto her group chat with her two best work friends.

Frank Simms

> What the shit is Dana doing here? 10:00am

Frank Simms

> Did we know she was going to be here?!
> 10:00am

Meg Malloy

> Do ya'll see who is here? 10:00am

Meg Malloy

> LOL exactly Frank 10:00am

Hazel Rogers

> I don't think many people knew judging from the SyncUp chat. I sure didn't. 10:01am

Hazel Rogers

> You know what this means... 10:01am

Frank Simms

> Something's up for sure. 10:01am

Hazel Rogers

> Get ready to be BUSYYYY! 10:02am

> I hate to say it but yeah, anytime Dana is
> here it means we're in for a ride. Schedule
> vacation time now. Looking at you Frank.
> 10:02am

DANA JESSUP, the CEO of FutureApp, was in their All Comms meeting. Her presence was a rare event and usually marked a significant change for the company. The Communications teams were disclosed to business shifts early. This was necessary as they were the ones who would plan out the cascade, forums, and tone of the rest of the communications for the entire company, and depending on the topic, stakeholders, and customers.

Dana started to speak, which kept her video feed the center of attention. The room stilled as everyone listened attentively. "Thank you so much for having me here today; it's always a privilege to be among our Communication gurus. You all represent the strategy and voice that keeps FutureApp strong, and that's true on multiple levels." She cleared her throat. "If I can have my slides shared, please?" Within seconds a presentation was on screen. "Thanks for that. As you can see, our customer satisfaction has increased year over year, and our clients continue to come back to us for their App development needs." People started celebrating in the chat and sending applause emojis. Dana continued, "Yes, you should be very proud of this! If you direct your attention to the chart at the bottom, you'll also see our brand recognition amongst the general public has increased by 62% this year. That's above our annual goal, and we've seen a marked increase in new customers due to this. We are so grateful to everyone, especially our external communications and marketing teams, for driving our brand recognition!"

Hazel's Chatter went off again. She assumed it was the group chat commenting, but when she glanced over, it was Sam.

Sam Pierce

I have a surprise for you. 10:16am

Hazel Rogers

Oh really? Well I'm sorry to say I didn't get you anything, I didn't know we were doing gifts. It's your fault, you've gotta tell me these things ahead of time. :P 10:17am

Sam was typing back, but Hazel turned her attention back to All Comms. The conversation there had taken a more serious tone. Looking at the new slide, she saw that Employee Satisfaction was lower than last year. It wasn't a massive decline, but she knew how seriously upper management took even a 1% change there.

Dana explained, "We value your feedback and dove deep to understand the decline here and what we can do to improve. This is why I'm here today. We believe we can make things easier on our employees and continue to increase our brand recognition and customer acquisition with one move."

Meg Malloy

"I'm so thrilled to announce today that we are retiring ICE. It has served us well over the years, but times have changed, and how we think about supporting our customers has to change with it."

The meeting chat was now a mixture of questions pouring in and people whooping in celebration. Dana watched the action. "I see your questions and that some of you are already excited." She smiled. "Your questions will absolutely be answered, but today you're getting the preview only. Without further ado, I introduce our new support strategy, CARE."

The slide was updated again with a large colorful CARE in its center. The acronym was spelled out; C for Capture the Vision, A for Align with Goals/Ideas, R for Review, and E for Execute the Plan. Dana continued to read through the slide, but Hazel had seen what she needed to for now and returned to her Chatter, which was exploding.

Meg Malloy

Frank Simms

Frank Simms

> I mean WTF was wrong with ICE?
> EVERYONE LOVED ICE! 10:24am

Frank Simms

> Didn't we just move to ICE a year ago?
> 10:24am

Hazel Rogers

> It seems really similar to ICE to me? Identify the Goal, Capture the Vision, Execute the Plan. It's only a different order and adding a Review section. What's the point? 10:25am

Meg Malloy

> I guarantee you the point is that CARE is a word we can use in marketing, it's all warm and fluffy for the customer to snuggle up with at night. 10:25am

Meg Malloy

> Nobody wants to snuggle ICE, we used it internally only 10:25am

Hazel Rogers

> Damn M, you're a genius at tying the message together. "Employee satisfaction AND name recognition." 10:25am

Meg Malloy

> Bingo! 10:26am

Frank Simms

> I just can't with more acronym changes.
> What was it before ICE? Can you
> remember? The three R's or something
> right? 10:26am

Hazel Rogers

> Yes LOL, Recognize Realize and Release!
> How could you forget the Rs?! 10:26am

Meg Malloy

> It's going to be tough to get people on
> board with this, we've got our work cut out
> for us with messaging. 10:26am

AT LUNCHTIME, Hazel closed her computer and went for her usual walk around the neighborhood. She lived in a unique part of town. The housing was older and a little run down, making it affordable, but it was also within walking distance to one of the bustling streets leading into the small city of Crestwood, North Carolina. If she turned left, she would continue into a historic district with large, old houses and maple trees lining the street, which were beautiful all year long. If she turned right, it would lead her to the busy throughroad and her favorite bakery. Today she turned left, influenced by the color change in the maple leaves and wanting to take their sight in.

The slightest tinge of yellow appeared at the tops of the trees. Hazel enjoyed the view as she strode down the sidewalk, but her thoughts about the All Comms meeting and CARE quickly overtook her mind. This was a big adjustment. ICE was the structure nearly every employee at FutureApp relied upon. The customer-facing teams who worked directly with clients used it, as did their coaches, the quality department, and the engineers. It was referenced constantly because everyone was accustomed to it and on board. Sometimes it felt exhausting, all the constant change inside the corporation, and what leadership didn't seem to understand was any migration like this…. Regardless of the consideration in communications or compelling training pieces, people would not be speaking the same language for a time. That was the hard part. Hazel sighed. Change was inevitable, and she even agreed with something Dana had said today. When times change, methodologies have to change to keep up. But was that the current truth? Frank was right when he said they'd only been using ICE for about a year now.

Her thoughts continued to swirl until she found that her feet had carried her back to her desk. She re-opened her laptop and checked her email and Chatter to ensure she hadn't missed anything on her walk. Her mail only held a few newsletters that weren't pertinent to her, Sam had still not replied to her from this morning, but a new message from Tamra appeared, "DM me when you're back." She responded right away and received a SyncUp link back from Tamra.

Tamra was in the room when she entered, "Thanks for coming in impromptu."

"No worries, you know I don't mind."

Tamra smiled. "I can still appreciate it! Anyway, I

wanted to give you the heads up on a couple things." Hazel leaned closer toward the computer screen. "Two projects are coming that are important enough I need you alerted now. In my last All Manager meeting, they discussed a pain point. Our retention for remote new hires has dropped while on-site new hires haven't. What ideas do you have about that?"

Hazel slumped back in her chair and put her hand on her chin. "Well, it's complicated, right? It's what I always say- I need more information. I wonder about the hiring profile, and I wonder about what conversations the recruiters are having. Has anything changed within onboarding, or is there a way to better prepare people for working remotely, or a better way for us to support them?"

"Mmmhmm," Tamra hummed, "I knew you'd have a lot to say about it right away. You're thinking along the right lines, and you're not going to like this part, but for now, the project is simply to build a How-To for successfully working from home."

Hazel's mouth fell open. "Are you kidding? It's way more complicated than…."

Tamra cut her off, "I know. I told you, you wouldn't like it. Do you know what I'm thinking?" She tilted her head down and gave Hazel a significant look. "This is something that could, *should* be taken very seriously by Training. You can make this compelling and then pitch it as a need to them for all the reasons you mentioned. Hiring profile, recruiting, literally the onboarding training. It's all related."

Hazel's hand was back at her mouth, and she directed her eyes upward. Her physical cues were easy to follow, and Tamra knew she was deep in thought. She allowed her the space to consider everything.

After a few seconds, Hazel let out a protracted whistle.

She nodded her head, "You're right. Okay, I will do some research and start drafting. When is it needed by?"

"Okay, so remember I said there were a couple of things?" Tamra grimaced; she shot her dark brown eyes up to the ceiling briefly. "You've been tapped for something else, and I don't have the details because I'm not disclosed for it, but it's going to be big. I imagine it's going to take a lot of your bandwidth." She rushed onward, "And before I forget, you can't exclusively research, Hazel. Anyone can look up best practices for working remotely. Only *you* can make this special. It needs to be researched, yes, but it also needs to come from you, your experience, and your knowledge of FutureApp. Make it unique."

Her eyes narrowed, and Hazel started, "I hear you, but let's go back to the disclosure project. What is it exactly? Who's it with? Please tell me it's not CARE?"

Tamra laughed. "CARE would be a good thing for you. The visibility of that project will be huge... but I really don't know. It wasn't even up to me. You'll find out more soon; I wanted to tell you, so you won't commit to anything else. Thankfully, the How-To due date is flexible because we aren't hiring until next season."

HAZEL'S BODY was filled with buzzing after her meeting with Tamra had concluded. She had too much energy and too many unanswered questions coursing through her to focus appropriately. It took her much longer to build her retro deck than it usually would have. A few times, she found she had come to a complete halt and was simply staring somewhere beyond the screen. After working through the final slide, she gave it a brief review. It was not her best work, but she couldn't apply more focus to it right now. She decided to move around for a bit, hopefully shaking off some of the lingering unease. She started a load of laundry and prepped for the dinner she'd be making later. The Chatter App sounded in the office as she sliced through the Brussels sprouts. Hazel popped a shaved piece of fresh parmesan into her mouth, looking forward to the Cacio e Pepe she'd get to enjoy later, and walked to her desk. Sam had finally replied.

Sam Pierce

> You got me there, but I think you'll owe me one. Can you SyncUp? 4:01pm

HE DIDN'T WAIT for a reply before sending the link to his room. Hazel also didn't reply before clicking to join the room. Sam looked up from his keyboard when she entered, flashing his teeth in a smile, "Sorry I didn't respond earlier. It's been busy like you wouldn't believe… umm, what's on your shoulder?"

Hazel followed his gaze and looked down at her left shoulder. She plucked off a rogue Brussels sprout leaf, frowning. "Brussels sprout."

They both laughed. "Send me the recipe for whatever you're putting together?"

"Sure, but you know I'm impatient. What is the surprise?"

"Nope, first I need an update on whatever is happening in *Belle's Beast.*" Sharing the details of the romance books Hazel was reading had become a recurring event between them. She loved it because she could squeal and gush about the exciting things happening without worrying about spoiling anyone.

Hazel cut her eyes but smiled indulgently. "Belle is

starting to catch feelings, and I have to say it's a little creepy because he's a literal beast, but she's starting to comment on his broad shoulders." Hazel couldn't help but notice Sam's strong-looking shoulders. Remotely, you only ever saw people from the shoulders up. She had wondered how the rest of him looked plenty of times before. A normal curiosity.

Sam cut in, a wicked grin on his lips, "So what you're saying is that you're a furry now?"

Hazel clutched at would-be pearls and put on an over-the-top look of disgust. "Well, I've never!"

They both laughed again, but Sam suddenly silenced and because serious. "Are you ready for your surprise?"

Hazel leaned in, and Sam changed his virtual background with a "Tada." It was the same image she had seen in the All Comms meeting of the rainbow-colored CARE.

"Oh, you got on CARE! That's exciting, it's obviously *the* project right now."

Sam corrected, "Not quite. *We* will be working CARE!"

She tried to reconcile the immediate conflicting feelings flooding her. This was a mission that would be difficult. It almost felt doomed. Yet, she would be working with Sam for the first time.

Finding her words, she said, "Wow, okay. Thank you… I don't know what to say."

For a single second, Sam's face appeared shocked, but as he was so great at doing, he quickly returned to a neutral expression. "You don't seem as excited as I expected you might?"

"No, Sam, I am. I'm so flattered to be part of such a major project. It's just…." She scrunched her lips together and looked for the words.

Sam prompted, "It's just…."

"It's just that, I mean, doesn't it feel like we cycle

through all these acronyms? It's busy work for us and only annoys the people living it." To her surprise, Sam smiled.

"This is exactly why I picked you for the team." Hazel blinked in disbelief as Sam continued, "I knew you would cut through the bullshit and help make this into something meaningful. Imagine if CARE was actually something our people could embrace instead of feeling annoyed by - which I'm sure you're right about!"

"You picked me for this?"

He nodded emphatically. "Yes. We need skeptics with experience and creativity to do this right."

She tried to suppress any visible results that her feeling of flattery might betray. "I am so flattered. Sam. Wow. But I have to be honest. I'm not sure how to add that value."

Sam sat back in his chair and put a hand up. "You don't have to know yet. I don't know either, but we need the best thinkers to figure it out together. That's how I tried to create the team."

"Tell me more about the logistics. What will my role be? Who else is on the team?"

"I will definitely fill you in, but first, you need to sign the disclosure agreements. I'll send them over now. You can sign them and then forward the entire thread to HR."

HAZEL SIGNED the agreements and sent them right away. She and Sam ended up speaking until it was time to go home. She learned a few basic things about the project.

1. She would be working on the internal communication plan for CARE (no surprise there).

. . .

2. There were several phases of launching CARE, and they were in charge of Phase 2. Phase 1 was already completed. They would hand off to Phase 3 and Phase 4, which would work simultaneously but focus on different areas. Phase 3 would be the All Employee Training, and Phase 4 would work on external Marketing utilizing CARE.

3. Phase 2 had two goals to accomplish, both lofty. They needed to get FutureApp leadership excited about CARE and ready to use it with their teams. They also needed to identify and update all the existing internal documentation that referred to ICE.

4. Phase 2 would culminate at the Leadership Summit in November, where Sam would be presenting on stage as one of the main events. Attendance would be required for all employees.

5. The core team was shockingly small. Just Sam, Hazel, and a technical writer named Lou, whom Hazel had never met. He was apparently an expert on FutureApp documentation. He would be helping update their Expert Database, where all their How-To articles lived.

Hazel still had a million questions when 5pm rolled around and started by asking why the core team was so small.

It was as if Sam was aware of her timezone, though, because his reply had been, "So we can work efficiently. We will have to take partners, of course. Lou will partner with Quality to update their forms and any other info. We'll partner with Training to keep them informed and ask their opinions and HR for approvals. Importantly, it's time for you to log out." He said the last line almost accusingly. "Brussels sprouts wait for no woman."

She chuckled, "I don't mind staying over a few minutes to learn more, besides it's still 2pm for you!" Sam lived in Oregon.

He shook his head. "I'm afraid we'll have plenty of late nights to be ready in time for the summit. Don't start them too soon."

Sam paused there, and Hazel was about to tell him goodbye when he continued, "You know, if I have to work after hours, I'm glad it's with you." Something in his tone made it feel a little awkward, and a slight heat rose to Hazel's cheeks.

She sang awkwardly, "Best work friends!" and they parted ways.

CHAPTER 3
MAKE FRIENDS

"There may be added challenges to forming friendships when working remotely, but they can be overcome. Trusted friends are necessary and will help you achieve and keep you sane."

The Calendar app alarmed on Hazel's computer, letting her know that Sanity Check would begin in 10 minutes. She always looked forward to these meetings. They had started as a series between Meg, Frank, and herself years ago when they had a large initiative they were all serving on. Its purpose was threefold: To ensure the branches of Communications they represented worked in a way that made sense, that their messaging didn't conflict, and to increase awareness of what other branches were doing. This arrangement, however, quickly evolved as they discovered how much they enjoyed each other's company and that they could trust each other implicitly. It became their space to share perspectives and air grievances with people who truly understood.

While each of them worked under the Communications umbrella, they were entrenched in different areas. Hazel and Meg both worked in Internal Communications, Hazel serving the Consumer Support teams while Meg was with Enterprise Support. Frank belonged to the small and relatively new group supporting FutureApp's Social Media presence.

Hazel logged into the meeting early and waited. Frank and Meg joined right on time, and they all burst into peals of laughter, pointing at their screens to each other. It had become a tradition to attend in some sort of unexpected way. There had been songs, soliloquies (Meg was a theater buff), costumes, pet reveals, and ridiculous backgrounds. One time Frank had even made his own shirt, emblazoned with "Frank Rules" in red sharpie. Today Hazel was donning every piece of FutureApp swag she had ever received all at once: two knit beanies, five t-shirts of various colors, a collared shirt, a lanyard, and an umbrella. Meg was wearing an unseasonable Ugly Christmas Sweater with garish flashing lights, and Frank had on a ball cap covered in small stuffed animals.

"Are those glued on, Frank? You put a lot of work into that!" Meg asked after the laughter had mellowed.

"Oh no, I would never be allowed to glue Brian's babies," Frank shook his head quickly, and the stuffies flung away from the hat, "I just had to be really, really still."

Hazel asked, "Aw, how is Brian?" Brian was Frank's seven-year-old son, who looked exactly like a miniature Frank. They both sported heavily freckled cheeks, expressive golden eyes, and dark blonde hair with a tinge of red.

While Frank gave the update on Brian by way of a hilarious tale about riding his hoverboard. Inside. With a cape. Hazel couldn't help but appreciate her friends. She chatted with Meg and Frank throughout the day every day, but being on different teams, she usually only saw them in Sanity Checks. Meg's room was never well-lit, making the lights on her Christmas sweater stand out, casting a red and green glare on her face. She was petite with long wavy dyed black hair. She wore heavy eye makeup, usually in pastel hues (Meg once explained this was so she had some color since so much of her wardrobe was black, grey, and white). She had a silver septum ring through her nose, which Hazel thought was the coolest thing ever.

"AHEM!" Frank cleared his throat loudly, and Hazel realized they were both looking at her expectantly.

"Geez, I'm sorry. What's happening?"

They cackled, and Meg said, "We were just asking what's up with you. You were at the end of the Q1 Comms Strategy. Do you know what's next yet?"

"Just found out! I had an interesting meeting with Tamra about it. She's tapped me to create a How-To for working remotely that we think Training might be interested in, and…. Okay, don't give me a hard time, and I can't say very much because I'm disclosed, but I'm on CARE."

Frank's eyes widened. "Holy shit, you're on CARE?!"

"Yeah. I have mixed feelings about it. You both know how I feel about the seemingly endless parade of rotating acronyms. Actually, Sam said he wanted me on the team *because* I feel this way."

Meg asked, "Wait, Sam brought you on the team?" Meg and Frank both reacted with distaste. Meg's lips thinned, and her nostrils flared with her breath. Frank frowned and narrowed his eyes.

Hazel sighed and looked up as if hoping for patience. "I don't know how many times I have to tell you both. Sam is a good guy, a great guy, actually! You have to get to know him."

"I'm sorry, we shouldn't have to get to know him. He

should conduct himself like less of a dick at work." Meg nodded, agreeing with Frank.

"I don't even know what you're talking about. I have never seen him act like that. Can you give me an example?" They'd had this conversation before, but Hazel had never thought to ask for an example. Maybe she could understand what they meant.

Meg's voice was cold. "He's a know-it-all, Hazel. No matter what, he thinks he's right. Ugh, and the way he speaks, you can tell he thinks highly of himself."

Frank added, "I once saw him giving a Customer Support Rep a hard time in a meeting because he asked a couple questions. He was unrelenting, started asking this guy permission to continue at every topic change to make him feel bad."

Hazel shook her head. She never knew what to believe when this came up. She'd been close to Sam since her start at the company. He was her assigned mentor all those years ago, and they never lost touch. But Frank and Meg were her confidantes; she had no reason not to believe their experiences. She repeated, "I've never seen him act like that. He's honestly always been there for me."

AFTER A WARNING TO watch herself with Sam, the conversation moved back to their personal lives. Meg was planning her wedding, which would take place next year, "I decided on a dress color; care to guess?"

Hazel and Frank both answered together, "Black."

Meg put her hand to her heart. "What, you think I'm some kind of monster?" There was a beat of silence then one side of her mouth quirked up. "Dark grey, though."

Frank 'Overcommitted' Simms lamented his decision to help volunteer with the PTA at Brian's school. Promptly receiving the usual advice from Hazel and Meg about knowing his bandwidth and being able to say no.

As both of her friends were in long-term committed relationships, they were in the habit of asking Hazel about her dating life. They relished the opportunity to roast these men whenever possible and reminisced about their favorite dates-gone-sour. When Hazel shared she hadn't been out on a date in the past month, they balked, "What happened to the last one? Who was he… the one with longer hair than you, right?"

Hazel's eyes went unfocused, and she subconsciously twirled a strand of her shoulder-length cut. "He did have Fabio locks. I don't know, it seems futile, and *frankly* (she emphasized the word and gave Frank a significant look), I'm exhausted of the constant stream of new names to learn. You both know how bad I am at learning names."

Sanity Check concluded, and Hazel had just brought up a tab for researching advice for remote workers when her Chatter went off. A DM from Meg.

Meg Malloy

Is everything really okay? 2:01pm

Hazel knew what she was asking about but didn't feel like discussing it.

Hazel Rogers

?? Regarding ?? 2:02pm

Meg Malloy

> Don't. Don't you dare play dumb with me. I
> saw your far-off look when we talked about
> long hair guy. 2:02pm

Hazel Rogers

> Okay I'm sorry, I knew what you meant. I'm
> fine I promise. 2:03pm

MEG APPEARED to type and retype her next message. Indicator bubbles would appear, disappear, then start again. The bubble dance.

Meg Malloy

> Don't give up, okay? You deserve
> happiness. 2:05pm

HAZEL DIDN'T KNOW how to reply, so she didn't.

CHAPTER 4
SCHEDULE SOCIAL

"For some people, working from home can feel isolating. Let's be real, though. Work is only one part of your life. Being intentional about your social schedule leads to a well-balanced you."

WHILE IT DIDN'T ENTIRELY MAKE sense to put on makeup for book club, Hazel liked to do it anyway. She knew the group would mostly come in clothes ranging from pajamas to athleisure, but what was wrong with pairing old stretched-out yoga pants with a dewy visage?

Her face was close to the mirror as she carefully applied eyeliner and a shimmering 'faun brown' shadow. She took a step back to admire her work. Not too shabby! She was sporting some comfortable black pants, a mustard-colored tank top, and a grey knit cardigan. Her makeup emphasized the rosiness of her complexion and the green of her eyes. She swept her hair up into a messy ponytail and checked the mirror one last time. Yes. This was the perfect arrangement for book club. She was comfortable and confident, ready to drink wine and discuss *Belle's Beast* before the conversation inevitably turned to other topics.

Hazel pulled into the long drive, gravel crunching beneath her car tires. They usually met at Amara's home. Which made sense because she had the largest living room and plenty of space in her circular drive for parking. As a bonus, her husband, Omar, seemed to have a sixth sense about when the wine was depleted and would sweep in to freshen their glasses. Over time he had even learned everyone's preferences for red or white. Omar For The Win.

She swiped through the chapters they would discuss today to review what she had highlighted as talking points while she climbed the steps to the porch. There was no need to knock as she entered the front door and made her way down the hall and into the living room. When she rounded the corner, she was greeted by cheers of "Hazel!" and smiling faces all seated around the coffee table.

Amara, Rosie, and Jessica were already sipping from their glasses. Rosie patted the space on the couch next to her, gesturing for Hazel to sit. As she settled in, Omar arrived with a glass of red and slipped it into her hand. "Thanks, Omar, you are truly a hero." He winked and pulled finger guns before backing out of the room. Hazel joined the conversation while they waited for their final member to arrive. Lydia walked in a couple minutes later, regaled by cheers of her name. She had a rosé delivered to her, and the book analysis began.

Rosie immediately declared that Belle had "A Classic case of Stockholm Syndrome." She was a captive who seemed to be falling for her captor. Rosie was interested to see if Belle would continue to have feelings for the Beast after being granted freedom in this rendition or not. Apparently, in real life, victims sometimes still feel love for their captors but are embarrassed about the emotion. Rosie is a Counselor and is full of this sort of knowledge.

Everyone agreed there was a strange disconnect between the story beginning to describe the Beast's body in traditionally attractive terms and their sensibilities. Everyone except Jessica, who staunchly disagreed. "Y'all are being way too real with this, it's a story, and his insane beast-muscles are hot… I bet he's great at giving head." Lydia choked on the wine she had drunk. Jessica continued, looking right at Lydia, "He's ravenous. I'd sit on his face." They all lost it and had to hold their glasses aloft to steady them as they shook with laughter.

When they had calmed enough to speak, Hazel said, "Sam would *definitely* call you a furry then. He accused me, and all I mentioned was that Belle was falling for him and had referenced his broad shoulders!"

"Wait, who is Sam?" Amara's question was dripping with intrigue.

Before Hazel could answer, Rosie cut in, "You remember Sam! He's the work husband."

Hazel glared at Rosie. "Not true!"

"How is it not true?" She countered, "You talk to him daily, seek each other's opinion, know about each other's personal lives, and mention him with us all the time."

Hazel sat in silence, thinking about how to disagree but her inability to immediately respond made everyone snicker. "Okay, okay, you might have a point."

This divergence in topic marked the end of discussing *Belle's Beast*, and segmented conversations began, Hazel, Lydia, and Rosie talking while Jessica and Amara carried on. They had been a group almost as long as Hazel had lived in Crestwood. Creeping up on around two years now, she realized. It did not seem real. At this point, they all knew each other so well that weaving in and out of discussion was effortless.

The fact their 2nd anniversary was upcoming struck Hazel so hard she announced it, "Do you realize we've been doing this for almost two years? I mean, I guess you all have been going for even longer, which is… it seems incredible."

"Incredibly awesome!" Jessica said, raising her glass. They all toasted.

Amara sighed. "It is strange thinking of all that's changed in two years. Aw, I'm so proud of us! Lydia, you got Teacher of the Year for the entire state. Jessica, your artwork was featured in Inked. Rosie opened her private practice. Hazel…" She swallowed and brought her wine glass into her lap. "When you joined, you had been through so much with the loss of your parents, and then…." She struggled to find the right words.

Rosie helped. "Then Sir Dickbag tripped and fell into his colleague's vagina the moment you were partially back on your feet, but look how strong you are."

Amara recovered. "Exactly!"

Hazel smiled at the room. These people had been a huge part of what had saved her. After Alex had left her only a couple months after her parents had died, she didn't have anything left in Chicago. She had looked for a smaller city that seemed slower, maybe even quaint, found Crestwood, and moved the very next week carrying everything she wanted to take in her car. It was the hardest thing she had ever done. When she arrived, her feeling of loneliness intensified. The therapist she had started talking to through FutureApp's Employee Assistance Program practically begged her to find a social outlet. She had seen Amara make a post about the book club on the Nextdoor App and reluctantly inquired.

"You know, that was the worst time in my life. You all pulled me through it." Hazel realized someone was holding her hand. "Looking back now, I'm so grateful. Alex…"

Rosie insisted, "Dickbag." They all let out a scoff.

"Yes, him," Hazel continued with a smirk, "We don't know what really happened with the colleague, but I'm honestly grateful he ended it. At the time, it was horror on horror, but I don't want to be with someone who doesn't love me, you know? And now I've found all you to love." While she was speaking, they had all taken each other's hands. They gave each other a squeeze.

Now things were heavy, which was not the typical book club vibe. There was an awkward silence for a moment until Jessica said in a protracted raunchy drawl, "Ravenousssss."

Everyone laughed, and the night continued with conversation littered with the term 'ravenous' and the phrase 'sit on his face.'

Rosie grabbed Hazel's sleeve as they departed, "We still on for tomorrow? Nick won't be there, but I'm still good for tea."

Hazel nodded her agreement. "We're going to Chai Chai, right? I'll see you at 8!"

THE WIND WAS WHIPPING the ends of Hazel's hair around as she cycled to Chai Chai. It was 7:45am, and the air was still cool and crisp. Knowing she was going to cycle there and not wanting her clothes to get stuck in the gears, she had thrown on jeans instead of her usual sweats. When she put them on, they made her feel dressed up. She grimaced, thinking she would need to somehow work that expectation into her How-To Work Remotely article. "After a while, your understanding of fashion may become misaligned with the general population."

She opened the door to Chai Chai, setting the bells on the knob jingling, and let her eyes sweep across the room. Rosie was already here. She had seen her car parked on the street. No sign of her in the front of the teahouse, however, and not many other customers yet either. Only one table had been occupied so far. Hazel went down the short hallway into the semi-private rooms and found Rosie seated on a pouf. She looked up at the sound of Hazel pulling back the sparse beaded curtain and threw her hands in the air in welcome.

Rosie pushed the menu aside. "I have to get the Chai Chai Chai, I know I get it every time, but it's too good. To be honest, nothing should be allowed to be this good."

"It is stunningly delicious. We may need to report it to authorities."

"Shhhhh!" Rosie waved her hands down, gesturing for quiet, "Mama didn't raise no snitch."

After a couple minutes of perusing the menu, Hazel said, "Ring the bell. I'm definitely getting the Sheng Pu-erh Mang Fei Shan."

Rosie looked at her with disgust. "The fermented tea, again?"

"The house chai, again?"

Rosie rang the tiny bell on the table to summon a waiter. Hazel often wondered if the waitstaff found this method enchanting, annoying, or a combination of both. After putting in their order, the kind words of best friends catching up began to flow, only briefly interrupted by the delivery of their tray.

As their teas' earthy and spicy smells wafted through the air, Hazel asked in a singsong rhythm, "How's Nick?"

Rosie's eyes brightened as the smile spread across her face, "He's doing well! He's packing right now. We're taking a long weekend to visit his family."

"Oh! Nice. Do you have plans, or just visiting?"

"No plans *that I know of*, although they love to surprise us. Last time we went, they had reserved us a table at this sensory-deprivation-tasting experience. It was limited seating, so since his whole family came, it was basically only us in the room. Then they turn off the lights, and you can't see anything. It was funny. Steph, one of his sisters, kept getting freaked out about not being able to see what she ate."

"Nick must get that from his family, then. He always seems to be doing sweet things for you. I bet he's packing for both of you right now."

Rosie snorted. "He is! He'll do a better job than I'd do for myself too." She shook her head in a show of disbelief.

"I love you two, I don't know how you found the perfect man, but I'm glad because you deserve him."

"Nobody is perfect. Don't get me wrong, I love Nick like I can't imagine loving anyone else. We still all have our imperfections. We compliment each other well, and we keep our romance alive, but Hazel," her face became more serious, "He has no sense of urgency about cleaning messes. Sometimes I get frustrated and leave a wrapper where I see it just to test him, but I'm always the one to give in first."

"Okay, I get that. Alex used to do the same. Maybe it's a dude thing? It used to feel like he must not see the same way I do."

"Ugh, don't get me started. It 100% is a dude thing in our culture. There have been studies! Turns out they do see the mess, but because our culture doesn't expect them to clean it (that's a woman's job) or judge them harshly for having a mess, they are programmed to be able to put it out of their mind. It's not urgent for them." She paused, "It's also probably unfair for me to test him this way, but that's what he has to deal with from me! See? Both of us imperfect."

"First off, gross. We gotta burn the patriarchy," They clinked tea cups, "Second, you've been together for so long now and still do the whole romance alive thing. That's special."

"You're right, but don't romanticize the perfect person either. They don't exist and never have."

Rosie changed topics by asking about Hazel's work, "How's the Sam project?"

Hazel narrowed her eyes at the title, "*CARE* hasn't started in earnest yet, but I think we will next week. I won't be able to tell you details."

Rosie swiftly amended, "I'll only request interpersonal details. You know I don't even understand what you actually do there, right?" She laughed.

This was true; most people didn't totally get Hazel's job. She tried to describe it but maddeningly, going into detail seemed to make it more confusing. She usually opted to keep it high level and let people assume what they would about Communications.

"I've got this other project too. It's making a How-To about working from home. Apparently, we've seen a tick-up in attrition out of new hires but only in the remote space. Tamra thinks if we package it right, Training could be interested."

"FINALLY!" Rosie's proclamation was so loud the customers who had settled in the room across the hall turned to look at them. "This is the best news. You've been looking for something with crossover for an eternity!"

Hazel looked at her tea and tried to suppress a smile. It had taken her some time to dare to believe she might have finally found a project Training would be interested in. Still, as she dreamed about the direction she wanted to take, she was becoming more convinced. "We'll see, but I do think there's a chance it could work."

She raised her eyes back to Rosie and was surprised to see that she was observing Hazel with a look of deep concentration. Hazel didn't speak but cocked her head to the side in question and waited. Rosie seemed to steel herself and asked, "Could I tell you something I would tell a patient? Just for a minute?"

Hazel braced herself by grabbing the back of her neck and massaging. She grinned, "Ah, so you're psychoanalyzing me?"

Rosie rolled her eyes but looked relieved at the humor in the reply, "Always, we really can't turn it off as a profession, you know?" Then she added earnestly, "But I won't without your consent."

"Alright, do your worst."

Rosie's voice was gentle; Hazel had only heard it that way a handful of times, "Do you ever think you might tend to build roadblocks to fulfillment?"

Hazel couldn't prevent the shock on her face. "Roadblocks to fulfillment?"

"Yeah. What you said about the Training project was… apprehensive regarding success."

"I can't control whether they're interested or not. I'm being realistic."

Rosie smiled kindly. "It sounds like you have some control. You're the one with the assignment and can tackle it however you want. Which means you could tailor it to make it more interesting to them, right?"

"And I will, but it's still out of my hands ultimately." Hazel shot her questioning look again. "You obviously aren't only thinking about the single sentence I just uttered. Out with it."

Rosie exhaled a heavy breath. "Something I've noticed is that you express your desires; You desire a position in Training. You desire a committed romantic partner. Then when you have the opportunity to pursue those things, you tend to find roadblocks."

Hazel opened her mouth to reply, but no sound came out. She felt hot, and the teacup she held in her hand was suddenly oppressive. She set it back on the tray. "You sure seem to have a great time at the expense of my "road-blocks" when I tell you how awful my dates have been."

Rosie swallowed and let her gaze drop. Both women began to talk at once. Their eyes met when they realized they were both hastily apologizing. They laughed, and Rosie scooted next to Hazel so they could share an embrace. When she pulled back, Hazel had tears sliding down her cheeks. "Oh no!" She extended her hand and brushed a tear away, "I love you so much, Hazel. You're my best friend. I do want to laugh with you about your horrible dates. Remember the one who brought the ferret?" They both smirked, then Rosie continued, "Exactly! I do want to laugh with you. I want you to be happy too."

Hazel nodded her head. "I didn't mean to accuse you of anything. I didn't expect to be considering deep truths this morning."

There was a pause, then Rosie added, "You have reason to see red flags easily. More than most... I get scared you might get in your own way by accident. And I could be wrong! I'm open to that. Nobody knows you like you!"

CHAPTER 5

LEARN FROM THE PAST

"It isn't simply living through experiences that makes us wiser or more capable. It's the awareness of those experiences that allow for growth."

TWO AND A HALF YEARS AGO...

HAZEL AND ALEX were in the backseat of an Uber headed to their apartment in Elmdale, a trendy area outside of downtown Chicago. They had gone to an upscale restaurant on a date to celebrate Alex's recent promotion, even ordering the wine-tasting menu to pair with their meal. Both of them were speaking animatedly. Loudly. Garnering annoyed glances in the rearview mirror from their driver that they didn't notice.

Hazel's phone rang.

She answered.

This was when her soul left her body.

Phrases pummeled at her, "Is this Hazel Rogers,

daughter of Larry and Elle Rogers?" "Can you come to St. Joseph's hospital?" "There's been an accident."

Every moment of that night was somehow a blur and a sharp unending pain. Alex had taken charge. Told the Uber driver to take them to the hospital, helped her out of the car and into the ER, and explained who they were there to see. He held her hand the entire time.

They were led back to a private room off the surgery wing and told a doctor would be in soon to update them. Waiting was agony. Not knowing what had happened was a constant needle being pressed into, removed, and pushed back into Hazel's gut.

There was a knock on the door, and two men entered the room. "I'm sorry. We did everything we could."

But this could not be real; Hazel didn't even know what had happened. She tried to explain they must have the wrong room. She had been called because her parents were here, but she didn't even know why yet, and she was waiting to talk to someone who would have that information.

Alex hugged her in a way that told her the truth. She didn't know the story, but her parents were dead. Hazel fell to her knees, sobbing and heaving uncontrollably. She vomited on the floor, on her hands. She didn't care.

. . .

Alex helped her stand and practically carried her to an office they were led to. Someone had cleaned her up. She sat there, empty and numb, as she was told her parents had been in a car crash. The surgeon explained their injuries and what he and his team had done to try to repair them, but none of it mattered. She heard them only vaguely, as if from a distance, as her mind swayed with disbelief.

The following days spent planning the funerals seemed to rush by in huge swaths until they were met by a solid wall of time and would screech to a halt. The first wall of time Hazel sped into happened while talking to the officiant, Jill.

Jill, Hazel, and Alex were seated around the dinner table. Jill asked logistical questions about the ceremony- the anticipated number of attendees, if any technology was necessary for a slideshow, if there would be portraits, and how the eulogy should be treated.

It happened when she asked, "Could you tell me about some of your favorite memories with them?"

Hazel saw her life in memories, and her parents were always there. They. Were. Always. There. Images swam in her mind of birthdays, Christmases, and graduations, but also dinner every night, reading together, and being bored on the couch. Even as an adult, she FaceTimed with her parents every evening after work. They had dinner together twice a week. She remembered their smiling faces from her phone and how goofy they would be dancing lamely with each other in the kitchen, gesturing for her to join. Her memories didn't seem to stop; instead, they changed to a sort of foretelling. She pictured every event in the future and what those memories would look like. She imagined her wedding without her parents, having kids without them, and buying a house they would never enter.

She realized her children would never know their grandparents. She realized she would never be able to ask them questions about anything.

Then she realized she must have been sitting in silence for a long time, here, at the kitchen table. Except she hadn't. Only a few seconds had passed.

EVERYTHING SEEMED MEANINGLESS, and Hazel was empty. She had stopped crying. She had stopped caring. She felt awash in a vast cruel sea, anchorless.

When she tried to return to work after her bereavement time, she found it impossible to sit through meetings or to put effort into anything. When she could think, she couldn't prevent her mind from playing the reel of what her parents and her would miss. She would settle into despair or anger, which would lead to guilt. Even though she wouldn't, couldn't, talk about it, her supervisor at the time obviously saw her struggle and referred her to a therapist through the Employee Assistance Program.

Alex had been the one who dialed the number for her. After she had not emerged from her office by 6pm, he had come in to find her motionless, staring at the screen. That therapist had determined to put her on a short leave while she worked through "the acute phase" of her grief and referred her to someone local to get the support she needed.

WHEN SHE STARTED SEEING ETHAN, her new therapist, it was less like she was going to see him and more like she was being bodily delivered to his office. Alex made sure she was on time for all her appointments. Slowly, surprisingly, for it seemed against all odds and even the nature of what Hazel knew to be true, she began to feel more energetic.

Time still jolted her, but she had enough energy to make coffee in the morning. She even wanted to taste the coffee, she realized.

With Ethan's encouragement, she began to reframe her thinking. Instead of 'my parents won't see their grandkids grow up,' she would think, 'my parents prepared me to be a great Mom.' This was not easy work, but she put her efforts toward it.

Weeks passed, and she discovered her gratitude for the experiences she had. This came at the cost of a few dark days when she shared the idea with Ethan, and he responded, "We have the most to lose when we have so many things we're grateful for. People who live in fear of loss do so because of their happiness and fulfillment." She knew he meant it as a way to validate her experience, but it struck her as a promise of loss in the future too. Still, she was grateful for being part of a close family and all the time they had spent together. She was particularly thankful they had at least met, known, and loved Alex deeply. They wouldn't be there for the wedding, which was tentatively scheduled for next year, but Alex was already a part of the family. They'd been dating for 5 years, after all. Then there was how he had taken care of her these weeks, making sure she bathed and ate, being patient and attentive.

She also started feeling grateful for her career at FutureApp. They had also taken care of her, first by granting her bereavement time, then by extending the EAP services and approving a leave of absence. There had been no doubting her, no requests for her to tie up loose ends, just unwavering support. When a month passed, she returned to work and was met with such a stunning force of kindness it overwhelmed her. Her friends had reached out immediately as if they were waiting for her status to turn to Available, not about work-related things, but checking in on her. Meg and Frank had made a collection of funny memes for her that they used to give an entire timeline of all the things that happened in the Comms department while she was away. Sam had invited her and Alex to have a virtual dinner with him. "It's your first day back. If you don't have plans, please let me order you some delivery, and we can eat and watch an episode of The Office together. Come on, end your first day by taking it easy." She couldn't refuse, and they had agreed to SyncUp at 6:30pm.

Alex returned from work at 5:30pm, and Hazel was sitting on the couch, waiting to tell him about their dinner plans. He turned toward the coat rack and started hanging his jacket. "How was your first day back?"

"It was actually really good. We'll be getting some delivery soon and…."

Alex interrupted, "I'm glad it was good." He turned to face her, and she knew something was wrong. Maybe he was exhausted from taking care of her for so long. Perhaps she hadn't looked at him properly since that night. Or could it be his promotion wasn't going well, and he had kept it a secret so she wouldn't worry?

"What's wrong, Alex? You look…." Dark, resigned, cold. She couldn't put her finger on it, "unwell."

His eyes swept upward, but he focused them behind Hazel. "We need to talk."

"Of course." She gestured for him to join her on the couch. She rubbed her hand on his back when he sat beside her.

"There's no easy way to say this. I'm…" he seemed to draw in determination to continue, "I'm moving."

"What?" Her hand dropped from his shoulder, "What are you talking about? Why would we move?"

He leaned away from her and stared at his feet. "No. I'm moving. It's part of the promotion. I have to move to Seattle."

"Well, I mean, this is big news, but FutureApp doesn't care where I work. I can move too." Panic flooded her senses, "Why didn't you tell me this before?"

"Hazel, I don't love you anymore." He said it quickly as if forcing it out hastily was the only way he could have spoken it at all.

The room was spinning.

He continued, "I didn't tell you before because of what happened. I couldn't leave you. You needed me. I asked them to postpone my start date, and I'll… I'll always love you in a way."

Hazel's voice was frantic, "No. No, why didn't you tell me before then? We celebrated. Went to dinner. We laughed in the car! We were happy…."

"I was confused." He swallowed. "I didn't know how I felt."

The doorbell rang.

"And you thought the best way to figure things out was to not talk to me at all about it?"

"I needed it to be my decision. This was the hardest decision of my life."

Hazel sat cradling her head in her hands. She couldn't bear to look at Alex.

The doorbell rang again. "Who is at the damned door right now?" Alex hissed. He answered it and found the bag of Chinese food Sam had ordered them.

"Sam ordered us takeout," she looked at the clock, then returned her vision to the coffee table, "We're supposed to be having dinner with him in a SyncUp in 15 minutes."

Alex turned to her from the door. "I don't know what else to say. I'll have my stuff packed by the end of the week. I'm… I'm going to go." And he left.

· · ·

She didn't know why she did it, but she grabbed the Chinese food and logged into SyncUp. She was several minutes early, so she queued up a random episode of The Office to stream.

"I'm going to have to start coming to our meetings earlier, so I can beat you in." Sam had joined seconds after she had selected the episode, also early.

Hazel quirked one side of her mouth up in a grin and intensified her gaze, "You'll never beat me! Bwahahaha!"

"Where's Alex?"

"He had to leave." She was feeling a familiar emptiness but fighting it. "We can go ahead and eat."

Sam's face was contemplative. He looked like he might ask something but said, "Okay, hit the play button, Hazelberry."

She guffawed. "What did you call me?"

Sam blushed. "Umm, do you drink tea, by chance?"

Hazel had no idea why he was asking about tea. "Yes, I mean, yes, I love tea, actually, but what does that have to do with anything?"

"Hazelberry is one of my favorite teas. It's a pu-erh." He shook his head. "I'm sorry; it just slipped out."

"It's okay. I don't think I've tried a pu-erh before. I'll have to check it out."

"They're pretty unique; fermented teas. Let me know if you like it. Anyway, let's watch!"

She pressed play, and they started eating their takeout and adding commentary to the show. Hazel felt The Office was a good pick for this evening, accidentally good, but it was easy to zone out with. It was natural to talk and laugh with Sam about it.

It *was* easy until Pam walked across a fire pit on the beach. Hazel's chest constricted. She had thought she had no tears left, but her cheeks were wet.

"Pause the show." Sam's voice was commanding but

tender. She hit pause. Hazel was searching for the words but was surprised when Sam spoke first, "When you said he had to leave… He left?" There was an understanding between them. Hazel nodded her head. Sam stood up, going off camera. She heard a loud clanging sound, a sharp inhale, then saw him run past the screen. He called to her, "I'll be right back!"

She couldn't tell exactly what was going on. Her curiosity distracted her enough that the tears stopped flowing. Sam returned and dropped back into his seat; she saw a flash of white on his hand, but before she could inquire about it, he asked, "What do you need? Do you want to talk, or not, or later?" He added, almost to himself, while he shook his head, "He's a fucking idiot."

Hazel answered in a sigh, "I honestly don't know what I need. It only happened right before we met, and I'm so, so tired." She shouted, "I'm so tired of feeling like this!" It was a truth, and saying it aloud, even in the freshness of the situation, sieved some of the hurt from her.

Sam looked at her with such care, his voice low, "How do you feel?"

"A thousand despicable things." Her eyes were fearful. "Empty, meaningless, unwanted, deceived, surprised, but mostly alone." Once she started talking, she found it hard to stop. It was a little embarrassing to lay this at the feet of her mentor and bosses boss, but the more she spoke, the more room she had for relief to rush in. The way Sam listened to her felt warm and safe, so she kept going.

It was two weeks later when she made the move to Crestwood. She had always loved living in Chicago, but it had nothing left for her. Hazel wasn't usually impulsive, but she yearned for new surroundings and a tabula rasa for her life. She had made a list of traits she believed she might enjoy. Somewhere smaller than Chicago, artsy, good food was a must. She located several candidate cities, but Crestwood stuck in her mind.

She took a week to sell her large furniture, packed her car, and made the 10-hour drive to Crestwood. She hadn't found a place to rent before leaving, so she checked into an Extended Stay America while she figured out living arrangements.

Hazel moved into a small, older house on the outskirts of town a few weeks later. She was carrying boxes up the front porch steps when her phone buzzed. Alex's Facebook status announced he was In a Relationship.

CHAPTER 6
BE ON CAMERA

"Being on camera is important for developing relationships and the culture in a remote environment. Seeing expressions and reactions humanizes us and helps us understand each other."

PRESENT DAY...

HAZEL WAS WEARING a formal-looking floral print top with a small ruffle on the high neck, had put on makeup, and adjusted her office lighting to look as professional as possible. She was also wearing blue pajama bottoms with penguins in Santa hats. The joys of working from home! In a few minutes, the CARE team and all their stakeholder contacts would be meeting for the first time. Hazel, Sam, and Lou were already in the SyncUp when the top of the hour struck. Other colleagues started filtering in, tinkling bells announcing each new entrant.

While the core team was limited to the three of them, the complexity of the CARE project was indicated by the sheer volume of stakeholders who entered the room. There were numerous people from Legal, HR, and high-ranking leaders from Operations and Services. Marketing, Regional Quality members from the states and the UK, Technical Writers and Training were also represented. Jasmond was the stakeholder from Training, and her heart briefly raced when she saw his name. They would be handing off to Training at the end of everything, and Sam would create the first leadership training. His role as a Sr. Change Management leader sometimes called on him to have substantial overlap with other departments this way.

Sam cleared his throat to bring the room to attention. His shoulders were relaxed and back, and he flashed a broad smile, causing his right cheek to dimple. Hazel wondered why she had never noticed before. He must have tweaked the lighting in his office too.

Sam began, "Thanks for coming today, everyone. This will mostly be a simple introduction for all of us who will be helping develop and roll out CARE. Before we make introductions, though, let's talk about our mission with CARE."

As Sam spoke about FutureApp's mission to support their clients in the way clients want to be supported and how they aspire to bring up the best Apps available, Hazel couldn't help but notice how he commanded the room. Sometimes in meetings, you could tell people were doing work in the background or idly engaging in another activity. The opposite was true here. Everyone stayed on camera, all hanging on Sam's words. "The continued growth and success of FutureApp hinge on our successfully implementing this change. It is no easy task that we embark upon today, but one that will demand our teamwork, our courage to speak truth, and our relentless pursuit to be the best."

Hazel broke from Sam's enchantment when he

switched the topic to role explanations. He introduced himself first with a chuckle, "I'm Sam, and I'm a Sr. Change Management Specialist. I'll be leading this project and will likely be working with all of you over these next months. I will specifically be working closely with Training, Legal, HR, and department leaders as I craft the initial Leadership Training for CARE."

He continued to describe Hazel's responsibility of creating the Communication Plan through the Leadership Training and how she would work closely with department leaders, HR, and Legal. Then Lou's tasks of updating written documents and the Expert Database and how that would require Strategic and Regional Quality and Technical Writers. "The rest of you will want to be aware of how CARE is developing for Phases 3 and 4, which we will hand off to after the Summit in November. We will be certain to keep you up to date and invite your feedback throughout our work."

He dismissed the meeting but asked Hazel and Lou to hang back. They did, but so did the Operations VP. Sam addressed her, "Did you have a question, Samantha?"

She made a short, breathy giggle. "Oh, no. I just wanted to say I know CARE will be a success with you at the helm, and I'm eager to help you with anything. Give me a shout anytime."

Sam gave her a nod. "Thanks for that."

Hazel found she was glaring at Samantha and quickly fixed her face to a neutral expression. Why was she hanging around?

Once Samantha left, Sam whistled and said, "Here goes something. I wanted to talk to you both to get our meetings on the calendar. We really don't have a lot of time." He opened his Calendar App to count the weeks. "The summit is scheduled the week before Thanksgiving, and it's September 12th today. We've got 10 weeks. What do you think our schedule should look like?"

Hazel offered, "The approvals will take the most time and are frequently bottlenecks. I'd suggest we meet frequently. We can give each other updates and then have working sessions. We might be able to seek several approvals at a time if we're smart about it."

Sam asked, "You think three meetings a week for us plus our update meeting for all stakeholders?"

"Yes, but let's do the stakeholder meeting every other week."

Sam's calendar was still on display for them, their attention shifted to it, and they all seemed to realize there wasn't much open time available. "I can make the Stakeholder event for today repeat at the same time alternating weeks. For our meetings, how about Monday, Wednesday, and Friday? I can do Monday mornings. As you can see, I'm pretty tight. Any issue with doing 4pm Wednesday and Friday? Actually, that's too late for you, Hazel. I'll rearrange…."

Lou interjected, "Is that Pacific Time on your Cal?"

"Yeah, I'm in Oregon, and Hazel is in North Carolina, so she's Eastern Time. Sorry, I should have asked, where are you, Lou?"

"Haaa, well, I'm in Cork."

Sam and Hazel both exclaimed, "Ireland!?"

Lou slowly nodded his affirmation. "So a 4pm Pacific Time meeting for you is midnight for me. Earlier morning meetings usually work best, 7am-9am Pacific."

They all gazed at Sam's full schedule for a moment longer until Sam said, "I know we can find some good time slots. I'll try my best to rearrange some things."

Hazel guessed he would be working on this right away and messaged him.

Hazel Rogers

Good intro there, you even made me feel inspired, like maybe we can pull this off! 11:14am

Sam Pierce

Well that's a relief- phew! 11:14am

Sam Pierce

and thanks! 11:14am

Hazel Rogers

You gotta teach me your trick where everyone is focused on you sometime. What are you thinking on the schedule though? 11:15am

Sam Pierce

Easy, act so confident nobody dares to disagree, physically take up space. 11:15am

Hazel Rogers

That's it? That's the advice? Excuse me while I SCOFFSCOFFSCOFF. 11:15am

Sam Pierce

Bless you! And yes, it's always worked for
me. What is not working for me is the
schedule... 11:16am

Sam Pierce

Monday is easy, and I can come in early
Friday. Wednesday is the problem, I only
have 4:30pm my time and that's 7:30pm for
you and the middle of the night for Lou.
11:17am

Hazel Rogers

I can do 7:30 on Wednesday. Maybe we
can focus on Lou's stuff on another day, he
obviously can't be here at 12:30am.
11:17am

Sam Pierce

Yeah... I don't know. I know you're out of
here at 5pm and how important it is to
maintain. You worked hard to get the
balance you have. 11:17am

Hazel Rogers

Stop that. This is temporary and it's one
day a week. Plus you just sent the invites,
don't think I don't realize you're coming in
at 6am on Friday. That's even worse.
11:17am

Sam Pierce

It is usually when I run, I'll have to skip the morning run but I'd be up anyway. 11:18am

Hazel Rogers

Gross. The point is we can make short term sacrifices as long as we know they're really short term. 11:18am

Sam Pierce

You looked really professional in there today btw, I like the flowery top. 11:24am

LATER THAT EVENING, Hazel's doorbell rang. She quickly brushed the almond flour off her hands before running to answer it. Rosie and Nick streamed in mid-conversation.

"…it was totally appropriate. You're just salty you didn't think of it yourself." Nick winked at Hazel as he passed her, heading into the kitchen.

Rosie rolled her entire head in mock exasperation and directed her reply to Hazel, "Nick's Mom snuck in like 50 of those little liquor bottles into mini-golf in her purse."

Hazel bit her lip to prevent the laugh.

"and how many did you partake in, my dearest wife?"

"That's beside the point. We got KICKED OUT OF MINI GOLF!"

"We were asked to leave," Nick corrected, "it's one of my proudest moments."

"I mean, it was pretty funny." Hazel knew this had been where the conversation was headed. Rosie loved to play a humorous devil's advocate, and both of them were all flirty smiles.

Hazel chastised, "How many times have I told you both to come right in? My house is your house." As proof of this, they had both made themselves at home in the kitchen. Rosie was cracking eggs into a measuring bowl. Nick had begun chopping vegetables for the quiche they were making for dinner.

"Our hands were full!" Rosie motioned her head toward the bags they had brought with them, no doubt filled with other delicious goodies they'd get into.

As the quiche was baking, they moved into the living room, Nick handing out iced ciders he had brought. Hazel flopped onto the couch and propped her feet up on the coffee table, Nick sat beside her, and Rosie was perusing the bookshelf. They chatted more about Rosie and Nick's trip to visit his family. Rosie asked for advice on what book she should select for the club to read next, as it was her turn to pick.

The oven timer sounded soon after, and Hazel moved into the kitchen with Nick behind her. He set the table, and she began inspecting the quiche. Rosie called in, "Hey, what's this?"

"What's what?"

Rosie rounded the corner and put a worn brown book on the counter. "This!"

"Ah, my Mom's journal."

"Wow, what a cool thing to have. I should write when we have kids." She met eyes with Nick.

Hazel shrugged. "I haven't read it or anything. It's her personal diary."

Feeling the intensity of Rosie's gaze, Hazel looked over at her. Rosie arched an eyebrow. "I'm sure she would want you to. I appreciate what you're saying, it was private for her when she was living, but now it's this insight into her adult life and perspective. It's a gift for you from her."

The conversation moved on while they ate dinner. Hazel updated them that CARE had started, and she would be working late on Wednesdays until mid-November. "You should have seen Sam in the kick-off meeting. Sometimes people think he's an imposing asshole, but he's so confident. He just demands all your attention, you know? Everyone was tuned in when he was presenting."

Nick hummed and nodded knowingly as he finished chewing a bite. "People confuse confidence for arrogance and assery a lot. Happens to me all the time."

Rosie added, "And if you're a confident woman, they'd call you a bitch."

Hazel knit her brows. "Too true. It's just that both of my work friends think so. It's weird, I can usually trust them with anything, but this doesn't add up somehow." She got up to clear the table (they had demolished the quiche) and continued, "After the meeting, the Operations VP stayed behind and talked to Sam. Said she was eager to help with anything and how she knew we'd succeed since he was on the job."

Rosie had pulled out Cards Against Humanity and was dealing hands but froze mid-deal. "She said that in front of you?"

"Yeah, me and Lou were still there. We were waiting to talk as a team and figure out our schedule."

"Brazen, I'll give her that."

Hazel glanced over the sink questioningly. "Why do you think?"

"She was obviously flirting with him! You were there. You didn't interpret it as flirting?" Hazel was quiet a moment. "Maybe. It was hard to tell; honestly, it could be she's trying to suck up too."

Rosie said out of the side of her mouth, "She's trying to suck something." Everyone laughed, including Hazel, though she had a strange clenching feeling she couldn't quite place in her stomach.

They played cards the rest of the evening. As Rosie and Nick were headed out, Rosie grabbed Hazel's hand and leaned into her ear. "When you're ready to read that journal, we can do it together if company makes it easier." She pulled back and gave her hand a squeeze. "Up to you."

CHAPTER 7

MEAL PLANNING

" It's trickier than you might think to stay healthy while working at home. Snacks are everywhere, and it's all too easy to go out for dinner for a nightly change of view."

DAYS LATER, the diary still lay on the counter where Rosie had placed it. Hazel was chopping broccoli and peppers on the cutting board and occasionally shooting glares toward the book. She felt as if it was mocking her. Its presence made her replay some of her recent conversations with Rosie and Meg. What the fuck kind of phrase was 'road-blocks to fulfillment' anyway? She sighed, put down the knife, and picked up her phone. A romance like in the books she read wasn't going to fall into her lap. Even if she was guilty of finding things wrong with everyone, she should still try, right? She opened the DateFinder App and started swiping. DateFinder; it was one of FutureApp's first big successes which helped put them on the map. Hazel had a free subscription to DateFinder as an employee. She wondered, had Sam ever used DateFinder?

Several minutes of frustrated swiping later, she still had not found someone she wanted to chat with. 'Roadblocks to fulfillment' was becoming a song in her head. Sighing to herself, she settled on sending a message to Paul despite the fact he didn't list anything personal in any section. Even his career was left blank (a definite red flag), but at least he was easy to look at. Curly blond hair partially obscured his right eye in the profile photo. It appeared to be effortless, but she wondered how long it took to primp in real life. One side of his mouth was pulled back into a cocky grin. Trying to ignore her instincts and be more open-minded, she tapped the Connect button. He probably wouldn't be interested in her anyway. Someone with a profile picture like his usually balked when they saw Hazel's snap of herself in an Octopus costume from last Halloween. She finished chopping her vegetables and placed them in a Tupperware, then made the sauce she would use to stir-fry with later. Before starting the workday, she could squeeze in a few paragraphs of the new book Rosie had recommended, *Deeper than Snow*. Even those short few lines gave her suspicions that the title might be a double entendre.

THEY HAD HELD their kickoff meeting for CARE, but today was the first working meeting, and she knew it would be rough. At the beginning of projects, ambiguity was a certainty standing in the way of building a clear path forward. She messaged Tamra after checking her emails

Hazel Rogers

Good morning! 8:36am

67

Tamra King

Hey, morning 8:37am

Hazel Rogers

Heads up CARE is starting in earnest today,
we have our first working meeting. You
know how it is. 8:37am

Tamra King

lol yes, you've got this though. Do you need
anything? 8:37am

Hazel Rogers

Not right now I don't think 8:38am

Tamra King

Give me a shout if I can help with anything.
I know CARE will take precedence but how
is the How-To coming as well? 8:39am

Hazel Rogers

I've done the research part, and it gave me
exactly what you'd expect. Not to say those
are bad things, they're good pieces of
advice. Things like having a functional
home office that you enjoy being in, taking
breaks... 8:40am

Something I've been thinking. When I think about how to succeed in a remote space it also includes things you'd need to succeed in a traditional office. I wonder if those are not obvious? Like, are people only looking to add different skills and let those skills that are necessary in person slip as if they no longer matter? 8:40am

Tamra King

Document it all. Even the things that seem silly, if they occur to you- write them down. We can sort it through later. 8:44am

HAZEL CHANGED her Chatter status to Busy and prepared for the CARE meeting. Today was not their usual hour block; they all had been able to clear their schedules and planned on spending "as long as it takes" to make the initial timeline for Phase 2. Their SyncUp started at 10am for Hazel, but that was 6am for Sam and 3pm for Lou. She was grateful to be in the middle time zone.

At 9:30am, Hazel received an email alert. It appeared to be a $5 Starbucks gift card from Sam with the note, "Fuel up!" She put her sneakers on and walked swiftly out the door, taking the right turn towards the street. More color had crept down the Maple trees, but she didn't have time to slow down and soak it in now. If she was going to get to the Starbucks on foot and make it back in time, this had to be an all-business affair. She ordered a grande coffee with room for cream, hastily poured in some cream from the serving station, then spun on her heel and returned home with 5 minutes to spare.

She logged into SyncUp and narrowed her eyes at Sam. He was already there sipping his own coffee. He was wearing a black athletic shirt that hugged his shoulders. It was impossible to know what someone's body really looked like when you only saw them from the shoulders up, but Hazel found herself wondering. He ran a lot; she knew it was a beloved hobby of his. When she got to see him in the sort of workout attire he wore now, his shoulders and neck seemed to indicate he was fit. Maybe even muscular. What did he look like? Was he tall or short? Lean? Cut? "I see you ran here."

He winked at her. "I couldn't let you beat me here. I admit I felt it was a close call."

Hazel smiled and raised her cup. "Thanks for the coffee. What are you drinking?"

"Coffee and cream."

"What, no sugar? I take mine the same way!"

"Yeah, the cream is enough sweetener for me. If I want a treat, I'll put in some agave sometimes."

"Well, you have excellent taste, sir."

SyncUp tinkled to announce Lou's entry. He looked surprised he was the last one in, "Good morning to you two, and afternoon for me. Thanks for the coffee, Sam. I didn't have a chance to cash in yet, but I will."

Sam replied that it was no problem, and although they all knew what sort of day was ahead of them, he placed no pressure on moving them into business. Instead, he asked about what they enjoyed outside of work.

Lou shared he spent every second he could with his wife and three-year-old daughter, Abigail. His face lit up with unfiltered joy as he spoke about his family. Even when he shared they were having a tough time potty training Abigail, it was with humor and love. "It's shitty times these days."

Hazel shared about enjoying cooking and that she was

in a book club. Sam smiled, flashing his perfect teeth. "It's about time you started a new book, right? What's on the agenda currently?"

"It's *Deeper Than Snow*. We just started it this week." She wondered how he kept so in tune with the reading schedule.

"Well, I'll expect regular updates as per usual." Then Sam offered, "As for me, when I'm not here, I like to be outside. Hiking or cycling, and I love to run. I try to sign up for the fun races as much as possible."

Lou scoffed, "I'm not much of a runner, but what's a fun race?"

Hazel nodded her head quickly, eyes wide in agreement.

"Like the Color Run or the Bubble Run, you literally run through archways of waist-deep foam. Even non-runners have fun. You should try sometime."

The work organically began, and they started by setting the due date. This was not the week of the summit but 10 days before, where they would need to present the final project and Training for approval, then make any requested changes before the summit. From there, they filled in known waypoints. This was the easy part. The difficulty came next when they were each creating their own plans. They could identify the tasks they needed to complete and put them in a logical order. However, they needed to estimate the time required to complete each step, gain approvals, and engage with other teams as needed. It was a lot of guesswork and reach outs in Chatter to confirm with their stakeholders as best they could.

They worked in silence, creating their own plans with only occasional questions to each other or exclaiming, "Gah!" when a potential bottleneck was discovered. Lou had the most challenging time with his Tech Writing stakeholders, who seemed reluctant to commit to any timeline for edits in the Expert Database. After nearly an hour of chatting back and forth with them, they disclosed they had a backlog of other changes.

Sam had an easier time because building the leadership training didn't require anyone else's time or effort. It mostly fell on Sam to complete, and he would schedule time with Training for their input and then get approvals from Legal and HR.

Hazel's communication plan timelines were dependent upon Sam's and Lou's. She tried to help them as much as possible, giving advice about what to expect from different departments. Nudging them to complete a step quicker if possible, or even breaking steps down to make them more digestible. She suggested Lou meet with the Technical Writers in a SyncUp regularly, given their current state of overwhelm.

Sam and Hazel began discussing their tone goals across the project while Lou was marking up the last of his time-line. "Oh, I know! Let's do a free writing exercise and see what words inspire us." Hazel excitedly explained, "I do this all the time when I'm brainstorming. Think about the tones we need to take through the project- how we want CARE to be perceived. Then you write those words that fly through your mind. Don't think about them. Just write a river of words. Then we compare!"

"Okay, I'm down. A river of words. How should CARE be perceived."

"Yep. Annnnd GO!" Hazel was already typing, the sounds of her keyboard floating through the mic.

After a few minutes, her typing slowed, and she looked up. Lou still seemed busy, looking off to the left of the camera, working on his 2nd monitor. Sam was staring at her, smiling softly, hardly enough to crinkle the corners of his eyes. He said, "What did that keyboard ever do to you? I didn't realize you were such a violent typist."

"Listen, I gotta get all this aggression out somehow. The keyboard can take it." She teased.

"Oh, I don't know. I'd be interested to know what other outlets you have. Pretty sure our IT department wouldn't approve." His dimple emerged when his smile broadened, barely visible beneath his dark facial hair.

Hazel fought the blush on her cheeks as the sudden rushing realization of how handsome Sam looked swept over her. It wasn't solely the well-fitted shirt on his shoulders, the bob of his throat, and the smile that could surely attract wildlife the way a Disney Princess could. It was everything. How had she never noticed before? The dimple. The stretch of his shirt across his shoulders. How his hair swept across his brow. The colors of him- tan skin, black hair, dark brown irises with those glints of gold. He was a whole palette. An entire aesthetic.

She quickly averted her gaze to her notebook and stumbled over her words, "We should compare rivers. Um, words now. Maybe some of them will… do what they're supposed to." She leaned her head into her hand and closed her eyes. "Which is to give us inspiration."

"Should we copy and paste them into the chat and go from there?"

"Sure, let me just…." They both put their lists into the SyncUp Chat.

Sam Pierce

Important

Urgency

Worthwhile

Exciting

Taken Serious

Sexy

Fresh

Easy

Comprehensive 11:45am

Hazel Rogers

Exciting

Easy

Eagles

Worthy

User Friendly

Stable

Horses

Strong

Marketable

Commercials

Approachable

Ubiquitous

. . .

THEY WERE each reading through the other's list. Hazel exclaimed, "Sexy!?"

"I stand by it. It should have, at moments, a sort of intriguing appeal." He moved his hands as if presenting the word and said, "Sexy."

Did he say that with a little growl?

Sam continued, "Besides, no judgment from you! You said Eagles and Horses. Are we in the wild west or something?"

"It's not my fault if you didn't understand the assignment. You're supposed to let your brain noodle on a topic; sometimes, weird stuff happens. It could even be useful later. You never know!"

Lou joined the conversation, "I'd say you both have important themes here, and I agree with them. We should think about how to garner excitement and curiosity, if we're lucky, even buy-in, before the training."

Hazel agreed, "Yes, and of course, it should be easy. I see that reflected all over in these words. Easy to understand, easy to use, and easy to discuss. Easy will make it marketable and reinforce its worthiness."

Lou nodded. "Good exercise. I think I finally got my timeline done. I'm not confident about it, but it will have to do for now. I nested it with the others."

They all looked at the timeline. Hazel puffed her cheeks and exhaled. "This is a lot in a short time, but it looks good. I'll add my Comms timeline in based on this later today."

Sam asked, "Should we send this to the stakeholders as a rough draft? It would kinda give them the idea we need to move quickly, I think. Subconscious little nod for them?"

They tweaked a few words for clarity, and Sam sent it to the group. They had started saying their goodbyes when a response email came through. "That was fast." Sam opened his email. "Samantha wants a word. Mind if I see if she can pop in now since we're still together?" Hazel agreed, and Lou gave a thumbs up at the camera.

SyncUp tinkled as Samantha entered. Her face immediately fell when she saw the room, but she recovered with a smile. "Hi, Sam. I thought it would be just you and I. Sorry to bother everyone."

Sam replied, "Hey to you, Samantha. It's no trouble; we were all already together. Did you have a concern or a question about the timeline?"

She seemed to suppress a smirk. "Please, call me Sam. Everyone who knows me does. Plus, it's a power name. You know what I mean." She spoke directly to Sam.

Hazel felt a squirming in her stomach. Why was Samantha here, blatantly flirting with Sam in full-out makeup? Did he like her? Was there history? She made an internal note to never call her Sam.

"Thanks for emailing us back, Samantha. How can we help?" Hazel asked because Sam had not replied yet.

Samantha reluctantly flicked her eyes to look at Hazel, a slight frown on her coral-colored lips. "Oh, nothing. The timeline looked well put together. I was impressed at Sam's leadership to produce something so swiftly."

Sam replied, "It was a group effort. I couldn't have done it without Hazel and Lou. Very glad you approve, though." He spoke the last sentence with authority. It had the feeling of dismissal.

Samantha flushed. "Well, great job, everyone, then." She focused on Sam once more and regained her confidence. "I'll be around. Don't forget I can help with anything. Two Sams' are better than one." Then she dropped from the SyncUp.

. . .

Hazel was angrily typing her Comms Plan and layering it into the timeline. The cursor wasn't selecting what she wanted it to, and she clicked the mouse with such brutality it hopped on the desk.

"BUH!!" She spun in her chair and stood up. "Sorry, you didn't deserve that."

She still had a lot of work to do, but she was flustered, which made her mad. And confused. Why should she feel flustered at all? She walked into the kitchen and turned the kettle on, thinking about some afternoon tea. The pitch of the water rose as she took some steadying breaths. It didn't matter about Sam being suddenly hot. Why should she care that Samantha obviously shared her opinion? The truth of the situation was clear, she thought as she made her tea. Sam was her friend at work, and it was as simple as that. It had to be because he was definitely her superior at FutureApp. He was even her mentor; from his perspective, she was probably like a fledgling business-person-in-training. Her finding him attractive was only a result of them spending more time together, a proximity crush.

Her phone buzzed. A notification from DateFinder let her know she had a connection and a message. It was Paul. "I've always had a thing for cephalopods. Dinner tonight?"

Hmm, maybe he was okay; it was a cute first line. Tonight though? Short notice. She glanced at the fridge, thinking about her stir-fry prep but typed, "Tonight's good, but no sushi." They made plans to meet at The Brink, a brewery and tapas place downtown.

Hazel felt calmer. Taking a breather to think things through logically had been a big help, and now she would meet Paul later. That was… something. She pushed down the repetitious "roadblocks to fulfillment" in her mind and thought again that meeting Paul was something good.

By the time 5pm rolled around, Hazel had finished making the last edit to her Comms plan. She was proud of the enormous task the team had completed today. Shocked they had gotten this far if she was honest. The timeline would invariably change as they progressed, but that was to be expected, and this looked like a solid beginning. She messaged Sam once she had incorporated the Comms plan into the timeline and closed her laptop.

Hazel was nursing a beer and reading her book at The Brink. Paul was late and had not messaged her. After 20 minutes had passed, she was beginning to think she had been ghosted. She decided to pay up and walk to Chai Chai to read in a quieter environment when he sauntered in. She saw him scan the room, recognize her, and raise his arm. He started wending through the tables toward her. He was wearing fitted pants paired with a brown blazer and button-up. His blonde curls were perfectly coifed, and if he realized he was overdressed, it did not affect his swagger.

"Hazel the purple octopus, right?" He said in greeting.

"That's me."

He settled in across from her. She wondered if he would apologize for being so late and started, "It seemed like you might not…" but he interrupted her, pointing at *Deeper Than Snow*.

"What are you reading?"

"Oh, it's a romance. I just started it, and so far, it's been a rough winter, but another blizzard is expected. I think they're…."

He rolled his eyes. "I bet two characters who hate each other will be snowed in together, am I right? So predictable."

Hazel rubbed her temple for a second. She could do

this. He was late and had already spoken over her twice, but it didn't mean anything. He's probably nervous. "Something like that." She answered. "Do you enjoy reading?"

He arched an eyebrow. "Nah, I'm too busy. I mean, you probably know already."

She was puzzled. "Know what?"

"Who I am. Most people know. My Dad is on all those billboards." Hazel continued to try to place him. "Paul & Peter. You know Paul & Peter, the biggest law firm in the state."

Recognition dawned on Hazel. "Oh, and you're Paul Jr?"

He smiled and pointed at himself. "That's me." He turned his head to whistle at a waitress, who noticed him with loathing but came to the table. "Can I get an Old Fashioned?" He turned to Hazel, "Do you want anything?"

"Yes, actually. I'm starving. Do you want to look at the menu?"

"No need. We can share the steak nachos." He handed the menu to the waitress.

Hazel addressed her before she could leave, "Could I get the Cauliflower General Tso's and a refill on the IPA, please?"

"No wonder you're starving. Are you one of those vegans?"

"I'm pescatarian. The General Tso's Cauliflower is incredible here. You can try some if you want."

His mouth was turned down in disgust. "I'll stick to the nachos."

It was silent for a few awkward minutes. Hazel tried to stoke the conversation, "What would the worst combination of monsters be?"

Paul grabbed his drink from the waitress's hands. "What do you mean?"

Hazel thanked her before continuing, "Like if there was a hybrid Werewolf slash Moth Man."

He squinted briefly but then smirked. "I don't know. But hey, do you believe in women's suffrage?"

Hazel rapid fired, "For me, it's the Zombie Vampire combo because vampires have been sucking blood their entire lives and are probably skilled at people hunting, and the right to vote belongs to all people. I think I'm going to go."

She stood up to leave, but he stood up too. "No, no, it was a joke! It was only a joke because suffrage sounds like suffering?"

Hazel pursed her lips and walked to the door. Paul followed. Staring at the downpour from under the restaurant's awning, she muttered, "You've got to be kidding."

Paul observed her. "Listen, I know this hasn't been the best, but let me take you home? You won't have to find your car in this. Mine is right next door in the garage."

The situation was impossible. Hazel gritted out, "I rode my bike."

"I can fit it in the back. Where is it?"

Unwillingly but unable to come up with a better solution, Hazel unlocked her bike and sprinted back to where Paul indicated he had parked. He opened the trunk of his oversized SUV and loaded the bike in. It was only a few minutes to get back to Hazel's house, but her head was swimming with doubts the entire way. Did she feel safe with Paul in his car? Was it okay that he would know where she lived? Is this how all murder mystery shows begin?

Paul pulled over in front of her house and, to her surprise, got out in the rain to help get her bike out. He rolled it up to her porch as she unlocked the door. She turned to him and said, "Well, thanks. Have a good night."

He grabbed her wrist. "No kiss?"

"Are you fucking kidding me? Were you on a different date?" She snatched her hand away and slammed the door, locking it as fast as possible. She watched out her window until he drove away before retrieving her bike."

HAZEL WAS STARVING. Remembering the stir-fry she had abandoned for this disaster of a date, she went into the kitchen and flicked on the light. Her Mom's journal was the first thing that caught her attention.

Rosie arrived in record time after Hazel's call. She smashed the doorbell several times, causing it to ring in urgent succession. "You always tell us to come on in but hark, whose door is locked?" She sang as she entered, holding a bottle of wine and a bag of leftovers she had thrown together in her own kitchen.

"It's a long story." Hazel filled her in on all the details of her terrible day and the date with Paul. At the same time, they ate a strange assortment of whatever Rosie had brought, including cheese tortellini, lo mien, bagels, and the last part of a sheet of brownies. Rosie had a way of listening and interjecting a lighthearted poke at precisely the right moments. The day and her date had started to feel comical as she explained it and received Rosie's commentary. They were laughing at 'Paul's suffrage' and wondering if anyone paid for the food and drinks (Hazel would make sure tomorrow). When she reached the part about getting home, Rosie became quiet, her face drawn. Hazel finished, "So he drove away, and I saw the journal and decided to call. Thanks for coming over; by the way, I already feel so much better."

Rosie's eyes darkened as she replied, "I can't believe

you got in his car. You can't do that, Hazel! He was already a known asshole. He could have done anything to you!"

"I… I knew it was a mistake as soon as we closed the doors."

"Then you should have gotten out right then. You should call me! Or anyone! God, Hazel!" Tears were threatening to streak down her cheek.

Hazel considered all the trauma Rosie helped her clients process and understood the reaction. "It was a stupid decision. I'm so sorry." Rosie sniffed and wiped her eyes with her sleeve. Hazel tried to lighten the mood. "You know, I think Paul isn't the one."

A wet laugh. Rosie dipped her head in agreement. "The perfect relationship may not exist, but we can do a hell of a lot better than a non-reading, entitled, conceited fuck-boy."

Hazel smiled. "I love you."

"I love you, too."

They moved from the couch to the table in the kitchen. Hazel opened the wine and poured two glasses. It was Rosie who picked up the journal and placed it in front of them. "You ready?" Hazel nodded once, and she opened the book.

~

Jan 1st, 2015

I've never really believed in New Years Resolutions but here I am, starting a journal on day one of the new year. Let's call it a coincidence.

HAZEL WAS RELIEVED. "That was boring."

"Most of day-to-day life is, I guess."

"She was right about a few things. They did remodel the bathroom, thank goodness, and this was the year I started at FutureApp. Alex didn't propose until 2018, though."

Rosie asked, "What's Botanica?"

"Oh, they were always volunteering with the botanical garden. Its name was Botanica. It was funny because I think Mom started volunteering to learn how to take care of the plants, but she hardly ever did that. They planned and hosted community events and tried to drum up visitors instead. They were both great at the outreach stuff."

They flipped through the rest of the journal. It seemed Elle had written intermittently and that her entries spanned from 2015 through 2019 when they passed. There were clusters of dates when she was in the habit of writing and then months of nothing until she picked up again.

"Do you want to read more?" Rosie asked.

"I don't think so, not right now. I'm glad we did this one." She smiled.

"You going to keep reading it later?"

"Yeah. Seeing it now, it feels approachable. I'm looking forward to it, actually."

Rosie tipped her head to the side. "Hey, so do we hate Samantha or what?"

It took Hazel a second to get there. Her head was so full of the events of the evening and the diary that this morning felt far away. "What? Oh!" She slyly looked at her glass. When she had recounted the day's events to Rosie, she had told her about the detailed work that took hours, highlights of the meeting, the coffee, and Samantha, but she had left out the part about how distractingly handsome Sam had appeared. She took a sip of wine to think about her reply. "I mean, I don't hate her. I don't like her throwing herself at Sam, either. He's my friend; he could do better."

Rosie seemed to x-ray her. "He could do better," she agreed.

As Hazel was lying down to sleep for the night, she couldn't help but think about how Sam always wanted to know about her reading. He would definitely have had an answer about the most formidable monster combination, too. She would have to ask him tomorrow.

CHAPTER 8

USE THE TIME BETWEEN MEETINGS

"There's going to be meetings all over your calendar. They're going to change frequently. Maximize your time by being prepared to be productive between meetings or when one cancels."

Hazel Rogers

Good morning! Hey, what would be the most fearsome combo if two monsters combined? 9:49am

Sam Pierce

Uoooh, I need a couple minutes to think on this very important question! 9:49am

Hazel Rogers

Time is ticking, SPierce. 9:50am

Sam Pierce

> It's a Kraken but with Alien technology
> 9:51am

Sam Pierce

> Which is already basically happening, by the way. Octopus are using sea trash as tools so this is only a matter of time.
> 9:51am

Hazel Rogers

> Damn, that's a good answer, but it's wrong. The correct answer is CLEARLY Vampire Zombies. 9:51am

Sam Pierce

> Mmm, I see where you're going there. Vampires have a lot of practice eating people already 9:52am

Hazel Rogers

> Exactly! 9:52am

Sam Pierce

> but once they're zombies, they're slow. Plus, mine is definitely going to happen 9:53am

Hazel Rogers

LOL, they could be fast and I really hope
not. 9:53am

Hazel Rogers

Not to change the topic to something far
less pressing, but I had an idea this
morning. SyncUp? 9:54am

Sam Pierce

I've got 6 minutes, is that enough? We can
get started anyway? 9:54am

HAZEL HAD SOMEHOW MIRACULOUSLY WOKEN up refreshed and clear-headed. She'd been brushing her teeth and thinking about the free writing exercise (okay, she may have been thinking about how Sam said the word 'sexy') when she had an epiphany.

Sam entered the SyncUp she sent right away. Wasting no time, Hazel said, "Teaser trailers."

Sam chuckled. "Okay, I'm listening."

"I was thinking about our lists from yesterday. We wanted to create a sense of urgency and excitement. That's exactly what teaser trailers do before a release of a movie. What if we built teasers to release to leadership leading up to the summit?"

Sam rested his chin on his thumb with his finger across his lips. "Okay, my heart is literally racing. This is an exciting idea. Can we pull it off? We only have a few weeks to get everything ready. Is it possible for us to also prepare and issue teaser items simultaneously?"

87

Hazel let a smile slowly creep upwards. "That's the best part. We're only teasing, right? It can be Eagles and Horses! I mean, it should be clear it's about CARE and that it's coming, but it can be fun and purposefully elusive to cause discussion and questions."

Sam's look was penetrating even through the screen. "If we make this work, it's a game-changing approach. We need to ensure we spin the discussion and questions to be positive and not fearful. Foreboding is the only risk I see."

"So we try it?"

"Mock it up. I'll see you tonight."

She muted all her alerts for unimpeded focus. Ideally, she would have some ideas ready by Friday's meeting. Sam was right about needing to decide and implement quickly. Even with just teasers, there would be approvals involved. The work began familiarly by considering the audience. She wrote everything she knew about FutureApp Leadership first. The fact they were mostly a tenured group was a pro and a con. It meant they would *definitely* talk to each other, but there were bound to be cynical voices amongst the crowd.

Another point that stood out was that these were, indeed, leaders. They would benefit from the 'ease' factor of CARE in usability and teachability. Eventually, they would be leading teams of people who would use CARE. If they could prepare them for the leadership portion and holding their teams accountable, it would be advantageous. Perhaps they could have a teaser about those aspects as well.

The method of delivery would almost certainly be email. They could either write or create a video to attach, or both. Hazel favored video because it was more visual, and there was less opportunity for miscommunication if done well.

Hazel reviewed the document she had been working on. Usually, she would talk to several leaders. She could not presume to know everything about their reality and wanted to fill in the blanks. However, she was limited to those disclosed on the project, which meant she needed Samantha. She would try to schedule some time with her and the other disclosed leaders after this next meeting. Until then, there was an awkward amount of time before the meeting started, and she was at a good stopping point. She picked up her Mom's journal and flipped to the next entry.

~

Jan 17th, 2015

Botanica is almost always this amazing outlet to me. I feel good being in the gardens myself, but then seeing the people learning about the plants and enjoying themselves is a tonic that cleanses meanness from me. Not today, though.

They were throwing a "Lunch of Gratitude" for the volunteers. Lar couldn't make it today, so it was me at a table with Janet and Charles. Every time someone would be called up and recognized for their contributions, Charles had some snide remark he whispered to Janet about them. I could hear a few of them.

Then Janet was called up for having recruited the most new volunteers. When she was up front, Charles leaned across the table. He told me Janet only got that many new volunteers because she was lucky and had a whole family interested. I was *disgusted! I told him she must be a great spokesperson to have a family wanting to help and turned away.*

How can he dismiss his wife's accomplishments like that?

I told Lar when he got home, and he figured Charles must be jealous of all these people. Just like Alex. It goes to show that what seems like something little can be something big. I'm grateful Lar and I see each other's wins as something to be proud of and celebrate.

Maybe I'll try to thank Janet next time I see her.

THE SECOND MIRACLE of the day occurred when she found a time that worked for Services, Enterprise, and Operations Leaders to meet with her that same afternoon. Hazel, Trent, Trevor, and Samantha were all in a SyncUp at 4:30pm. Hazel started, "I want to thank you for your availability on such short notice. I respect your time, so I'll try to be brief, and if you think of something later, you can email me."

Samantha asked, "Are you starting without Sam? Shouldn't he be here as the Project Lead?"

"He isn't available currently, but I will catch him up with everything we cover. The reason we're here is to learn about your experiences and your leader's experiences. I had an idea we are trying to work up. A sort of series of teaser trailers for CARE to get our leadership excited, engaged, and looking forward to CARE."

Trent and Trevor seemed to be paying close attention as Hazel spoke, but Samantha had begun typing and was looking at other things. She hadn't even bothered to mute herself. Hazel continued, "Essentially, I want to know everything I can find out about your leaders. What makes them feel safe, what excites them, and what are their fears? Has FutureApp done anything that affected them in a bad or especially good way? Do you think they'd be enticed in a positive way through teaser information? Anything you can think of!"

When Hazel opened the floor to discussion, Trevor immediately offered insights into his team. He led the conversation, verifying what Hazel had expected but adding information regarding the Enterprise leaders being under pressure the past 6 months to improve efficiency. The new goals left a sour feeling because they seemed unfeasible. Trent was following along, agreeing, and inserting the Services perspective. Their ability to speak to their teams so well warmed Hazel's heart. This was the sign of good leadership she loved to see.

Samantha had not rejoined the conversation. When Hazel was coming to a natural close, she opened the floor to her again, "Samantha, do you have any insights from an Operations perspective? I know this is short notice, so there is no pressure. If not, you can always email me, or we can meet up later."

Samantha let out a lengthy sigh. "I'm sorry. I'm shocked nobody has pointed out that there isn't time for this." Hazel could have sworn she saw Trevor roll his eyes. Samantha continued, "Operations will roll with whatever punches are thrown. If they have teaser trailers, fine. If they don't, fine. Another indication that it's a waste of time."

Hazel unclenched her fists below her desk. "I hope we will have the bandwidth to launch this in the most advantageous way for everyone. Thanks for your time, everyone."

Hazel Rogers

> Does anyone know Samantha Swann from Operations? 4:55pm

Meg Malloy

> I haven't worked with her directly but I have heard some things. She isn't well-liked in Enterprise. 4:56pm

Frank Simms

> We can't be talking about the same person then. 4:56pm

Hazel Rogers

> Blonde straight hair. Looks perfect all the time. 4:56pm

Frank Simms

> That's her. I worked with her a little last year. Tangentially, though, we were both stakeholders for a project. She was a good contributor. 4:56pm

Hazel Rogers

Well, I just had the absolute worst meeting with her. She was downright hostile? Can we do a Sanity Check? I need to talk about this. 4:57pm

Meg Malloy

I'll schedule it and see what I can find out about her. 4:57pm

Meg Malloy

You okay? Hostile sounds intense… 4:57pm

Hazel Rogers

Yeah, I'm… Shocked, I guess. I mean, I was kinda put off by her for other reasons before, but she at least seemed eager to help with CARE, then when I called on her for input she told the whole meeting my idea was a "waste of time" 4:58pm

Frank Simms

She used those words? That's some shit 4:58pm

Meg Malloy

What the hell is wrong with your calendar, Frank? You literally don't have available time? 4:59pm

Frank Simms

Okay, so don't lecture me, but I was tapped for something big. I'll tell you about it when we meet, you can schedule anywhere and I'll make it work somehow. 4:59pm

Hazel Rogers

Big things shouldn't mean you're overextended! 4:59pm

Frank Simms

Tell me you aren't working late on CARE. Go ahead. I'm waiting... 5:00pm

Meg Malloy

Y'all are hilarious smh 5:00pm

Hazel Rogers

Only Wednesdays starting tonight until the project is done and I still have breathing room on my Cal! 5:00pm

Meg Malloy

I can verify that! Invite incoming 5:00pm

IT WAS the first night Hazel would return to work on CARE after hours. With that in mind, she padded to the kitchen to prepare dinner. The stir-fry prep from the previous day still looked fresh, so she began collecting ingredients for a sauce. As she got the sesame oil and chili crunch, she wondered how the meeting tonight would go. Should she tell Sam about Samantha's behavior? She'd need to be careful about it, she didn't want to start drama, and maybe Samantha was having a terrible day. Everyone has an off day sometimes. She organized her talking points in her mind. She could give an update about what she had learned from Trent and Trevor about their teams and share her vision for the actual teasers. It wasn't complete yet, but she was well on her way! He would also need time to update her on where he was, and he may even have updates from Lou to share.

At 7:20pm, Hazel logged into SyncUp, confident she would be the first in the meeting. When the room opened, however, Sam had already logged in but wasn't at his desk. She looked at his background. There was a bookshelf filled with books and some pictures spotting the shelves. It was too far away to read the spines of the books; a few covers looked familiar, but she couldn't quite place them. There was an acoustic guitar on a stand in the corner she had never seen before. Sam ran on screen. "I'm here!" He spun around in his chair and flourished his hands.

"I'm not sure it counts as beating me in the room if you weren't actually here."

"I assure you, it does. I had to open the room to enter, you know?"

"But then you left. It was more like your computer was here first. Doesn't count."

Sam harrumphed and said, "Okay, I'm going to reluctantly agree, but only because I intended to be here. I realized I had forgotten my water and went to rescue it." He shook his water bottle.

Hazel smiled and nodded. "Hydrating before meetings, you are wise." She gestured toward the guitar. "You got a new toy?"

"Ah yeah. I've always wanted to learn how to play and figured I'd start at the busiest possible time at work."

They both chuckled. Hazel asked, "How's it going so far?"

"Oh, I'm abysmal! Really, really bad... I've always considered myself okay with my hands, but even the first chords you're supposed to learn are proving me wrong."

"I'm sure you're great with your hands." Hazel blushed, hearing herself. She quickly looked away from the screen. "I mean, learning new things is always hard- difficult."

When she looked back at the camera, she was surprised to see Sam's cheeks were rosy, too, and he was grinning wickedly for a moment. She probably imagined it. He said, "Thanks for your confidence. I know you're on late, so let's dive in. I figured you could update first, then I'll share what I have, and if there's anything we can work out together, we'll allow that to naturally occur. How are comms coming? We only talked about your teaser trailer idea this morning, but if you have updates, let's hear those too."

Hazel shared that her first planned task was on schedule and inquired if Lou had left any updates. Some of her upcoming comms depended on the status of his functions. Sam pulled up the email Lou had sent to him and reviewed it. "He says meeting with the Technical Writers in person was a good idea and seems much more effective, by the way."

She hummed knowingly and pressed her lips together. "Always meet in a SyncUp if you need a commitment."

Reviewing Lou's email led to Sam giving his updates. He shared the presentation he was building with Hazel. "This is only the beginning of the deck, but my intention is to flesh it out into the full leadership training." She watched as he flipped through the slides, occasionally stopping to ask her opinion or share his.

After taking in what he had so far, she offered, "My overall takeaway is that this is missing some of the fun, especially when we break down CARE. Each part should draw the audience in."

Sam smiled a flash of white. "I agree. I also thought the teaser trailers could be recapped at the beginning. Almost like the training is a reveal?"

"I love this idea! Okay, let me tell you what I have so far." She updated him on her process and what she knew about the leadership. "I met with Trent, Trevor, and Samantha this evening to hear about their teams straight from them."

Sam sat back. His mouth opened as if he had put something together. "Hmm, okay. That's what Samantha was messaging about." She noted he hadn't called her Sam.

"What does that mean?"

"I'll tell you, but first, how'd it go in the meeting?"

Hazel glared. This changed how she wanted to approach the conversation. "I'm going to be candid. Trevor and Trent were great. They gave me a lot of information about their teams. They were easy to talk with and seemed excited about trying something new."

"And Samantha?"

She gazed out the window of her office. "Look, I don't want to be unfair. She might have been having a terrible day or something, but she didn't participate in the conversation at all. At the end of the meeting, I told her I'd like to hear from her and that she could email me if she thought of anything. The meeting was short notice, it's true. But then she said the idea was a waste of time. It felt a little vicious. I didn't know exactly how to reply, so I ended the meeting."

Sam pressed his fingertips together and leaned his lips against them. It was clear he was considering how to reply. Finally, he said, "It was inappropriate for her to share negative feedback in a public place."

"What did she say to you?" Hazel asked.

He scanned his Chatter. "I told you I'd let you know, and I will. Before I read it, I want you to know I haven't gotten to talk with her, and I disagree with what she said." He cleared his throat and began, "At 1:32, she said, 'Do you know about this meeting Hazel pulled me and the other Sr Leaders into? Her head seems in the clouds. She isn't prepared to hold this conversation.'"

"I… what?! That's… I mean, it's preposterous. Sam, I would never." She took a beat, inspecting her fingernails. "Wait, 1:32 your time? We were only 2 minutes into the meeting!"

"Really? I'm not sure how she could form an opinion so swiftly; that is surprising. Like I said, I haven't even responded yet. I wouldn't have brought it up at all, except Samantha has a bit of a reputation, and I want you to be aware."

Hazel was unsettled. Her professionalism had never been called into question before. "Are you freaking kidding me? All these reputations to keep track of. *You* have a reputation, too, you know?"

Hazel started apologizing, mortified, and at the same time, Sam began responding. They both stopped simultaneously. "Me first," Hazel said, "I'm so sorry. Nobody has ever complained about me. Ever. I'm so frustrated and annoyed, and I don't know how to make it better. And now

I'm thinking I might deserve a complaint because what I just said to you was so uncalled for."

Sam shook his head. "You can say anything to me. We're friends, not just colleagues. Samantha… likes to feel like she's involved. When I worked with her in the past, I learned consulting her, even for trivial things, made her feel included. That got me on her good side."

"I'll keep that in mind. She does seem to like you. A lot."

Sam let out a throaty chuckle. "So I have to ask. What's my reputation?"

"Ah," she considered, "Well, you have two amongst my friends. My book club friends call you my 'work husband,'" Sam's face erupted into a huge smile which crinkled the corners of his eyes, "and my work friends think you're… hard to work with." The smile slid from his face. She added quickly, "Obviously, I disagree, and I'm always telling them they're wrong."

A half quirk of his lip, but he turned serious again immediately. "You never want to get known for the wrong reasons. There have been times I was not pleasant to work with. I regret my behavior from then."

Hazel cut a questioning look at him, but he didn't extrapolate, instead saying, "You know, my friends call you my work wife."

She tried to suppress a grin by biting her lip, failed, and looked down instead.

CHAPTER 9
KNOW YOUR BANDWIDTH

"In a remote workspace, the visibility of all you do may be minimal. You must be able to know and represent your bandwidth to continue to perform at a high level."

HAZEL AND ROSIE were seated in their usual spots on Amara's couch, wine in hand, discussing *Deeper Than Snow*. They were already in stitches, but when Jessica asserted, "Undoubtedly the best way to keep warm in a blizzard is in reverse amazon." Then Lydia googled 'reverse amazon,' and her face flushed to match her pink sweater; the laughter turned into loud whoops.

The whooping was exacerbated when Omar popped his head around the corner, observed the all-out hysteria, and promptly left. Amara pointed after him and wheezed, "I can't breathe."

Once they had calmed down, the discussion shifted toward work. Lydia and Jessica quickly stole the show whenever careers came up. As a 3rd grade teacher and a tattoo artist, they had appealing stories of all kinds.

Tonight, Lydia regaled them with a recent parent-teacher conference that would have been appalling if it wasn't so funny. Jessica ranked her favorite tattoos of the week. The top spot belonged to "a witchy little ginkgo branch."

Amara turned to Hazel. "And how is the work husband?"

She straightened herself by shifting back and forth. "It turns out I'm his work wife, too!" Hazel had expected laughter or cheers at this, but the group gaped at her. "Why are you all looking at me like that?"

Rosie did laugh then and replied, "It makes things a lot more real. His friends know who you are!" Hazel had considered this. It became one of the two things ringing in her mind when Sam told her. She played out what he might have said about her and to whom. She wondered if his friends, like hers, would ask for updates like these. "That is necessarily true." She smirked.

To everyone's surprise, Lydia went for the question first. "So, are you going to date him or what?"

"Oh, I couldn't." The ladies surrounding her and Omar in the doorway hissed. Exasperated, Hazel continued, "You don't get it. I literally couldn't. Sam is…" Dreamy, kind, considerate, a great listener. "in Oregon and…."

"And people make long-distance relationships work all the time these days." Amara inserted.

"And he's my boss's boss. I don't even know what the HR implications would be! Plus, we're working together on this project. That's a big deal. The optics are bad. Like someone could get fired bad."

Rosie swirled her wine. "Let me ask you this. Would you want to date him if none of those barriers existed?"

"I, umm," Hazel really considered it. She saw vivid imagery of what it would be like. Sharing work stories, poking fun at his early morning runs, eating takeout together at the table instead of across the country, and kissing him on the cheek as she went to book club. She whispered the admission, "yes."

The faces around the room were solemn yet determined. Jessica broke the silence, "You should ask your HR person as a hypothetical." Her friends were nodding. Amara added, "People move all the time. You both work remotely already... Though, mind you, he should move here." Hazel pointed at her head to note the idea and smiled.

"Time out, everyone. You're all making it seem very easy. It's not. He probably doesn't like me romantically anyway, so let's all calm down."

Rosie replied, "But he does talk about you with his friends. That's 'necessarily true.'"

On the way to their cars, Hazel asked Rosie for a word, and they piled into Hazel's old car. Rosie asked, "What's up?"

"I've been reading Mom's journal. Most of the entries are like the one we read, sweet little snippets of her life, but there was one where she said something weird about Alex."

"Oh? What did she say?"

"She was writing about a couple she sat with at the botanical gardens as they were doing this awards-for-volunteers luncheon. I guess the guy was a prick and made all these ugly comments about the recipients. He even said something downplaying his own wife when she was recognized."

"Ouch, the world-class dick award goes to this guy."

"I know, right? But then she talked to my Dad, and he figured this guy was jealous of other's success, but then she wrote, 'Just like Alex.'"

Rosie hummed in thought. "How do you feel about that?"

"Confused! I can't stop thinking about it. Alex was supportive, and I always thought my parents liked him."

"Well, a couple things come to mind." She strummed her fingers on the dash. "First, maybe she's referring to something else, and we're misinterpreting her writing. This was a casual personal journal, not exactly refined and edited. A three-word sentence doesn't mean they didn't like him. Second, let's say she was comparing Alex to jealous guy. Oftentimes people perceive others differently. Maybe your parents saw something about Alex that wasn't on your radar." Hazel flattened her lips. Rosie continued, "I'm sorry. I know it isn't exactly a mystery solved."

"No, it's okay. I remember us all being so happy. I remember, after they died, I was so glad they had met him and approved. I mean, obviously, it ended up not mattering anyway."

"It does matter. Even though it didn't work out. I didn't realize approval was a big thing for you?"

Hazel slumped. "I never realized it was until they were gone. They weren't going to be at the wedding, but I was so grateful they already knew Alex."

Rosie smiled sadly. "It makes sense that would bring some small solace." They were quiet, watching a squirrel scurry up a tree in the porch light. "I get the feeling they trusted your judgment. I know I never met them, but hearing you talk about them... It just sounds like they did."

Hazel's head was hung, but she nodded in agreement.

"Good morning Hazel! Good afternoon Lou!" Despite it being 5am his time, Sam seemed exuberant.

Hazel waggled her finger in the air. "Listen, I am a morning person, but you're bringing this to extremes even

I can't stand for. Who hurt you?" Lou snickered, and Sam looked around as if to verify she was addressing him.

Lou said, "I hate to start the business topics first, but I could use some help." He provided his updates. Things had been looking promising to meet their timeline goals for the Expert Database edits; however, one of the Technical Writers quit. "I'm going to have to pick up the slack on the edits personally, which I think I can do, but anything you can take off me will help me achieve that."

Hazel was thoughtful. "Is there some way Sam and I can see what's ready to send for approval? We could keep them moving."

Lou shared his screen. "It's a bit manual, and I'm sorry to say the real-time updates have been unreliable, but this is the best we have." He navigated through a shared spreadsheet, explaining the columns and how they could continue to track each article's progress and submit them for approvals with the various departments."

Hazel's jaw dropped. There were hundreds of articles. "Lou, this is... enormous. I knew you had a lot to do, but wow."

"Yeah, I mean, if you think about it, ICE touches everything. It's mentioned all over. These you're seeing are only for our internal Expert Database. There's more for me to do in other internal sites, and when we hand off to the next phases, they'll be tackling the customer-facing sites."

Sam made eye contact with Hazel. "We've got you, Lou. We'll keep the approval train moving and the spreadsheet updated."

When it was Hazel's turn to update the team, she briefly caught Lou up on the idea of teaser trailers for CARE and what she had learned from Trevor and Trent. "So here's what I'm thinking. We make three email comms, each with a very short video. They can relate to ease of learning and usage as it pertains to leaders. Like this, check your mail."

Sam and Lou began focusing on their Mail, and she even heard the incoming mail sound through her speakers. She had sent a mockup of the first two ideas. The first was an animation of turning on a light with a voice and caption, 'Teaching your teams CARE is easy as turning on a light.' The second was a video of a berry pie being taken out of an oven and placed on a counter, 'Inspecting your expectations with CARE is as easy (and delicious) as pie.'

It seemed to take them a long time to react. Hazel said, "If you hate them, of course, we go in another direction. These are first drafts."

"They're perfect." Sam was beaming. "I had no idea you actually made mockups at all."

Lou's mouth was slightly open. "These look professionally done. People are definitely going to want to know more."

She looked up, feeling gratitude and relief. "I'm so glad you like them! I'm stuck on the third. I feel like we need a third to keep the talk going, looking at timing. I keep thinking of connection, how everyone will use CARE or how we'll be connected to it together, but I'm getting nowhere."

They all considered until Sam snapped his fingers. "It's gotta be from Dana!" Hazel and Lou stared at him. "Yes! Dana can do the voice. It might be a tiny bit longer. We start with the Milky Way or a spider web or something to represent the connection, and then it's Dana coming on, and she says something like, 'With CARE, FutureApp teams are more aligned than ever before.'"

Hazel stumbled over her words, "Dana... Jessup?"

Sam shook his fists in excitement. "It has to be, yes, *that* will get everyone's attention."

Hazel managed, "Well, yes, I'm sure it would, but how do we even ask her to do it?"

He considered, moving his head from side to side. "She could say no, but I'll ask her. No big deal."

Lou regained his voice, "You're friends with Dana? The CEO Dana?"

Sam seemed to grasp their reaction. He relaxed his face. "I mean, we aren't friends-friends, but I can ask her a question, for sure."

Hazel Rogers

You're on casual asking questions terms with our CEO? 9:01am

Sam Pierce

You're making it into a big deal, she's just a person. 9:01am

Hazel Rogers

I'm going to start watching my mouth around you 9:01am

Sam Pierce

Please don't 9:01am

Sam Pierce

Hey I was thinking, since we're helping Lou and we need to be extra careful since the spreadsheet is not always reliable, my number is 503-085-2067 9:02am

Hazel Rogers

Mine is 828-143-1002 9:02am

Hazel's phone buzzed. Sam started a text thread with her, "It's me."

Hazel Rogers

Haha! I programmed you in. 9:03am

Sam Pierce

Likewise! What a day to be alive :) 9:03am

Frank was late to the Sanity Check, which allowed Hazel and Meg to rib him. They sent him repeated giphy messages of phones ringing, alarms going off, and search and rescue dogs until he arrived.

"You both sure know how to remind someone of a meeting," Frank said as he entered the SyncUp. He looked a bit sickly. Sallow and bags under his eyes.

Meg took off her black and grey striped elf hat that included pointy ears on either side. "God, Frank, are you okay? You look awful."

He laughed. "Thanks, Meg. I'm fine. A good night's sleep will fix me up."

Hazel tilted her head to shoot a side-eye at him. "Don't think I haven't seen you working late every day. You were still in available even on my scheduled late day when I logged off. And look at you, you didn't even wear anything fun!" She put the giant stuffed lion she had been displaying on camera off to the side and sat in her chair.

"Yeah," Meg agreed, "What's the big project anyway?"

Frank put his hands up in a stop motion. "Not yet; we're here for Hazel."

In truth, Hazel was bursting to talk about Samantha and see what her friends had found out, but she also wanted to hear from Frank. "No, Frank, we'll talk about that after. What's the project?"

His face seemed to brighten. "Okay. It's *so good!*" He practically squealed. "I'm running a pilot to determine if emoji usage is beneficial in our Social Media support space. It's everything I love. Learning about the history of images as language and researching how images help express emotion and meaning across written communications. Plus, I have complete control over the pilot design." As he spoke, the tiredness and yellow tinge seemed to evaporate and was overtaken by radiance.

Hazel said, "I love seeing you love your work." Both she and Meg were taken in by Frank's fervor. "But Frank, can you request that some of your other responsibilities be taken off you temporarily?" He made a dismissive gesture, but she continued, "I'm serious! When I got put on CARE, Tamra reduced my load and even cut back our 1x1s to give me more time."

Frank said with severity, "Holly isn't like Tamra. Wish she was, but it's not like that over here." He shrugged, "I'll get to present my findings and recommendation at the summit."

Meg's mouth fell open into an O. "This *is* a big project! Congratulations."

Frank quickly amended, "Just in one of the workshop rooms, but still!"

After thoroughly celebrating Frank and urging him to at least try not to overwork himself, it was Hazel's turn to share. Now that she had her friends in a SyncUp, she gave them the complete recap of what occurred in the meeting. She was relieved they didn't think she was reading too much into the situation.

Meg waited until Hazel finished, then immediately jumped in, "Alright, here's what I found. She plays favorites, but it's like a crap shoot. Nobody seemed to know *why* she likes some people and apparently loathes others. Still, they all agreed about her behavior toward those groups. If you're on her good side, she will lift you up, praise you endlessly, and advance your career. If you're on her bad side, she will actively make your life hell."

Hazel considered this information. "That would explain why Frank seemed to have a good experience with her. Sam mentioned she likes to feel included, too. I'm going to try to ask for her input more proactively if I can." She started to speak again, hesitated, but decided to plunge on, "There's something else. It's purely speculation, and at the risk of being gossipy, so please don't repeat any of this." She sighed. "Exclusively facts first. She has stayed after our meetings and urgently requested to meet with Sam just to tell him good job. Now my perception. She seems disappointed when Lou and I are also in the room, but it doesn't stop her from being flirtatious with Sam."

Frank buzzed his lips. "I don't have much for that."

Meg tapped her pen against the desk. "Could she be jealous of your relationship with him?"

Hazel deflected the question, "Isn't it strange she would overtly come on to him in the first place? I've never seen anything like it. It's like, harassment adjacent."

Meg lifted a brow. "I haven't either, but if it's not making Sam uncomfortable, then it's probably fine, but a bit uncouth to do around you and Lou."

Hazel chose her words carefully, "Would that even be allowed? If they were into each other, I mean, could they be together?"

Frank said, "I think they'd be fine. However, there are rules. I know some of them because our department is small, and we had an incident." He rolled his eyes. "Since they're in different departments, I think it'd be okay."

Since Sam and Hazel were both in Communications, they could never, then. She had never wanted to transfer to Training more.

CHAPTER 10

ESTABLISH HOURS OF OPERATION

"There are times in your career where long hours will happen. Holiday seasons, launches, and promotions; you'll spend more time at work during these events. Those are the high tides- make sure you're in low tide during normal run-the-business times."

∽

April 20th, 2015

I sometimes wonder if I'm too risk averse. What would life be like if we had left Illinois and lived somewhere else? If I had gone to school for photography? If I had applied to all the jobs I had ever wondered about without regard for being highly enough qualified?

~

HAZEL CHECKED HER PHONE AGAIN, a kernel of self-loathing for it festering in her stomach. It was the weekend. Sam wasn't going to work over the weekend, and he might not message her anything about it even if he did.

She chucked her book on the nightstand and rolled across the bed, trying not to crave his conversation or think about how his voice rumbled. She sat bolt upright. He could have a girlfriend! It was none of her business. He wouldn't necessarily say anything about dating someone. She racked her brain. They had talked about her dating life, but that had been a long time ago. He had never mentioned anything. They talked about everything else, though. A warm feeling circled up her as she recalled teaching him how to propagate plants (he was amazed and sad about all the ones he had purchased), the time he went to visit his Dad and surprised him with birthday donuts (his favorite donut was jelly, gross), and the time he had volunteered to work a 10k instead of running and how he lit up reminiscing about handing out water cups (he had lost his voice from cheering the runners on by the end).

Her phone buzzed beside her, and she knocked it off

the bed in her rush to flip it over. Cursing, she hung off the side to collect it. It was only an email.

She should message him! But how? The truth would not work. She imagined sending, "Hey, I know I'm your low-level colleague, but I can't stop thinking about you. What's up today?" Plus, he had only given her his number for the Lou thing. Maybe? It seemed a little sketchy, to be honest. Why wouldn't they use Chatter like normal?

Hazel pulled on a hoodie and headed outside, turning right toward the historic district. She hoped the maples, which had reached their peak coloration, and the slight chill in the air would loosen the tightly wound feeling in her center. She closed her eyes as she walked the sidewalk, listening to the sound of the leaves crunching beneath her sneakers, feeling the temperature on the exposed skin of her hands and face. She came to the bottom of a hill where the road curved to the left and ascended. Her favorite tree, which she had named Breezy, was on the other side of the hill. Breezy was massive and, for the next few weeks, would be so violently colored she would appear as if she was on fire.

Hazel was in jeans. She had not planned to run but felt compelled to move her body. She grabbed the waistband of her jeans to prevent them from falling down and ran up the hill. Is this how Sam felt when he ran? Probably not; she was already wheezing and wondering why she had decided to do this. She kept going; she was a quarter way up the hill. Halfway up. Her thighs burned as she crested the apex. She saw the great tree lying below, flame branches licking the sky. She ran down the hill- thankfully easier than uphill. She stopped beneath Breezy, inexplicably laughing, rasping to regain her breath.

The bands that had been constricting her loosened. She took the phone from her hoodie and typed to Sam.

Hazel

> Sorry to message you on the weekend, I was thinking about Lou's situation and I realized we didn't say when we would start working the shared sheet? I want to be available to help if you try to start early. 11:15am

She pressed send and started walking back home, but her phone buzzed immediately.

SPierce

> I'm glad you messaged, I was thinking the same thing. Let's start Monday. 11:15am

She frowned at the phone. This was fine. Professional.

SPierce

> What are you up to today? 11:16am

Hazel beamed.

They continued to chat frequently throughout the weekend. Hazel found it easy conversations, and though there were breaks when he was practicing guitar or when she was cycling to the store, it was also natural to pick up where they left off.

Hazel reached for a bundle of cilantro when she felt another buzz in her pocket. She retracted her arm to fetch it and again found herself smiling and tapping away at the keyboard.

SPierce

Thanksgiving is coming up. What are your plans like? 10:02am

Hazel

Undetermined. If Rosie and Nick are in town I'd spend it with them. Sometimes they go visit family. What's yours like? 10:02am

SPierce

I'll go to my Dad's. He and my stepmom do the whole traditional turkey thing. 10:03am

Hazel

That's nioo :) and you bring the jelly donuts? 10:03am

SPierce

HAH to Thanksgiving? No, Summer would
murder me. My jobs are to bring the pie,
which I make the day before, and then I go
over early to help them with sides. Kale
salad, sweet potato rings, cranberry sauce
sort of things 10:03am

SPierce

One year I convinced them to let me make
elote. It was perfect. They hated it lol
10:04am

Hazel

You're making me so hungry! I didn't know
you cooked! 10:04am

Hazel

How could anyone hate elote? It's literally
one of my favorite grilled things ever.
10:04am

SPierce

Ah, they don't appreciate heat. I rib them
for it all the time ;) 10:05am

> My parents were adventurous eaters. The first Thanksgiving I took on pescetarianism was a proper disaster. My Mom tried to surprise me by making this meatloaf dish, but it was salmon, and she shaped it like a turkey, which didn't work out at all. It was so disgusting but sooo funny. 10:06am

"Excuse me!" Hazel was nudged by a customer trying to get to the parsley she was blocking.

"Oh, sorry." She moved out of the way.

"Hazel!" Amara, with Omar trailing behind, was hustling to her from across the store, arm waving in the air. "Fancy some shopping buddies?" She asked as she pulled her cart up beside Hazel.

The three of them continued together, pausing to get items off the shelves as they went. Amara and Omar were infectious. They didn't make shopping feel like a mundane task at all. Omar bopped along to the songs, sometimes doing glides down the aisles. Amara used countless boxes and bottles as microphones, shaking her head and lip-syncing. They both seemed to have an ongoing sort of basketball game where they would throw soft items into their basket from a distance. Omar made a particularly spectacular shot with a bag of mini marshmallows, earning him a squeal and a smooch on the cheek. As they approached the registers, Hazel said, "I'm so glad we ran into each other. I can't remember the last time I had so much fun while shopping!"

"Most of life is mundane if you let it be. Omar taught me that mundane is just one option." Her face glowed as she looked at him. She winked. "That's why I married him."

SHE WAS UNPACKING her groceries when she noticed several messages were awaiting her.

SPierce

> Sounds… awful. But how cool that she tried! 10:06am

SPierce

> What do you usually make for Thanksgiving as a pescatarian? 10:06am

SPierce

> You should figure out your plans, Hazelberry. It's important to have things to look forward to- besides the summit. We'll get to meet in person! 10:11am

OH! How had she never thought about this before? This would be Hazel's first time going to the annual summit. The logistics of it had not occurred to her. She would see many of her colleagues (Sam, most notably) in person for the first time. God, and they would see her! What would she wear? Pajama bottoms surely would be frowned upon.

Hazel

1. It wasn't the only disastrous dish she concocted, though most things turned out great. 2. OMG there are so many great recipes for Thanksgiving! Quinoa stuffed Acorn Squash, Roasted Butternut, Pomegranate and Wild Rice Stuffing, Balsamic Roasted Brussels Sprouts, and Roasted Carrots over Farro with Creme Fraiche! 11:22am

SPierce

Who is making who hungry now? 11:22am

Hazel

3. Even if Rosie is away, I always make something delicious, one of my other friends will adopt me, and the next day I put up a little Christmas tree 11:23am

SPierce

Wasting no time to bring in Christmas season, eh? 11:23am

Hazel

Hey, Thanksgiving is officially done! 11:23am

SPierce

I love it haha! 11.24am

. . .

Hazel and Sam started working through Lou's Expert Database approvals on Monday. Despite the many steps necessary, even for a single change, they immediately fell into a rhythm. Hazel progressed any pending action first thing when she arrived, then Sam would update everything when he came in. They would both check midday, then close out the day with Hazel updating before she left and Sam doing the same before he did. All the while keeping in touch with each other in Chatter.

Hazel had been right about her suspicions that Chatter would be the place for it. Even so, she was grateful they had exchanged phone numbers because their texts had also not slowed. It had become a bright spot in her day every time she heard the phone buzz, and she found it was Sam.

Thursday morning, Sam messaged Hazel and Lou in Chatter, "I know it's not our meeting day, but I have news. If you can SyncUp come now." Hazel had been working on the How-To article, but she was finding it hard to dedicate enough time to it with CARE at the forefront. She had never worked slower on anything, and it was always a grind to get started on it. She knew her priorities, however, and wouldn't miss a chance to see Sam, so she jumped into the SyncUp.

"Good morning!" Sam greeted her when she entered. She could tell the news must be good because his energy vibrated with anticipation. He was wearing a well-fitted hunter-green polo, and his facial hair was longer than she had seen before. It looked slightly wilder and suited him, she thought. "It looks like Lou can make it in, but he needs 5 minutes. Want to guess the three words I'm going to share with you?"

How many times had she heard "the three words"

pertaining to I love you? In every romance she had ever read or watched, that's how many. "Oh, I don't know, Kraken Aliens Found?"

His eyes glittered every time he laughed as if that deep sound was internally connected to them somehow. "Not *yet*, I'm afraid."

SyncUp made its tinkling chime as Lou entered. "What'd I miss? Something funny?"

They both shook their heads, and Hazel said, "Just a silly joke."

Sam looked as if he would burst with excitement and said, "I have three words for both of you," He paused dramatically, tilting his head to the side, "Dana said yes." The impact was instantaneous, with both Hazel and Lou's jaws dropping. Sam chuckled and said, "You're such a good audience!"

"I didn't even know you had asked her," Hazel said, stunned.

Sam replied, "Oh, I'm sorry about that. Actually, I asked her right away. Immediately after our meeting, I figured it would be a given."

Lou nodded. "We should have known."

Sam went on, "There is a sort of catch. She wants to record her part tomorrow." Lou let out a long whistle, shaking his head.

Hazel felt her jaw drop again. "Tomorrow, tomorrow? When tomorrow? We aren't ready at all!"

"I know, but I can stay on tonight and work if you can, we can knock it out in no time." Sam soothed.

Hazel steadied herself, "I'll tell Rosie to let the club know I have to skip tonight. It's worth it. Dana, wow."

WHEN HAZEL CALLED ROSIE, she was met with affectionate school-yard teasing, "Oh... So you're abandoning us already for your boyfriend? I'll be sure to tell everyone." Then, "I'm kidding. Of course, I'm so excited the fucking CEO is supporting your idea! That's huge! Remember me when you've made it, okay?" Her reaction drove home that this *was* an accomplishment.

Eating was not an option. Hazel's stomach churned with acid, nerves, and determination; there was no room for food. She sat at the dinner table with a pen and notebook and jotted down idea after idea, most non-starters, but she prayed some of them could spark something. She had filled out two pages when the time came to meet back up with Sam.

She logged in only a minute early and was surprised to find she still beat Sam. Only by seconds, he joined almost immediately after. He didn't know that, though. "Slow today, SPierce. Losing your touch."

"You have a point. I lose track of time when I'm practicing guitar. Look at this!" He raised his fingers close to the camera. "Calluses!"

"Does that mean you're a real guitarist now?"

He nodded. "I think so."

"I should have done something more creative also. I was trying to list out ideas." She held up the notebook, pages flipping.

"Look at you, using real paper!"

She chuckled. "Yeah, when it's important, I crave tangible notes."

"What did you come up with?"

"Honestly? Pages of nothing, possibly." She inspected her writing. "You'd mentioned space or a spider web, I put those on here, and I think they work. Others that seemed okay were social networking, highways, and family trees?"

Sam rested his head on his hands in concentration. "We're going for connection as the theme of this one. I like the idea of family because, naturally, we want employees to feel like a family. I like the imagery of highways because it's so visual."

They tried to tie them together, but none of their ideas felt right. They both knew it. After an hour of going in circles, Hazel suggested, "What if we start with what we want her to say? What's the most compelling thing to hear from Dana?"

Sam leaned back in his chair. His broad shoulders took up the length of the screen. Did she see an outline of a pec? Hazel chewed her lip, distracted.

He asked, "What are you thinking?"

"Hmm?"

"You look deep in thought. Any ideas about Dana's script?"

Hazel was thinking about how his calluses would feel on her thighs while Sam held her against a wall. She shook her head to refocus. "Is it too cheesy if she talks about family? What about, 'Connection is important in the FutureApp family, and CARE will... something?"

Sam considered with a one-sided frown, "What if it's a play on CARE like we CARE about you as individuals?"

Hazel slapped her desk. "I've got it! The imagery! We start in the galaxy and zoom into Earth. We zoom all the way into California, to San Fransisco, to the campus, and into Dana's office. She says something amazing, then we zoom out to a globe and show where FutureApp employees live on the map. It would show our interconnection via location. See what I mean?"

"Yes! Yes, I'm with you! We can use the directory for employee locations. It'll have to be mostly anonymous, but maybe we can get the stakeholders to sign a waiver to use their image to make it more personable."

"Brilliant, okay, and Dana can say...." Hazel gestured to fill in the blank.

Sam filled it in, " As we zoom in, she says, 'FutureApp

cares about our place in the universe. We care about our world. Our cities. We take pride in our campus.' Then we zoom out and start pinpointing our locations, and she says, 'I'm Dana Jessup, CEO of FutureApp, and I'm here to tell you I care about you. Our people define who we are. Enable us to make a difference in every area we inhabit. CARE will make us stronger and more impactful in our communities and world.'"

Hazel had leaned forward toward the camera, her mouth slack and eyes wide, staring at Sam. "We totally just cracked this thing open, didn't we? That was great!"

Hazel started working on the visuals using their internal stock images and royalty-free clips they could get approved. Sam figured out a way to export employee locations from their directory and started organizing them by region. They worked in near silence for another hour until they began combining efforts. It was as if they had been making videos together for years. They supported each other's efforts seamlessly, making editing recommendations as they went. They worked late into the night but created something they were proud of, something they would present to Dana so her script would make sense.

As they watched it play one final time, Sam whistled, "I can't believe we did that."

Hazel was stunned, too. "I've never done anything like this in a single night."

Sam smiled so genuinely that Hazel felt it in her chest. "We make a great team." He paused. "Sorry you had to skip book club. Want to lay it on me?" The right side of his mouth curled up.

"Ah… well…" Hazel flushed. "We're nearing the end of *Deeper Than Snow* now, and I'm afraid we're to the real smutty part."

Sam tipped his head back in laughter. "Well, in that case, I really need to know!"

Hazel provided the back story, explaining how Snow was both the surname of the ex of the main character, Darla, and a description of the weather. "At this point, Darla is snowed in with three dudes, and they're all love interests. One of them is older and has the security factor, and one is younger and has the hot guy thing going, but he's also a golden retriever. One is her age but is kind of a bad boy."

"Mmhmm, and which one will she end up with?" Sam asked.

"Ohhh, well, she's already done bad boy and daddy, so I'm thinking this is a reverse harem situation."

"I see," Sam pressed his lips together, suppressing a smile, "and if you were Darla, what would you do?"

"Psht. The characters in this book have different attractive traits that make them interesting. If I was Darla, I'd be pissed I couldn't find a singular man with all the qualities I appreciated."

"A fine answer, but also, you're cheating. What would it be if you had to choose between security, golden retriever, or bad boy?"

Hazel challenged him, "You have to answer too, then. On three. One, two…"

"Golden retriever," rang out in unison, followed by a chorus of laughter.

Hazel didn't think before she blurted, "Are you seeing anyone?"

Sam's eyebrows raised, and Hazel's heart stood still. Why did she ask that?! "Uh, no. I haven't dated anyone in a long time. What about you? Still out there on DateFinder?"

She could not stop her face as it washed with relief. "Oh, no, not recently. The last one I had was the worst on record." She filled him in on Paul's Suffrage, leaving him aghast. "And don't tell me I was stupid to get in his car, I already know, and Rosie about killed me."

"I gotta meet Rosie one day. I have a feeling we'd get along."

"You would," Hazel yawned, "too bad you're so far away."

Sam focused on something beyond the screen, but he snapped back his attention, "It's so late for you- go to bed!"

CHAPTER 11

ERGONOMICS

"You're going to be typing. A lot. Not only will you be typing what you normally would on the job, but chat and emails are primary modes of communication when working from home. Take care of your body by creating an ergonomically aligned workspace."

TAMRA WAS UPDATING Hazel about what the rest of the team was up to and reminding her to fill in her annual performance review self-assessment before next Friday. Hazel was patiently awaiting the moment the floor would be open to her so she could share all the news about the teaser trailers. "That's it for our team. What do you have for me?"

Hazel's brows shot up, "A lot. First, let me start with I'm meeting Dana later today to record her for a teaser trailer regarding CARE."

Tamra raised her hands as if motioning for her to stop. "Way to sit on that news! You're meeting with Dana?!"

Hazel nodded excitedly. "It's been speedy, to say the least. We asked if she would help us, and she agreed yesterday but then said she needed to record today! You can imagine the scrambling. Sam and I worked laaaate to get ready. I can't show it to you before release, but I am so stoked for you to see these!"

"I'm sure they're incredible. Teaser trailers. Can you tell me more about the concept?"

Hazel spent the rest of her time explaining the idea and what goals they sought to accomplish through them. Tamra's response was promising. Even without knowing the details, she was eager for more.

As they were wrapping up, Tamra shot her a wink and wished her good luck with Dana. "I think you'll be surprised at how down to earth she is when it's not a large formal meeting she's presenting."

Hazel tore through the clothes in her closet, searching for the right thing to wear to a meeting with your CEO, wherein they were participating in your crazy idea. What that was, she didn't exactly know. After minutes of deliberation (much more time than she usually spent deciding what to wear), she put on a navy blue dress with a lacy detailed sleeve and neckline. She did her makeup and clipped back her hair. She stood back to admire herself in the mirror and told her reflection, "You've got this!"

She and Sam entered the SyncUp 15 minutes before the start of the meeting to run through everything and ensure their screen shares and sound were working flawlessly. Sam's face transformed in the final moments before Dana entered the room. He had been joking with Hazel, but now the intensity of his stare hardened. "Listen. This is a slam dunk. You take the credit that is due to you."

"Why would I...." Hazel started.

"Don't give me more than I deserve. I mean it."

SyncUp performed its tinkling announcement, and

Dana joined them. Sam resumed his usual business look. Calm and confident. Gentle but commanding. How did he do it? "Dana, welcome in! Thanks for your time today. Having a good one so far?"

Dana's smile was generous and warm. "Yes indeed, and it's so good to see you again, Sam." She focused on Hazel, "And nice to meet you one-on-one, Hazel. Sam has said wonderful things about you."

Hazel returned the smile and tried to match Dana's demeanor. "Thank you. I'm flattered. It's nice to meet you as well. Sam and I have prepared the teaser trailer you'll appear in, except for the part we'll record today. We would like to start by showing you if that's okay?"

Hazel shared her screen and stepped through the trailer, explaining where Dana's voiceover would be and how they would zoom into a video of her. At the conclusion, Dana said, "It's rare that I see such high-quality work on such short notice. I didn't expect there to be anything created before our meeting." Hazel rapped her knuckles on the bottom of her desk in excitement. Dana went on, "I do have one concern before we record my part. At the end where we're zooming out and showing the locations of FutureApp employees on the interconnected web. The anonymous markers are no problem, but have the people you're using an image of signed their image rights waiver for this project?"

Sam spoke up, "Not yet. Those are all our stakeholders for this project, and we plan on asking them to sign later today. Of course, we'll remove their photos if they choose not to participate."

Dana's wide smile lit her face again. "I knew you'd be all over it. You know, you haven't asked me to sign one. Send a waiver to me, and you can use my photo, too."

Hazel breathed, "Wow, thank you so much. We will!"

They helped Dana set up her sound to maximize clarity and captured the recording with only three takes.

Sam said, "We'll send you the completed video before anyone else so you can see it. And you should know the idea for teaser trailers was all Hazel. She did almost all of the visuals too."

Dana replied, "This is impressive work, and you've made my part painless- enjoyable! And Hazel," Hazel focused on Dana, "People tend to think I'm too busy to reach out to. I'm not too busy. My door is open to you any time."

Dana dropped from the SyncUp, and Sam and Hazel stared at each in silence for a moment. Sam broke it first, "Well?"

"Well, that went better than I could have possibly even imagined, and now I don't know what to do with all the energy in my body." She laughed. "Plus, *when* did you talk to Dana about *me*?"

His dimple made an appearance. "Oh, before. Don't worry about that." She gave him an incredulous look. His gaze in return was something like sad admiration. She wondered why he would be sad after such a success.

"Everything okay?"

"Better than." The hint of melancholy gone. Maybe she had imagined it. "I'll email the waivers if you want to incorporate Dana's footage."

"You know me too well. I already started." Hazel admitted.

By the end of the day, they had collected enough waivers, had sent the full-length trailer to Dana and gotten her blessing, and had sent it to HR for approval. This was the hairy part. If they wanted to stick to their ideal schedule, they would need to start issuing the teasers by the end of next week. Hazel's most detested part of working in Communications was the hemming and hawing about approval for word choice. In her experiences, it had sometimes taken months to agree on how to present a basic idea. It would make their timeline much tighter if they had to rework anything. She felt queasy thinking about it, so she closed the laptop lid, gathered her Mom's journal, and picked up her comfort read, *A Clan of Fog and Destiny.*

~

June 3, 2015

Frustrated with Lar doesn't even begin to cover it today! I swear he watched me clean everything and do all the laundry without even considering that he might have helped. Then he went to the store to pick up asparagus, and I asked him to bring home half and half, and he forgot. Then when I checked the mail, we had an outlandish charge on our credit card. I have no idea what it could even be.

I went to confront him about the card, and when I got to the kitchen he poured me a glass of wine, had dinner set, and had a candle lit on the table. He stopped me dead in my tracks, and the look on his face, like he had never seen anything so beautiful. All of it just melted away. He reminded me of what was important.

⁓

HAZEL WAS clean and wrapped in her blankets in bed, reading *A Clan of Fog and Destiny* for the fifth time. Her brain was doing funny things against her will. Whenever the love interests (impossibly muscled, beautiful, and tattooed Fae) were worshiping each other, she pictured them looking like her and what she imagined Sam must look like. She was nearly asleep, trying to banish the thought of Sam's strong arms lifting her onto the bed as if she weighed nothing. The motion he made, taking off his shirt to reveal lean, cut abs, and patches of dark curly hair at his chest and beneath his naval, leading down.

Her fingers started to swirl around her clit over her panties. She felt a sense of unease about fantasizing about Sam like this, but she couldn't stop. It had been so long, too. She nudged her panties aside and writhed at the touch of her index and middle fingers, slowly exploring her sex.

She closed her eyes to a scene playing like a movie. Sam's pants dropped to the floor, joining his shirt. She let her vision follow the trail of hair downward, and she gasped at the length of him. He playfully pounced over her on the bed and wrapped her in his arms, rolling them onto their side. She could feel his hands caressing her shoulders and arms. They both reached down, exploring each other. Stroking and dipping.

Her hand was moving faster and harder, and she felt wetness on her fingers. She was soaked.

In her mind, Sam was back on top of her, thrusting into her. He filled her completely. Perfectly. She wrapped her legs around his back. He leaned in to kiss her, and his tongue parted her lips. He nibbled her lower lip, then moved down her neck, her shoulder. Every part of him was touching every part of her.

Hazel arched and shuddered, release tingling through her body in waves.

Hazel

Kind sir, do you have any tattoos? 10:30am

SPierce

Three, but you'll have to guess where. 10:30am

Hazel

Easy. Jelly donut on your chest. Mom Heart on a tricep. Some sort of Hermes winged foot on your ankle. 10:31am

SPierce

Wow. Ummm, I hope you think I have better tastes than that hahaha! How about you? 10:31am

133

Hazel

I have one. 10:31am

Hazel

but wait, you're not going to tell me?
10:32am

SPierce

Perhaps we can trade information?
10:32am

Hazel

A rather unequal trade, but you can owe me
;) 10:32am

SPierce

Sounds dangerous… but okay. I have owls
on both calves, one day and one night, and
an 8-bit heart gauge under a collarbone,
kinda like Legend of Zelda if you ever
played that. 10:33am

Hazel

"If I ever played that." Are you kidding?
Hours! Hours! When Ocarina of Time came
out it was all I played for a year. Aiming the
arrow while riding that freaking horse was.
the. worst. 10:33am

SPierce

Wow okay, how long did the water temple
take you? 10:33am

Hazel

Okay, so I know people think it's the
hardest of all time, and it was hard, but the
Spirit Temple though! 10:34am

SPierce

I had no idea I was working with a fellow
nerd this whole time. I mean, I did know. I
just didn't know it also included gaming.
10:34am

Hazel

Hah! Well, I don't play as often anymore,
but such nostalgia, and I do pick up the
Paper Mario and Yoshi titles. 10:35am

SPierce

This is amazing. But I fear we've skipped
something… Trade right? 10:35am

Hazel

Ah yes. Okay, I've always been curious
about tattoos, and then when I became
friends with Jessica (she is quite an
accomplished tattoo artist), it made sense
to have her give me one 10:36am

WHEN HAZEL LOGGED in Monday and checked her email, the least likely thing to have happened had occurred. She read and re-read the email, dumbfounded.

"Did you see the email?" She had joined the SyncUp for the CARE team meeting. Sam was already there, but she didn't pause to let him gloat.

His lips curled knowingly. "I did, of course. You're surprised?"

"Of course I'm surprised! Are you kidding?! This stuff takes weeks if you're lucky. We sent the trailers off Friday, and it's Monday morning now. When did they even have time to approve it?!"

Sam sat back and strummed his fingers on his desk. He started to say something but was interrupted by Lou joining. "Dang, I thought I might beat one of you in today. Why are you both always early?"

Hazel and Sam laughed. Sam replied, "It's a bit of a game we've been playing for years now. I can't remember exactly how it started." Hazel wondered if he was being truthful about not remembering. The intensity of his face seemed to tell her he wasn't.

Lou continued, "I saw the approvals come in for your teaser trailers. Congrats!"

Hazel jumped at the renewed topic, "Yes, we were just talking about that, actually. What were you going to say, Sam?"

"That when Dana is an active participant in something, it nearly implies approval. I'm sure the rubber stamping began as soon as they saw her in the video."

Hazel pushed off her desk and made her chair spin 360 degrees. "That's all I have to say about that."

The meeting continued with everyone sharing status updates and actively working through Lou's approval sheet together. Sam shared his screen to cover the most recent edition of his proposed Leadership Training. He said, "Now the trailers are officially approved, I'm going to work them in up front. I'm hoping it will almost be like a recap of the excitement and wonder they cause leading into the culmination of the training. Hazel, you should present that part."

"I can do that. When are you presenting to stake-holders?"

The look on his face told her she had missed some-thing, "We'll start the run-throughs on it at the next Stake-holder Meeting, but I mean at the summit."

Her vision tunneled. "At the summit?"

"Yes. At the summit. These are your babies. You should take that part. Lou, you should also be available for recognition, and you can direct everyone to resources at the end." Lou simply nodded his agreement.

Hazel needed to digest this. She was comfortable deliv-ering any update in a remote conference. Still, She had never physically stood on a stage in front of all the leaders plus many more employees. The prospect was harrowing, but at the same time, this was at least Training adjacent. It was *part of* the Leadership Training. If she could present this well, package the idea for teasers, and complete her How-To all with a nod to Training, it amounted to a lot she could speak to. A lot of potential involvement with them.

Sam sensed her hesitation. "I can see your brain work-ing. I'll help you practice, don't worry."

CHAPTER 12

HAVE A DEDICATED WORKSPACE

"Remote workers struggle with taking work home or feeling like they are always at work. It can help to have a dedicated workspace. Entering that area becomes going into the office, and leaving it becomes going home."

HAZEL WAS TRYING to schedule a meeting with Samantha. Applying Sam's advice, she aimed to bring Samantha in on the trailer approvals. She planned to ask if Samantha thought it would be better to send the first email on Tuesday or Wednesday. In truth, Hazel wasn't attached to a particular day out of the two. The issue was that Samantha kept declining her invitations. Hazel had been sure to check Samantha's availability and had chosen a slot that seemed open on her Calendar three times now. Yet, each time Samantha would decline the event without commentary.

Hazel Rogers

Whelp, I'm trying to schedule time with Samantha to ask her opinion about something, and she can only decline all my invites. I tried. I'm done. 9:38am

Meg Malloy

Yuck! The worst! You could always wait until she's in Available on Chatter and ask for an impromptu? 9:38am

Meg Malloy

Or you could do the whole "I'm having trouble finding time on your Calendar, but I will make time to meet with you. Could you find some time that works for us?" Kinda put the ball in her court 9:39am

Hazel Rogers

I don't know, it's not like I WANT to meet with her either. But it would be nice to have a good working relationship. I've never been in this situation before. 9:39am

Hazel Rogers

She can't be bothered to even recommend a time that works after three invitations. It's a clear message in itself honestly 9:40am

139

Meg Malloy

You're right. Maybe forcing it isn't the best solution. It's a tricky one. @Frank Simms, you got anything? 9:40am

Frank Simms

Catching up, one moment. 9:43am

Frank Simms

Geez what a garbage move from her Hazel. Could her Cal be broken? I've had weird issues before. It's rare, but we gotta assume positive intent right? 9:45am

Hazel Rogers

You know what, that's actually pretty helpful! 9:46am

Frank Simms

It is? I mean… glad to be of service… 9:48am

Meg Malloy

LOL 9:48am

yes and lol. I think I'll combine approaches, maybe reach out and say I'm having some trouble getting on her Cal and I've had Calendar issues in the past so I thought I'd reach out. Takes any would-be blame off her 9:48am

Samantha didn't reply until the end of the day. She had typed back, "I'm swamped. Will this take long?"

Hazel replied, "It shouldn't. I just wanted to get your input on a date. No biggie if you're too busy, we've all been there. If you're free now I can SyncUp?"

There was a 10-minute pause, then, "OK."

When Samantha joined the SyncUp, Hazel started, "Thanks for giving me some of your time when you're busy. I'll jump right in." Samantha gave a curt nod, and Hazel continued. "I know you weren't totally convinced about the teaser trailer idea, but we were able to get them worked up and approved. I really think you and your teams will enjoy them. We are going to start sending the series next week. I wanted to ask your expertise on if we should deploy Tuesday or Wednesday."

Samantha was scowling, but her lips pursed in satisfaction as she began to reply, "Have you considered Friday instead? The sooner, the better, right? You've already gotten the approvals."

Hazel had not anticipated this. "I see your point. In Communications, we make it a practice not to send emails on Friday or Monday. Both days are more likely to get lost as people try to leave for the weekend or catch up for the new week, and they're the most commonly used days for vacation." If looks could kill, Hazel felt confident she would be a bloody stump by now. Since Samantha had become deathly quiet, she continued, "We were thinking Tuesday or Wednesday because they're earlier in the week to create that buzz about them."

Samantha finally retorted with slow, silky venom, "You asked for my advice, and I gave it to you. Take it or leave it."

Hazel's stomach dropped. "Listen, if I did anything to offend you ever, it wasn't intentional." She considered her following words carefully. "I want us to work together well. Is there anything I can do to make amends?"

Another stretch of silence followed. Then, "I don't know you. How could I have possibly been offended by you?"

Hazel began to reply but was interrupted by Samantha adding, "Since we're being real, you're nobody."

"What?" Hazel asked.

"Perhaps you're not used to getting constructive feedback. I shared my views about these trailers, and you pursued them anyway. I gave you my opinion for the launch date, and you don't like it."

"Only because, as I explained, from the Communi…."

"You're impertinent. Interrupting."

Hazel's fingernails were digging into her thighs. She felt reckless. Pushed to her limit. "Would you speak to me like this if Sam were here?"

Samantha smirked. "Be careful with that one. I've given you my answer." And dropped from the SyncUp.

It was another disastrous encounter with Samantha. Hazel replayed it over and over but couldn't think of much she could have done differently. She had an inkling Samantha wanted her to fail. Friday and Monday emails were a standard practice to avoid even outside of Communications, but why would she want that? And what did she mean about being careful with Sam? For the first time in her career, she half-wished FutureApp recorded their meetings by default. Yet, apart from being rude, Samantha hadn't threatened her or harassed her or anything. She wasn't sure if this qualified as a hostile work environment. Maybe? The easiest path forward seemed to be avoiding Samantha. She comforted herself by thinking she didn't have to work with Samantha directly anymore, and CARE would be over in a few weeks anyway.

She messaged Rosie to ask if she wanted to meet at Chai Chai and got a time and a smiley face in response. "See you there."

Evenings at Chai Chai were a different vibe than mornings. When they opened the door to enter, the sound of drumming music and jingling hip scarves spilled into the street. There were customers at every seat; some stood, enjoying the belly dancers' performances. They wended their way through the crowd to the semi-private rooms. They were so busy that additional poufs and tables had been added to the rooms. There was one spot remaining. The couple sharing the room squeezed closer to their table to let Hazel and Rosie pass.

Hazel opened her text message thread with Sam and wordlessly handed it to Rosie. She shot a curious look at her but accepted the phone. Rosie started scrolling, her eyes wide, then she punched Hazel in the shoulder. "Hey! That hurt!"

"I should do it again! I can't believe you didn't tell me there was this much flirting, and you're texting now!" Rosie's voice got progressively higher as she spoke.

Hazel glanced at her feet. "It is flirting, isn't it?"

Rosie smiled at her friend. "It's the definition of flirting. And it's both ways." She scrolled up slightly and gestured at a message from Sam. "Look here, you say you prefer sweet to savory breakfasts, and he replies that makes sense. Can I add the fact you're chatting about breakfast preferences alone is already encouraging!"

Hazel hesitated. "Well, we were talking about the summit and the breakfasts they serve there, so...."

Rosie's hair swayed as she shook her head and grabbed Hazel's hand. "No. Enough with the wild justifications. He likes you." Hazel blushed. "So tell me everything. We can pour this tea while you spill the tea."

Hazel did tell her everything. How the realization of how attractive he is crashed into her suddenly. That she felt addicted to talking to him. How she imagined what he might look like in person. All about his family. The way she could picture their lives together. That she was nervous about meeting him.

Rosie was listening, beaming, encouraging Hazel to keep talking. When she finally sighed and stopped, Rosie asked, "So what are you going to do?"

"I don't know. Frank said relationships in the same department weren't allowed, and he's several levels higher than me. I'm angling harder than ever at Training, but it might not happen. I've tried to not think about him. I always tell myself not to, but I just can't."

"What if you talk to him and, you know, ask?"

Hazel swallowed. "I want to, but I can't, at least not until after CARE wraps up. We still have to work together daily right now, and I can't risk exploding anything."

"Okay. Here's something. What if you finally see him at this summit and there isn't any chemistry, or maybe he looks totally different than you imagine? I don't think it likely to happen, but it is possible. Maybe it's a blessing in disguise you have to wait until you do meet, and you can make a more informed decision?"

"I have to present at the summit's main event with Sam and gauge our physical chemistry. No pressure." Hazel brushed her shoulder's off. "There is something else, too," Hazel told Rosie about her meeting with Samantha.

Rosie asked, "She seems unprofessional. How did she get to be so high in your leadership?"

Hazel shrugged and sipped her tea. "I don't think she's like this with everyone. I've heard she plays favorites, but I have no idea why I'm the most hated for her now."

"Oh, I mean, it's because she's jealous of your closeness with Sam. Definitely."

Hazel looked skeptical. "I don't think so. I did consider that because of her over-the-top flirting before, but she wouldn't know we're particularly close."

Rosie frowned. "She's not flirting with him still?"

"Not that I've seen. She hasn't stayed after meetings or replied to our emails anyway."

"Well, I would tell Sam about the meeting and her behavior toward you. Remove your personal relationship from this. He is the project leader. It seems like something you would tell the leader, right?"

Hazel replied, "You're right. I would usually bring that up. I don't know, it feels sticky, and I'm nervous about it." She paused to think. "It's the only thing I can come up with. It's that or say nothing."

Hazel resisted the temptation to put on makeup before her Wednesday after-hours meeting with Sam, but she did put on her favorite top. A green satiny scoop neck that made her eyes pop.

She brought dinner (a bowl of tortellini soup and bread) to her desk and logged into the SyncUp 15 minutes early, satisfied to see she was the first in. Sam entered 5 minutes later and snapped his fingers at the sight of her. "I had a feeling you'd beat me today."

Hazel held up a finger and chewed the bread she had

put in her mouth as fast as possible behind her other hand. She swallowed. "I was determined!"

"So determined you ate dinner in your office?! What are we having tonight? You brought me some, right?"

"Bowl of soup and a slice of challah."

"You aren't supposed to slice challah. That's blasphemy." Sam wrinkled his brow into a concerned expression.

"It's already done, I'm afraid. Slicing is very convenient."

"Surely not more convenient than pulling it apart, as god intended. You know, tearing it keeps it fresher too. Anyway, pass me a bowl."

Hazel lifted her bowl to the camera as if to pass it through, and Sam raised his hands to accept it. "I wish I could; it won't seem to go."

Sam sighed dramatically. "Maybe next time."

They began working, comparing notes. Hazel explained she had decided to send the first teaser trailer out next Tuesday when Sam said, "Oh yeah, that reminds me. Good job asking Samantha her opinion on timing. A perfect case for including her."

Hazel was confused. "Did she say something about that?"

"Oh yeah, she was very complimentary about you. Seems like you turned her around."

Hazel stuttered, "I. This is." She twiddled the spoon inside the bowl, her brain working overtime to figure out what was happening. "That doesn't make sense. Sam, this makes me uncomfortable."

Sam alerted at the word and sat up straight. "Okay. I want to help, and I never want you to feel uncomfortable. Tell me more if you can?"

Hazel took a steadying breath. "I did meet with her. During our meeting, I asked if we should issue the first trailer on Tuesday or Wednesday, and she insisted we do it this Friday. I explained why we wouldn't do it on Friday or Monday, but she doubled down for Friday. Then I asked if I had done anything to upset her because of the way she's acted toward me, and she said I was impertinent and ignored her advice." Hazel was shaking slightly. "I left feeling like she wanted us to fail, or me at least. It doesn't sound as bad explaining it to you, but it was awful."

Sam's voice was low, "No, it does sound awful. Nobody should speak to you so disrespectfully."

"I don't understand why she told you it went well. I promise you it did not. I mean, I wish it did. That was my goal… Why would she tell you something else?" They were both quiet for a moment.

Finally, Sam said, "I don't know. Maybe she regretted her behavior and didn't know how to apologize to you?" Hazel knitted her brows. Sam asked gently, "Have you considered going to HR? I would support you."

"I have, but I don't think I should. I mean, she was rude to me, but it's not exactly clear-cut. Not harassment or discrimination. I'll probably never have to work with her again after a few weeks. Plus, now I feel crazy! Her compliment to you. Maybe I'm totally misreading everything?"

Sam's lips were pressed together in a thin line. She could tell he was reluctant, but he nodded, "Okay, but let's not have you in a room alone with her. If she acts like that again, we need witnesses. Preferably me."

"Ready for a 'Rosie Conspiracy Theory'?" She made finger quotes.

The mood lightened as Sam asked, "Oh, these are a whole official thing? I'm so ready."

"She thinks Samantha is jealous of our, uh, friendship." Sam sat back in his chair, hand to chin, thinking. "I mean, she does seem to like you. You know? It feels like she's trying to be in a room with you as much as possible."

He cleared his throat and sat back up. "She is…

demanding. She recently requested a one-on-one with me to give her updates. I agreed, but after the first meeting, we were clearly duplicating information from the regular Stakeholder Meeting. I told her we should cancel the series, and if anything popped up that involved her department, I'd let her know proactively."

A sense of calm fizzled through Hazel. She tried not to show it when she asked, "So, you're not interested in her?"

Sam burst out laughing. "No." More laughter. "Oh, that's a good one. No, she's not really my type. To be honest, I wondered if she was trying to flirt with me or if she was trying to take credit for the success of CARE. Position herself to maximize her impact. Maybe she's gunning for a promotion?"

Hazel burned to know what his type was, but it felt like too much to ask. Instead, she replied, "Yeah, after working with her, I couldn't really see you two as a couple."

Sam faltered, "Yeah, I…." His focus adjusted into a long stare. Hazel saw that hint of something in his face again. Melancholy? She wanted to reach him, feel the scruff of his beard in her hands, and kiss him. Just as fast, he was back. "That'll never happen. I know what I want."

BEFORE LOGGING OFF, Hazel noticed Frank was yet again on late. She messaged him, "GO BE WITH YOUR FAMILY," and closed her laptop.

SPierce

The green blouse is beautiful. 9:01pm

SPierce

> I remember you were stressing about
> summit clothes. Bring that one. 9:01pm

HE HAD MESSAGED her almost immediately after their meeting ended. Though it was chilly in her old house, Hazel's whole body seemed to warm reading it. She steeped tea and daydreamed about him ending his mysterious sentence with one additional word, 'I know what I want. You.'

Hazel

> Thank you! And noted, it's on the packing
> list! I can't have you making me look
> underdressed. 9:02pm

SPierce

> I don't think that could ever be at risk. If
> anything it'll be the other way around.
> 9:02pm

THE BOOK CLUB had started reading *Stocking Full of Love*, a holiday-themed romance Hazel was unabashedly enjoying. It was like watching a Hallmark Christmas movie but reading one instead, and she loved it for its tropes. Not everyone agreed. Jessica's exact words to kick off their conversation were, "I bet Jolly Old St. Nick makes a magical appearance later on, and we don't even get to see his dick."

Rosie spewed a fine rain of wine that covered the coffee table, part of the edge of the couch, and Hazel's legs. Rosie stood up, apologizing. She ran out of the living room to the kitchen, but Omar was already on his way with cleaning supplies.

Amara, who did not seem bothered about the mist of wine covering her furniture, started chipping in with comments. "Yeah! Sugar Plums or get the fuck out!" and "We need Santa's candy cane!"

Lydia, blushing furiously, said, "You never know, maybe it's a twist, and Santa turns out to be the love interest."

As Omar graciously offered Hazel a towel to dry herself, she said, "I actually really like this book. It's seasonal. It's a feel-good. And yeah, I could predict what's coming," Jessica cut her off, "Not Santa." The laughter renewed, and Hazel plunged on, "She's going to leave her dumb city job she hates and end her engagement to find love in her small hometown. But that's okay with me. I'm here for it."

While Lydia agreed with Hazel and cited some of the scenes she found most cozy, Hazel felt a buzz in her pocket. She retrieved her phone stealthily, but not stealthily enough. Jessica exclaimed, "Oh ho! Is it the work husband?"

Rosie shot Hazel a significant look that she understood meant she didn't have to share unless she wanted to. Jessica caught that too. "Oh my God, it is, isn't it?! You're texting now?!"

Hazel couldn't prevent one side of her mouth from quirking up. She quickly filled them in, skipping over some of the finer points, and ended with, "But things remain the same. There are literal and figurative mountains between us."

Lydia's soft eyes met Hazel's. "The best part of books like *Stocking Full of Love* is you know everything will work out. There will be hardships to conquer, but you know, in the end, everything is happy. It's what keeps me reading." Hazel knew she wasn't talking about the book and the earnestness in her voice made her throat constrict.

CHAPTER 13

HAVE A DEDICATED WORKSPACE... BUT MOVE AROUND AS NEEDED

"It's contradictory, but different things work for different people! Working from home allows the freedom to change your view, which can help with creativity."

THE FACT that CARE was on track despite losing a Technical Writer and adding the teaser trailers was nearly a miracle, and the team was garnering a lot of attention for it. The Tuesday the first trailer launched was also a Stakeholder Meetings day. As people joined the room, there was a buzz of excitement. Everyone joining was gabbing about the video and its effect on their teams.

Sam cleared his throat and called for attention. The room instantly silenced. "I can tell what's on your minds, and I'm thrilled to hear it. In our update today, Hazel will tell you more about this email series. It was her brilliant idea." He tipped his head at Hazel and shared his updated Leadership Training presentation.

"Thanks, Sam. Before we begin with today's run-through, let me echo Sam. I'm overjoyed at your reaction to the first trailer this morning. Our goal in creating these was to create a buzz. Get people talking about CARE and how it's a positive change that will serve them and make their lives easier as leaders. We'll be formally collecting feedback on the approach after the summit. Now, you lucky people will get a sneak peek of the other trailers because they are highlighted in the training."

Hazel was aware of the room hanging on her words. They were behaving as if Sam was speaking. Dialed in. Attentive. She felt powerful and intimidated at once. She gave the cue for Sam to start the presentation and the trailer videos began to play silently. Hazel spoke over them, nailing her timing. "CARE isn't just another acronym. It's an approach designed by FutureApp for FutureApp. Every consideration was given to the ease of learning and use. For leaders. For representatives. For customers. I think Dana says it best."

As the video of Dana started, and its sound kicked in, delivering her message, there was an audible gasp from someone whose mic was turned on. The SyncUp chat exploded into action, with people applauding and exclaiming. Hazel felt like she was having an out-of-body experience. "Now I'll turn it over to Sam."

Hazel barely registered Sam as he presented his portion or Lou as he demoed where the resources for CARE could be found at the end. When they asked for feedback, it was nearly all glowing, with some minor changes recommended. Jasmond specifically complimented Hazel, "The timing of your phrases with the video. How many times did you practice that?"

"More than I'll admit."

"Well, it was worth it. You nailed it. I know it's not easy." He paused and nodded. "I hope we see more of you at the summit."

Hazel was somewhere in the stratosphere. She, Sam,

and Lou were hanging back as the other stakeholders dropped from the meeting to compare notes. When the last person had exited, Hazel squealed with delight, and Sam said, "You crushed that, Hazelberry." His face exuded pride. A softness in his eyes met her like a tender caress.

SyncUp played a door-closing sound jolting Hazel back to earth. It was the sound of someone exiting the room. She looked at the attendee log and found Samantha had dropped from the room but had reentered unbeknownst to the three of them, likely masked by Hazel's squeal of celebration.

Why did she come back in? Why did she drop again without saying anything? Did Sam call her Hazelberry in front of Samantha and Lou? She told herself it was nothing and tried to calm her mind, which was suddenly spinning. She felt nervous but couldn't exactly explain why.

Hazel asked, "It looks like Samantha came back in. Should we message her to see if she has questions or feedback?"

Sam quickly replied, "I'll take care of it. Let me Chatter her."

～

December 24, 2015

Will I be excited the day they inevitably get engaged? Hazel is so happy with Alex. I see it in her face all the time. I saw it today at Christmas Eve dinner. She adores him in every way. And Alex is a good man. I believe he loves Hazel, but it's not the way she loves him.

Their love feels unequal to me. I want to protect her so much, but it feels like there's nothing I can do. I feel so judgmental. Why should my feelings even matter if my daughter is happy and safe? Maybe I'm wrong!

Yet there are times that I see him speaking over her. There are times when she is celebrating, and he makes it about him. He speaks of her career as if it's something cute. These little things bother me.

~

HAZEL HAD PICKED up her Mom's diary between meeting times, expecting another peek into her parents' everyday lives. Certainly nothing like this. She set down the brown book and paced the kitchen but then returned to it and fumbled through the pages looking for entries toward the end.

~

May 15, 2018

Alex finally proposed. It was a beautiful proposal. He had arranged a floral archway in Botanica, which was exceptional in so many ways. Not only gorgeous, but having Lar and me in on the secret was special, we got to help build the archway.

~

SHE FLOPPED into the chair at her kitchen table and rested her head in her hands. She felt... Okay, she realized. Stunned, yes, but overall she was okay. A feeling bloomed in her chest. She felt her mother's love for her and a confidence. She did deserve those things.

Alex wasn't a bad person. He just wasn't her person. She thought about him, and wished him well, and felt free.

THE FEELING in her chest remained all day and into the next. She felt creative and productive, so she decided to work from her bedroom to fuel the creative spark. Jasmond had messaged her in Chatter to further congratulate her, saying he couldn't stop thinking about her delivery and asking if she was presenting at the summit. He was pleased to learn she was. She'd also made headway on the How-To Work Remotely article. Polishing the actual piece so it complied with FutureApp style guides and starting on a presentation she hoped would continue to wow Jasmond. Her idea was to create a piece of training which could be used in the Onboarding sequence. If she made it complete enough, maybe Training would be so interested they could incorporate it with minimal adjustments.

When Hazel logged on to meet with Sam later that evening, she noticed Frank was still online. She navigated to their DM.

Hazel Rogers

You're literally going to make yourself sick. I'm concerned about you Frank, you aren't even chatting with Meg and me in the group chat this week? 6:45pm

Frank Simms

Gah I know, I'm behind on everything. We're almost there, just a little more push! 6:45pm

Hazel Rogers

How are you? How's the pilot? 6:45pm

Frank Simms

Not going to lie, I'm tired but okay. The pilot is AMAZING. Are you going to come to my session? I can't wait for you to see it! 6:45pm

Hazel Rogers

> OF COURSE I'LL BE THERE! Are you
> kidding, I would not miss it! 6:46pm

Frank Simms

> Actually, do you think you and Meg could
> sit for a run-through of my presentation? I'd
> like your feedback. 6:46pm

Hazel Rogers

> I'm honored. Put it on the Cal! 6:46pm

HAZEL FLUFFED the pillow behind her back and logged into the SyncUp.

Sam greeted her with a wink that made her knees weak. It was a good thing she was sitting. "I thought you might not make it."

"Well, I'm only 13 minutes early, so I see why."

Sam leaned in toward his camera and peered around Hazel. "Where are you? This isn't your office."

"Ah no, I worked from the bedroom today. Change of scenery and all." She picked up her laptop and aimed the camera around to give him the tour.

"Wow, I love the wall. Did you do that?"

"Hah, yeah! A little bit of painter's tape and some color, and you've got yourself a geometric masterpiece."

"I intended to talk about and maybe practice for the summit and celebrate a little if you're interested, but now I'm thinking I should change my scenery too." He stood up, picking his laptop up with him. He walked through his

158

home; Hazel caught glimpses of a dark hallway, what may have been the front door area, and finally, a sitting area. Sam sat back on a blue couch and placed the laptop on a table that must have been there. "Welcome to the living room!" He spun his computer around so she could better observe. She was surprised to see how comfortable a place he had arranged. There was a blanket slung over the back of the couch and some mismatched squashy-looking cushions. He had some modern art pieces on the walls, alongside some pictures. A shelf beneath the television had some candles and knickknacks decorating the space.

"Wow, Sam! I'm loving the vibe. Those art pieces especially. And the blanket. Having a comfy blanket at arm's length is always important!"

Sam chortled, "I pride myself on the ability to keep you- anyone warm."

They continued on, discussing the summit. Sam explained how the stage would be set up, including details down to where the entrance was for presenters, what stairs she would come up, and where the podium would be. Hazel would walk onto the stage by herself to start the presentation since her part was at the beginning. There would be a device that controlled the projection behind them on the podium, and all she would need to do to start was press the button.

The logistical information made Hazel feel a greater sense of security about the task ahead of her. The idea she would be kicking it off by herself, however, not so much. "I feel like I'll be okay once I get started. I know the script, and we'll practice more. Walking out alone, though, I don't know. Couldn't you come out with me? Or all three of us?"

"What would Lou and I do while you presented? Our presence would distract the audience because we don't have a job." Hazel knew he was right. "Besides, you absolutely can do this. And you *will* nail the presentation, but when you're on stage, you're going to tend to rush the timing. When we practice, let's develop waypoints for you to check your timing. For example, you'll know you should be saying the words 'every consideration' when the light-bulb scene first begins."

They worked together to define the waypoints and practiced Hazel's script until she could not prevent the boredom from coming out in her voice. In her last practice, she adopted a robotic voice with Sam doing robot arm movements. They were giggling at each other by the end. Sam said, "You know, I think we've got it for the night. Do you want a little nightcap with me to celebrate the Stakeholder meeting?"

"Absolutely! What are we having?"

Sam's dimple flashed. "I believe you prefer reds, so I got a cab. Meet back in 3?"

"It's going to take longer than 3 minutes to have a cab drive you cross country, you know, but if you mean cabernet. Yes, I'll go grab some from the kitchen."

They returned, each holding a bottle of garnet and a glass. Sam raised his tumbler toward the camera. "To the instant hit of teaser trailers and a successful first run-through." Hazel raised her glass to meet his, and they drank.

Hazel was feeling relaxed. Dangerously relaxed. Glancing at the wine, she realized they had consumed half a bottle each and had the slightest idea she should call it a night or risk saying something she wasn't ready for. Yet, when Sam poured another, her heart beckoned her to join.

They gave each other tours of their homes, noting their favorite rooms and areas. Sam set up the computer in his bed after showing her around the bedroom. It had been a grown man's bedroom. Not some bachelor pad or frat house replica, but a sensible and comfortable place.

Hazel imagined it smelled clean and of evergreen. A book on his nightstand looked so much like the cover of *Belle's Beast* that she almost asked about it, but she commented on his extensive shoe collection instead. The shoes had been the only shocker for her on the tour. "You have more shoes than me, friend." She took another sip.

"They're almost all running shoes. One fact I can share with you about running. If you wear the right color shoes for the particular day, your run will be better."

"Fascinating. How do you know which color is right for the day?"

"Gut feeling, but you need the full rainbow because you never know." They both laughed, and then silence fell between them for the first time. Hazel tried not to look at Sam and played her fingers along the stem of the glass instead. Out of her peripheral vision, she thought she saw him take a gulp of wine, but when she turned to him, he was looking at her with such intensity it made her cheeks heat.

He barely whispered, "Can I ask you something personal?"

Hazel alerted. "Of course," she breathed, "You can ask me anything."

Sam's throat bobbed once, twice. "How is it that you're single? You're just… I mean, it just seems unimaginable."

Hazel's mind was racing with answers she wouldn't speak. Because I can't stop thinking about you. Because I compare everyone to you, and they all lose immediately. Because I love you.

Shit. Shit, shit, shit. Did she love him? No, she had too many glasses of wine. They'd never even met in person before. There was no way she loved him. Except did she? She was staring at him. Not answering. She giggled nervously but tried to play it off as dismissive laughter. Her mouth found and repeated his words to her, "I just know what I want." Yes, that would work.

He nodded knowingly. Hazel wanted to ask him something personal in exchange. Her mind was reeling with so many questions she combined two in a malaphor-esque way, "What did you do that you regret wanting?" It was some horrible combination of 'What do you want in a partner?' and 'What did you do in the past that you mentioned regretting?'

Sam looked confused, and she shook her head. Only one of those questions was okay to ask. "I mean, you mentioned before you regretted some of your past behavior at work. I can't even imagine that. You're so professional, a great leader, and lovely to work with…."

Sam looked down, then grabbed his bottle of wine and poured the last glass. He blew air through his lips. "I don't know if I should tell you… but I will if you really want to know."

Hazel realized this was meaningful for him. She dipped her chin and leaned in to listen.

"I have to preface this. I know I was being selfish, and my experience was nothing compared to what you were going through. God, you're going to think differently of me." Hazel's curiosity peaked. How was she a part of this story?

His eyes clouded, but he continued. "Please understand. One day, we're getting close to it being three years now; you were gone. I had no idea where you were, but you weren't responding to my messages. I thought you might be out sick but then a week passed. I emailed you, but you didn't reply there. I was afraid. I was so afraid you were…. I searched for you online and started asking people about you, but I had to be careful. You know how we are about privacy. I tried to strategically mention that you weren't in office or that I hadn't heard from you in a while, but weeks passed, and nobody said anything. No hints I could pick up on."

He took a sip from his glass. Hazel was staring at him. "I became distracted. I missed you, and I was so worried, Hazel. And it's not an excuse, I know, but I let all that manifest in terrible ways. There was one meeting. I was leading an information session on opportunities for the new Social Media team, and this guy was there. Greg. He asked some questions that sent me over the edge, he was grating on me, I perceived him as a know-it-all, and I…. I let him have it."

His eyes were shining bright now. "I tortured him through that meeting, making him a public spectacle. I directed every question asked to Greg in the most condescending ways I could come up with. I knew I was doing it, but I kept going. People were DMing me in Chatter, telling me to stop, asking what I was doing. I ignored them. I dismissed the meeting at the end by asking Greg if it was okay if we left. I hated myself afterward. I logged out mid-day. I pondered resigning. The next day I logged in and had a Calendar invitation from Dana first thing in the morning. I went into her SyncUp, knowing I would be fired before I could resign. Knowing I deserved it. But Dana. Her first words were to say she wasn't firing me or accepting a resignation today."

He took on that far-away look she'd seen before. "I remember she was so steady and calm. Her voice was like some sort of medicine. I told her everything I could. That you were missing, and I didn't know if you were safe and that I hadn't been sleeping. That I had no way of contacting you outside of work. How I felt sick about the way I had treated Greg and what all the people in that meeting must think of me. She said, you know, she couldn't share personal information about a colleague. She said she wouldn't put me on disciplinary action if I apologized to Greg, but I couldn't do anything like that again."

Sam drained the rest of his wine and wiped a tear sliding down his cheek. "I found Greg immediately after that meeting. I've never apologized to anyone the way I did to him. I wanted him to know I was deeply hurt by my own actions. Ashamed. That it was nothing he had done. Greg is an amazing person, it turns out. He forgave me even though I wouldn't have blamed him if he didn't. A few hours later, I got a text message from an unknown number that linked to your parents' obituary."

Hazel didn't know how to reply; she looked anywhere but the screen. "I need to think for a minute."

Sam quickly said, "When I realized why you were out. My heart broke for you. I wanted to help, but I didn't know how. I'm sorry for not being there. I'm sorry for not immediately getting your contact information when you returned... There are so many things I would do differently."

Hazel was horrified she would say something wrong. In her wine-fueled haze, this felt like Sam was confessing something, yet she could feel the effects of the wine slowing her cognition and knew she could not trust her own brain for the truth. She struggled to reply, not wanting to confess anything and make a drunken fool of herself. She said gently, "Sam. I don't think any less of you. I know how stress can wear down a person and make us behave in crazy ways, and I've worked with you for how long? You're.... Wonderful. Kind, funny, caring, handsome, fair, so smart, and just the best. The fact you were so worried about me... I'm grateful to have you in my life."

Drinking more than a couple glasses of alcohol always made Hazel sleepy. By the time it was 1am, paired with the fact she had consumed an entire bottle by herself, Hazel was going to sleep whether she liked it or not. She yawned and stretched. "I think I'd better get to bed, but I enjoyed our celebration. Thank you for hanging with me!"

"The pleasure is mine, Hazelberry. Sweet dreams."

"Goodnight, SPierce."

HAZEL WAS grateful to already be in her bedroom. Even the steps into her bathroom to brush her teeth felt like too much effort. She immediately fell asleep when she returned to bed and dreamed they were still talking. They both said, "I know what I want," simultaneously, and in her dream, she knew they both wanted each other.

CHAPTER 14

PROOFREAD BEFORE SENDING

"One benefit of writing as a primary mode of communication is that you can check for clarity and edit your thoughts before responding."

DESPITE THEIR CELEBRATIONS the previous evening, Hazel woke early, mind sharp. She craved time to think over her morning coffee and flew through her routine to get there. When she was finally perched on her porch chair, snuggled tight in layers, she watched her coffee swirl in her cup. The steam spiraled up to meet her face. There were lingering rumors about Sam being an asshole because he had been distraught about her absence and acted out. What did that mean?

It had been years ago now. They were close at work then, using Chatter nearly every day, but not all day. He said he was worried about her. Even losing sleep. He had said he wished he got her contact information sooner, didn't he? Her dreams of them were making her question some of her memories. She remembered the feeling that he had been looking for her to return. He was one of the first people to message her to welcome her back the day she returned from leave. At that time, she didn't think much about it, except that he was a kind friend, but thinking about it now… Her DM with him would have been at the very bottom of his Chatter App due to disuse. To see her in an Available state would have involved some scrolling.

She tapped her fingernails on the sides of her mug. Last night when she listened to him, she had seen and heard the emotion in his face and voice; it had felt like something hopeful. As if maybe he felt the same way about her. Revisiting the memory now didn't feel as clear-cut. He hadn't said he liked her, never said he was interested. It was abundantly clear he valued her friendship and thought about her outside of work if he lost sleep. He had said the part about wanting her contact information sooner, it was interesting, but it could also mean he's innocently enjoying their friendship and not fantasizing about slamming her against a headboard or how their hands would fit together perfectly in a movie theater.

Even if he did! Even if he did reciprocate, the other sad facts remained. FutureApp would disapprove. They both had lives on opposite sides of the country. Maybe Dana could help in some way. Hazel felt confident she was the one that messaged Sam about her parents. Could she show clever flexibility in other ways? Could Hazel imagine moving to Oregon, leaving Rosie, her friends, and Crest-wood behind?

Her phone buzzed in her pocket. She knew it probably wasn't Sam when she reached through several layers of cardigans to retrieve it. It would be 4:30am his time, which was early even for him.

SPierce

Hope you're still having a great time in dreamland. Thought I'd send you my Dad's hangover cure for when you have to rise n shine 7:32am

Hazel

Don't you ever sleep? How in the world are you up at this hour? 7:32am

SPierce

Oh no! I didn't wake you did I? I need a long run this morning. 7:32am

Hazel

lol, no you didn't wake me. I'm enjoying coffee on the porch. No hangover here :) What color is today? 7:33am

SPierce

Phew- good! Get an egg and cheese biscuit anyway (that's the cure) just because they're delicious. 7:33am

SPierce

Green today! 7:33am

Hazel

My favorite color! 7:33am

SPierce

I know :) 7:34am

SPierce

Hey, what do you think about doing a
Turkey Trot with me Thanksgiving morning?
The 10k I'm doing has a 5k portion and
there's a virtual option. 7:38am

Hazel

Well, I tried to run up a hill a few weeks ago
and nearly died, so could I do virtual yoga
at the same time or something? 7:38am

Hazel

How would it work? 7:39am

SPierce

The race starts at 8am for me, 11am for
you. We could call each other and run, or
text if you prefer. The bummer is I'd get to
run with a lot of people, and you'd be on
your own- well with me sort of. You totally
don't have to. I saw the virtual thing and
you came to mind 7:40am

Hazel

> Aw that's sweet! I'm a little scared. If we called you'd just hear my wheezing and cursing and nothing else 7:40am

Hazel

> I'll try it, but you have to do a yoga with me some time too. 7:41am

SPierce

> Deal. I won't make fun of your cursing wheezing if you don't make fun of my flexibility-or-lack-there-of 7:41am

Hazel

> MMMMMM, IDK, I kinda love the idea of making fun of you. Might be worth it to take some heat 7:41am

OVER THE NEXT FEW DAYS, Hazel noticed how their relationship had changed. Something had shifted since their late-night cabernet. If possible, they were speaking more than ever, consulting each other on mundane things. It was also impossible to deny that their interactions were dripping with flirtation, even innuendo. Hazel had officially scheduled their yoga time for the week after Thanksgiving. Sam responded by asking about her favorite Christmas movie and suggesting they have an Elf watch party. That meant they now had three non-work-related events planned together.

. . .

THE LAST TIME Hazel had lamented what to wear to the summit, Rosie had cleared a Friday afternoon and declared it an emergency shopping situation. First thing Friday morning, Hazel checked her Calendar to make sure nothing had changed. It was surprisingly packed for a Friday, but she could still meet Rosie on time if she left right after her last meeting. With this in mind, she got ready for their Target and Starbucks date. She was mindful of everything from the underwear she put on to how she applied her makeup. If she was shopping for the summit, she wanted to look and feel how she would be at the conference. She put on a comfortable but cute pair of matching panties and bra that she knew would let her move freely but complimented her figure. She selected a slightly darker shade of lipstick than she usually wore, a deep mauve called 'No Cry,' and paired it with light pink eyeshadow for a splash of color. She wore the green satin top since she knew it represented the style she would be going for.

She logged into the SyncUp for the morning CARE meeting 9 minutes early. Sam was already there with his head down, typing on the keyboard. Without looking up, he said, "Beat you!" She could tell he was smiling even with his head tilted because the corner of his eyes crinkled. "One sec, almost done with this email." His hair was perfectly mussed today, dark, wavy, and clean, moving slightly with each move he made.

He looked up mid-sentence, "annnnd finish…" he had stopped suddenly. His mouth was open, and his eyes were bathing in her. Searching and memorizing every angle of her face, every strand of hair. Hazel grinned and coyly looked to the side. His voice was deep, "You look… You stole my words. Beautiful."

Hazel blushed. "Thanks. I'm shopping for the summit later and wanted to feel like I was there, you know?" They stared at each other. Sam's eyes darkened as he continued to take her in. He wet his lips, biting the bottom one. Hazel breathed heavily, her eyes trained on his lips, imagining his teeth on her.

Lou cleared his throat. "I didn't mean to interrupt anything."

They were both red in the face, shaken from the moment. Hazel inhaled. "Not at all." The meeting progressed in their usual business rhythm. They were only 2 minutes into working through the last approvals for the Expert Database when Hazel received a Chatter notification.

Sam Pierce

> If you come to the summit looking like that,
> I think I might be in trouble. 9:00am

Hazel Rogers

> Looking like what? 9:00am

Sam Pierce

> Now that I have my words back.
> Resplendent. Holy. Dazzling. Literally
> stunning. 9:01am

HAZEL TYPED and erased over and over, deciding how to reply. She wanted him to say more. She wanted to leave this meeting and dive into his arms. Her heart beat so swiftly it made working through the spreadsheet unbearable.

Hazel Rogers

Sam Pierce

WAS SHE DREAMING? The warmth in her body was threatening to overwhelm her. She could barely focus her eyes to navigate the approvals.

Hazel Rogers

THEIR CHAT WAS INTERRUPTED when it was Sam's turn to give the updates on the training. Hazel followed up by covering the rest of the Communication plans, adding more about their handoffs to Phases 3 and 4. There were only two weeks left before the summit, and they were crammed with additional actions and meetings. "Next week, we have our usual Stakeholder meeting and the big show for the extended upper leadership for the final sign-off. The week after, I've scheduled all our handoff meetings in your calendar so you can color-code them. We'll have more of those continuing after the summit. Then, of course, we'll see each other there."

The meeting closed with polite goodbyes and Lou eyeing both of them. "You two kids have a good weekend."

The rest of the workday was a blur of meetings. Sam did not chat her back, and it made Hazel feel nervous. She pushed the feeling aside as she sprinted out the door to meet Rosie.

The Starbucks inside Target was bustling with customers. Hazel and Rosie stood in line, and Hazel filled her in on the details of the morning. "Ever since Wednesday night, things have felt like we're together. Like we're a couple even though we aren't, but now he suddenly hasn't talked to me since this morning."

"He probably doesn't know what to say, is all. Where do you go from the near foreplay level of dialogue?" Rosie looked thoughtful. "Plus, he's in the same boat as you. You are questioning his interest because he hasn't outright said he likes you. Despite him practically screaming it," she rolled her eyes, "but you haven't told him anything explicit either."

"Hi, can I get a grande cafe latte and a grande mocha, please?" Hazel ordered for both of them, then turned back to Rosie. "You've got a point. Maybe he's trying to wait to meet me in person too."

Rosie laughed. "I don't know. He did say he'd do more than make you blush, right?"

Hazel fished her phone out of her purse and messaged Sam, "Out with Rosie doing the summit shopping. Hope you had a good rest of your day." She was putting her phone back in the bag when it buzzed. Rosie peered over her shoulder to read with her.

SPierce

> Still in it over on the West Coast but it's good. Have a great time shopping- HI ROSIE! 4:12pm

Rosie put her hand on her chest, "He said hi to me! HI SAM!"

Hazel

> She says hi 4:12pm

SPierce

> Listen, I'm sorry about this morning. I was too forward. 4:13pm

Hazel fumbled the phone as the barista called her name. "What do I say to that? I don't want him to be sorry!"

Rosie shook her head and handed her the latte. "I don't know. You're either going to validate that it's okay or not. You just said he shouldn't feel sorry, so validating it's okay seems like the way to go."

"Yeah, but what do I say?! 'Please, Sir, I want some more,' with an image of Oliver Twist?"

Rosie laughed so loudly that other customers glanced their way. "I mean, it would get the point across." Seeing Hazel's face, she added, "Don't panic. Let's shop, and we'll think about it."

They slowly strolled through the women's clothing, picking items and holding them up to Hazel, then either putting them back on the rack or over the side of the cart to try on.

Rosie gave a thumbs down at the silky pink blouse with puffy sleeves Hazel was inspecting. "I've never seen you this way about a guy. Sincere and excited look good on you."

Hazel placed the blouse back on the rack. "That reminds me, will you and Nick be around for Thanksgiving?"

"How about this?" Rosie held up some fitted black pants with a decorative seam up each side. "No, we're going to see my family," she sighed, "I'm sure to have tons of drama to share with you, at least."

"Put those on the cart. And yes, you know I'm an addict when it comes to your family drama llamas. Seriously, it'll be good for you to see them."

"I'd rather it only be us, to be honest. You, me, and Nick. It'll be good, though. You're right. How did I remind you to ask about Thanksgiving?"

"Sam and I have been comparing holiday traditions. His family still hides Easter Eggs for each other. So cute."

Rosie looked impressed. "It's nice he's still close with his parents like that."

Hazel agreed, "It is. His Mom died when he was young, but his Dad eventually remarried, and they all seem like a tight-knit group. I can tell the way they tease each other from talking with him. Let's head to the changing room. I think we've seen everything."

Hazel started working through the small mountain of

maybes they had put in the cart, exiting the changing room to get Rosie's commentary after every new piece.

"That skirt is a yes. It really compliments your *assets* if-you-know-what-I-mean." Rosie winked at her twice, and Hazel chuckled. "What if you replied something to bring it back to flirty, like, 'I always enjoy our banter.'"

Hazel stopped and leaned on the doorway to the changing room, "Hmmm… I like that. It's kind of welcoming the continuation but without admitting everything."

"You are still planning on sharing the truth with him if you feel chemistry in person, right?"

"Oh, I don't know if I could keep myself from doing so. The bigger risk is we meet, I instantly feel it and proclaim my undying affection to the whole company."

"So you're saying we should see if they have a mega-phone for you to pack, too?"

HAZEL PUSHED her bags into the backseat of the car. She messaged Sam before turning the key.

Hazel

Outfits attained! No need to apologize, I've always enjoyed our banter. 5:58pm

SPierce

:) Heard. What did you find? 5:58pm

> I guess you'll have to wait to find out
> 5:58pm

SPierce

> Torturous! 5:58pm

Now that CARE was nearing the end of Hazel's phase, time seemed to be in quite a hurry. The weekend was over in a blink, except for one prolonged 30-minute period where Hazel went for a run. She was looking forward to joining Sam for this Turkey Trot, but not because of the running. When she told Sam she had barely made it, he simply replied she was wearing the wrong color shoes and that he would teach her pacing techniques.

Monday was their last regularly scheduled Stakeholder meeting. An event that Lou referred to as "The dry run for the run-through" because they had their final presentation (and hopefully approval) on Friday.

Although Hazel had practiced her script and had the timing down perfectly, she felt particularly nervous about this meeting. She couldn't shake the feeling they weren't going to get approval and could be stuck with a hellish week of re-work with simultaneous handoff meetings. She decided to go for a walk before the meeting to cool down her nerves. She grabbed her coat and took the familiar left turn onto the street.

She walked quickly, wanting to burn off some of her anxiety. She focused on her breathing, long inhales and exhales, and tried to relax her mind. Whenever an unwanted thought would drift in, she imagined inspecting it briefly and then sending it down a river away from her. She walked past Breezy. The tree had lost most of its leaves, but a few bright spots remained amongst her lower branches. Hazel decided to stop and sit beneath her so she could close her eyes and focus.

Hazel was broken from her reverie when a splash of something hit her cheek. She didn't need to open her eyes to know it was pouring rain as she continued to feel the pelt of drops across her face. She started running back home, glancing at her watch every few minutes. How had she not checked the forecast?! The position she was in now was embarrassing. She wouldn't have enough time to dry off before the meeting. Her calm disappeared and was replaced with irritation at herself and desperately considering alternatives, none of which would work. She slipped on a patch of wet leaves going downhill and fell hard on her right hip and forearm. The rain continued to come down, and Hazel limped the rest of the way home, miserable.

The fall had slowed her considerably, and there were only three minutes until she was due in the SyncUp when she opened her door. She threw off her coat, thinking at least she had the good sense to have worn it. She fell into her desk chair, turned on the camera before entering the meeting, and straightened her hair as best she could. She was soaked through and freezing cold. There was nothing else for it; she would have to be off-camera for this meeting. It was not ideal for her presentation, she knew it wouldn't hit the same way, but it was better than everyone seeing her hair drip onto her keyboard. She turned her webcam off and logged in.

Hazel Rogers

> 911, I can't come on camera today
> 10:59am

Sam Pierce

> Why? Is everything okay? 10:59am

Hazel Rogers

> No, I got caught in a freaking storm, I look
> like someone rescued me from drowning
> 10:59am

Sam Pierce

> Okay we'll roll with it. 11:00am

Sam Pierce

> Going to need the full story later ;) 11:00am

SAM KICKED off the meeting as he always did, explaining their agenda and expectations. Unfortunately, Hazel being off camera was noticed and became a distraction. Trevor used the SyncUp chat to ask if she was okay, causing other concerned comments to follow. As Hazel was typing back to the chat that she was okay, Sam started to address the comments, "Hazel is fine. I miss seeing her face too, but she will remain off-camera today due to some unexpected circumstances." Hazel was relieved he had explained it so elegantly, excluding saying she was not presentable.

Samantha promptly made two comments that changed Hazel's mind about everything. She chatted, "How can we, as stakeholders, know she'll be prepared to present at the summit if she can't be prepared today?" Then, "Have you worked her too hard, Sam?"

Hazel lost all sense that she was shivering with cold and instead felt as if her skin was on fire. Samantha was coming after her and disguising it with professionalism, but accusing Sam of anything was too much.

Hazel glared at Samantha, loathing the smug look on her face. She turned on her webcam, hair plastered to her face, still visibly dripping onto her shirt. Several things happened at once. The audience reacted, some laughing, some shocked, and others looking curious. Hazel said, "I don't know if you've ever worked with Sam, but he would never. I'm more than prepared for this presentation and the summit. I just got caught in a downpour." And Sam typed into the SyncUp chat, "Jesus, Hazel, how wet are you? ;)"

It was his typed message that derailed the meeting. The room suddenly stood still, but Hazel could feel the attendees typing. Samantha's face looked triumphant (but why?), and Sam, for the first time Hazel had ever seen, was speechless and red in the face. He mumbled something barely audible that sounded like, "Sorry, wrong chat."

Lou called the meeting back to order, "Hey, hey, everyone. Let's get back to our agenda. I believe we were set to go through the Leadership Training first. All your recommended changes have been implemented, so keep an eye out for them. In the end, we'll ask for your final feedback as we seek approval at the end of this week."

As if in defiance, they presented the Leadership Training flawlessly. When everyone was dismissed, and only Hazel, Sam, and Lou remained in the room, Lou again broke the awkward silence. He said soothingly,

"Don't worry about it too much. Everyone's chatted in the wrong room or been on the mic when they intended to be muted. Everyone will move on; it'll be the gossip for a day."

Sam let out a long exhale. "It's my first time, and I'm… mortified. Thank you, Lou, for getting the meeting back on track. I'm so sorry to both of you." Lou exited, leaving only Hazel and Sam. Sam repeated his apology, "I'm so sorry, Hazel, I thought I was typing in our DM." When she laughed, the relief that washed his face was so comical it made her laugh again.

She replied, "You know, the worst part was the winky face. There'd be plausible deniability if it wasn't for the wink." They were coming terrifyingly close to a conversation that would change everything. The possibility thrilled through her body before she tried to stamp it out. It was too soon. CARE wasn't over. The summit was still to come.

Sam stroked his beard, and Hazel imagined how it would feel to her touch. "I'm embarrassed. I guess I should try to keep work chat to work topics." He was watching her but suddenly alerted. "You're freezing! Go dry off!"

CHAPTER 15

CHOOSE THE RIGHT FORUM FOR COMMUNICATION

"The ability to shoot off an email or chat with someone in seconds is a blessing, but it's also so easy it's a temptation to use in all circumstances. A virtual meeting is necessary for constructive feedback, asking complex questions, or having difficult conversations."

~

April 2, 2016

I made the horrible mistake of re-reading some of my entries. I tend to think of myself in a good light. Not that I'm perfect or even anyone very important, but at least I am fair-minded, have some patience, and am decent to be around. Reading my own diary entries has me doubting that.

~

THIS PASSAGE, even more than some of the ones about Alex, made Hazel long to speak to her mother. She would assure her that she was a kind, loving person whom the community respected and looked up to. Sometimes, being caught up in trivial things was normal, but her values were apparent. That she shouldn't doubt or feel embarrassed.

SHE WAS STILL FEELING the needling in her heart from the journal entry when she logged into the Sanity Check for Frank's presentation. Idly wondering about what the important things were to her. They had agreed to forego their quirky tradition today to give Frank their full attention. When Frank joined the SyncUp, all her attention went to him. "Oh, Frank. How can I help?"

Frank grimaced. "That bad, eh?"

"You're literally wan. Like a 16th-century peasant or something."

SyncUp played its tinkling sound announcing Meg's

entry. She looked at Frank and drew herself back in shock. "Dude, have you slept, like, recently?"

Frank looked down at his desk and nodded, "Yeah, I know. I've definitely overdone it and am honestly not feeling great. I keep telling myself it's almost done. Plus, it's so good. I can't wait to show you ladies. This shit is awesome!"

Hazel's face softened. "We can't wait to see it, either."

Meg said slyly, "It's true, I'm definitely stoked to see what you've sacrificed yourself for, but can we address a rumor I heard first?"

Frank's eyes had been dull but sparked at the question. "You know I'm here for the gossip. What'd you hear?"

Meg said, "Maybe you could ask Hazel?"

Frank looked confused for a moment. Hazel figured Meg must have heard about Sam's mistaken chatroom, but Frank had not. Frank snapped his fingers. "Something to do with working with that asshole. Did he finally show his true colors to the CARE team?"

Meg played with her tongue inside her cheek and tried to stifle her giggles but couldn't quite. "You're right on one count! Hazel?"

Hazel briefly considered where to start her answer. "Sam told me about the meeting where he was an asshole. He's haunted by it. He immediately regretted it and almost resigned after it happened. Did you know he apologized to the guy he went after the very next day? How about this? Do you remember when that meeting was?"

Neither of them expected her to reply this way; she could tell by the dazed looks on their faces. Frank replied first, "I mean, I was there. It was probably a few years ago now."

"It was while I was on leave. Sam was worried about me and couldn't figure out where I was or why I wasn't in office, and he let that worry overwhelm him."

Meg exclaimed, "Oh my God! It's true you're together. I thought it was a half-truth when I heard…."

Hazel cut her off, "Hold on, we're not together. I assumed you heard about what happened at the Stakeholder's meeting. What did you hear, exactly?"

Frank jumped in, "Wait, I'm so behind! What happened at the Stakeholder meeting?"

Meg ignored him and continued, "I did hear that. He said something in the SyncUp chat about how wet you were with a winky emoji? Hearing you now, I'm guessing the rest was an assumption. I heard you two were dating but not talking about it."

Frank's eyes were saucers. "Go back to the comment, *please*. Why is he talking about you being wet?"

Hazel braced herself. "I was literally caught in a rainstorm. I had been off-camera because I looked a complete mess. Then Samantha asked how they would know if I was ready for the summit if I wasn't ready right then, and accused Sam of overworking me, so I turned on the camera anyway."

Frank hung on every word. "This is amazing. And hilarious. Wait, why would he say that with a winky face anyway?"

"I mean, he didn't mean to chat it in the SyncUp Chat. He meant to send it to me as a DM in Chatter." Frank narrowed his eyes for her to continue, and she did. "And I'm not totally surprised at the message because we've gotten really close and… things have gotten pretty overtly flirtatious."

Meg huffed and repeated, "'Pretty overtly flirtatious.' I'd say so!"

The conversation seemed to be the most fun Frank had ever had. "So okay, why aren't you dating? You both like each other. He's accidentally saying sexual things. Apparently, he loved you years ago? Fill. In. These. Blanks." He clapped at each word.

Hazel held up her hands. "Whoa, okay, I wouldn't say he loves me, and you know why! You're the person who told me you can't date if you're in the same department!"

They all sat silently. Meg said softly, "I don't know. It sounds like love to me. You'll figure it out." Sometimes Meg was surprisingly soft for someone who only wore shades of black and grey.

"Mmm, we should let Frank amaze us with his presentation." Hazel nodded toward him.

Frank only said, "I guess." However, he shared his slide deck and delivered a genuinely interesting and well-researched presentation.

Hazel and Meg asked questions along the way that they believed were likely to come up from HR. Frank had clearly anticipated these and was able to answer all of them succinctly. He finished with a strong recommendation, "You've seen the industry research, the psychological advantages, and historical precedent for using emoji in communication. Those, and our pilot's results, led us to strongly recommend emoji usage in client communications such as social media and chat messages. To minimize liability concerns, we recommended approving a subset of 10 emoji and building parameters for when they should be used. We have prepared what those emoji and parameters could be and will work with our Quality and Training teams in P1 to document and roll out."

Both women applauded in front of their webcams. Hazel told him, "Frank, that was legitimately one of the best presentations I've ever seen. I'm so proud of you!"

"Thanks, Hazel!" Frank let out a squeal. "Okay, what can you tell me about improving? I'm most concerned about timing. I finished this with you in 25 minutes, but I have 45 minutes at the summit. Having an audience will make it take longer naturally- more questions and the activity I skipped with you."

Meg requested that he talk them through the activity and led the group looking at rearranging the order of his slides. Frank only made minor changes but was visibly relieved this dry run had gone so well. "I can't thank you enough. This almost feels like an I'm-too-close-to-it situation at this point."

Hazel scrunched her nose. "I know about that feeling! Let us know how the final approvals go."

Frank's presentation for approval was Thursday, the day before Hazel's. He updated Hazel and Meg immediately.

Frank Simms

ITS A YES! 2:01pm

Meg Malloy

AH! Great job Frank! YESSSS! 2:01pm

Frank Simms

Well, pending some tiny changes, but nothing material. 2:01pm

Hazel Rogers

BRILLIANT! Frank! I'm so excited for you! 2:02pm

How will you celebrate? You've earned it.
2:02pm

Frank Simms

I need to make these little tweaks first but
then I think I'll take out Liz and Brian,
maybe have a nice dinner and go by a park.
2:03pm

Meg Malloy

That sounds lovely. Try to get some short
work days in too. Rest up before the
summit. I wouldn't expect it to be a very
relaxing experience. 2:03pm

Hazel Rogers

Good to know, Meg. Apart from the
presentations, what usually happens?
2:05pm

Meg Malloy

I've only been once but there's usually a lot
of socializing. Some of it's built in- dinners
and mixers. Some are people being
together who generally don't get to be.
They hang out all night, go out clubbing.
That sort of thing. Plus there's always
something scandalous. 2:06pm

Meg Malloy

> Remember last year when everyone was
> talking about that team leader Mickey?
> 2:06pm

Frank Simms

> Oh yeah, I do remember! 2:06pm

Hazel Rogers

> I don't think so? 2:07pm

Meg Malloy

> The rumor was that he hooked up with
> Alice and Lynn. It was a whole thing.
> Anyway, I feel like the event is a rumor mill
> every year. 2:07pm

HAZEL DIDN'T SLEEP SOUNDLY Thursday night. She jolted awake several times feeling as if she was late to get somewhere. At 5:30am, she gave up and set off for the kitchen to make some tea and read the end of *Stocking Full of Love.* She would finish it slightly earlier than the club's schedule, but it was better than tossing and turning.

The last few chapters entranced Hazel. She rested in a way that sleep had not provided. She journeyed with the main character, discovering her belief in Christmas magic, receiving thoughtful stocking stuffers, and having a mightily long night of lovemaking under the Christmas tree. The book made a satisfying papery clap as she closed it.

. . .

Sam Pierce

Ready? 9:45am

Hazel Rogers

Yes. 9:45am

Hazel Rogers

Oddly enough, I'm less nervous than I was
at the last meeting. 9:45am

Sam Pierce

Do I jinx anything if I say me too? I'm at
least comforted I won't make a spectacle of
myself. 9:45am

Hazel Rogers

False. You're always a spectacle unto
yourself with how you command everyone's
attention. :P 9:46am

HAZEL WATCHED as the attendees streamed into the
SyncUp. All the usual Stakeholders were there, but today
they were also joined by additional high-ranking leaders,
including Dana. As each of them filed into the room,
Hazel felt her confidence grow. She imagined their
impressed faces at the end. The final boost came as Dana

entered. She seemed lit from within, as if she would rather be here than anywhere else. She greeted Sam, Hazel, and Lou personally, "Sam! Hazel! I'm so glad to see you again. Hazel, your idea for teaser trailers has been all anyone wants to talk to me about these past few weeks. What an enormous success we owe to you. Lou, we haven't met personally before, but I have heard such wonderful things about your work, and it's a pleasure to meet you today." The warmth of Dana's greeting swelled in Hazel's chest. They were going to crush this. Hazel could feel it.

They planned to perform everything exactly as they intended to present at the summit. Hazel started them, imagining herself on a large stage alone in the spotlight, which fueled her. She felt all eyes on her and did every-thing in her power to maintain the audience's attention. Hazel sensed she was doing it; she was commanding the room as Sam had done so many times. She hit every mark perfectly. Her sense of pride and accomplishment soared around her as she handed off the presentation to Sam.

Sam was electrifying. Even though Hazel knew the material by heart, she couldn't take her eyes off him. He was sparking with energy and passion for the training he had built. When he asked for volunteers, every hand was raised. When he revealed each step of CARE, the chat-room exploded with cheers and gasps. Hazel had never seen anyone read and react to a room as well as he did. Seeing his mastery at work made Hazel's heart pound in her ears, and her blood rushed to other parts of her body as well.

Sam handed off to Lou to close out the presentation, and he, too, seemed buoyant with confidence. He spoke to the changes of the How-To articles with such graceful ease he received very few questions when he opened it up to the floor. Sam returned to center stage. "That concludes our Leadership Training. Thank you all so much for being such a captive audience. We will now open the floor for questions and concerns. Please speak up now with anything you may have, as this is our final planned meeting for approval."

There was a tense few seconds of silence where everyone seemed to be waiting for someone else to start the discussion. Hazel felt alive. Wired. Then everyone began silently applauding; their microphones were off, but she could see hands clapping together in almost every video feed. The impressed faces she had imagined starting the meeting shined back at her. Sam started to talk, but Dana interrupted, "I usually wait to say my piece because it tends to put an end to others' feedback, so let me ask first, does anyone else have feedback?" Nobody replied, and Dana's face erupted into her wide smile. "Then I will say I see nothing that could be improved. If you all present so well at the summit, it may well be the most meaningful training we've had. This is undoubtedly due to countless hours working together and applying feedback you've already received, so my thanks are also extended to you amazing Stakeholders."

Once everyone had exited, Hazel, Sam, and Lou gaped at each other. Sam started, "Never. Never even once have I presented something for approval that required no changes. It has been such an honor working with you two. We should all feel extremely proud."

Lou was stunned. He shook his head and said, "I can't believe how well that went. Incredible job, everyone. I don't know what to do now."

Sam gave a throaty ha and said, "We should all go home for the day, and I'm totally serious. Go celebrate."

Before Hazel had logged out of the SyncUp, she heard her Chatter alert.

Sam Pierce

> Get your phone, I need to talk to you
> immediately. 12:01pm

She picked up her phone, feeling it buzz in her hand as
she lifted it.

SPierce

> You were incredible. I've never seen anyone
> so captivating. It was watching magic.
> 12:01pm

SPierce

> How did you erupt with light? 12:01pm

SPierce

> I could drink you and I would glow.
> 12:01pm

SPierce

> Can I drink you? 12:01pm

Hazel's breath caught. She could only hear her heart
resonating in her ears. She typed yes, and the phone rang.
She answered.

Sam's voice, guttural, barely restrained, greeted her, "Hey."

"Hi." She hardly recognized her own voice, a low rasp that met his.

He rumbled a hum. "I'm picking you up and bringing you to your bed."

"I wrap my arms around your neck and my legs around your body. I'm kissing your neck."

"I lean you onto the bed. My body is pressing against yours. I kiss you deeply, nibble your ear, lick along your clavicle. I pull you up to sit. That shirt has to come off."

Hazel bit her lip. "Not before yours comes off. I grab the back of your shirt and glide it over your head, then remove mine."

"I unclasp your bra and run my tongue down your chest. I suck at your breast, then continue down your abdomen. I'm unbuttoning your pants, pulling them off, and tossing them in the corner."

Hazel could imagine the look on Sam's face. The tension in his voice told her he was about to take her. "I'm running my hands along your back. I slip off my panties."

Sam groaned. "Spread your legs for me. God, you're beautiful. I'm tasting you slowly. Licking your labia. You're so wet you're making my dick throb. I flick your clit with my tongue, then suck it gently." He paused. "Are you touching yourself?"

Hazel hummed an mmhmm. "Are you?"

"Not yet." She could tell he was grinning.

Hazel said, "I'm running my fingers through your hair, grabbing it, and tugging while you make me squirm."

"I can't get enough of your pussy. My tongue swirls along every part of you, and I start fingering you. You're so tight, and I feel you flex against my fingers. I'm increasing my pace."

Hazel gasped, quickening the motion of her own hand

She could see the scene in her mind. Feel it. "I don't want to come yet. I need you in me. I need to feel you in my mouth first."

Sam replied, "Do you want to taste yourself?"

"Please."

"I'm kissing you. Our tongues are learning each other. Your lips are so soft."

"I'm pushing your chest to roll you onto your back. It's my turn. I unbutton your pants and pull down your underwear. Your cock is gleaming, gorgeous; I've never felt anyone so hard. I'm teasing my hand along it, then lick you from base to tip."

"You're making me squirm with anticipation. Nobody has ever taken their time like this with me. I'm grabbing your shoulders and playing with your hair."

"I take you all the way in my mouth, swirling my tongue around you with every move. I flick your frenulum and hum as I take you in."

"Goddamnit Hazel. Can I have you?"

"Take me. I need to feel you in me." Hazel's voice was breathy.

"I leap on top of you and press my dick into you. You're so soft. I feel your wetness drip along me. I dip down to kiss you as we slowly find our rhythm."

"I'm meeting you with your thrusts and swivel my hips slightly from side to side. I nibble your earlobe after we break our kiss and breathe along your neck." Hazel's voice cracked, "I'm going to come."

"I'll go with you. I lean into your body and grab your ass. Our pace increases."

Hazel moaned, "I scratch down your back. I can feel you everywhere, inside, against my clit. I flex my internal muscles, begging for you to come."

She could hear him stroking his length. Sam erupted

with a roar. Hazel relished the sound, and it sent her over the edge, release flooding her.

Hazel laughed, unbridled. Breathlessly, she said, "I've never done anything like that before."

Sam spoke with a gentle purr, "Me either. But we aren't done. We're laying on our sides spooning. I'm stroking your silhouette."

"I lean back against you. I want to feel you everywhere."

"I whisper in your ear. You're the most beautiful woman I've ever seen. Hazelberry, how is the best sex of my life over the phone with you?"

Hazel stilled. What had she done? "I… It was great for me too."

Sam sensed her pause. "Don't be afraid, Hazel. I can't wait to see you. Only one more week."

CHAPTER 16
DON'T JUST PARTICIPATE

"Participation by itself can be hollow. Remote workers have an important voice in the workforce. We must move past participation to check a box and toward being present and engaged in meetings, with our teams, and in every aspect of our work."

PLEASE PICK UP, please pick up, please pick up. The mantra in Hazel's head repeated as the phone rang. "Hey-zel, everything okay?" Rosie's voice shimmied on her name.

"I messed up. We were high after our presentation, and we had phone sex. Now I have no idea what to do or where we stand, and he told me not to worry, but what does that even mean? What does he think we are? What happens at the summit?" Hazel rapid-fired everything clanging around her brain.

"You did *what?!* Hazel, slow down. It sounds like you're speeding through every worst-case scenario possible. Worst-case is not likely where the truth lives. I've got another session today; I can be there in a little over an hour. Try not to doom spiral."

The phrase doom spiral struck Hazel as so accurate and funny that it did actually help, though perhaps not in the way Rosie intended. She tried to organize her brain. Digest what had occurred as neutrally as possible, then sort through her emotions. She quickly realized the pesky feelings were the problem.

Rosie was there in 70 minutes flat, sitting on Hazel's couch and listening to the whole story. When Hazel reached the end and began to fret, Rosie grabbed her knee. "I understand this is a big event, and it's super fresh. Do you regret it?"

"No… Maybe?" Hazel made a frustrated sigh. "I don't regret it because it was honest and so natural. It was amazing! I'm not sure it was even avoidable. At the same time, I'm so scared. I have no idea if we're on the same page or even what page I'm on."

"What questions do you have for yourself?"

Hazel considered and said, "I want to know what I have the right to figure out. The answer to all these same questions I've had. I'm ready to overcome these 'roadblocks.' But I can't even ask myself these things because I have no clue where he stands!"

Rosie nodded. "So you're saying you want a relationship with Sam?"

"Yes. I'd also like to know that I feel the same about him in person. Though I'm sure that I will." Hazel squeezed the throw pillow on her couch.

"Okay, and what questions do you have for Sam?"

"What all the flirting means, and what the phone sex means. Is this how he treats a friend, or are we friends with benefits? If he is interested in being together, what are his ideas about how we'd work?"

Rosie dipped her head again. "So you want to know where you stand and hope that he feels the same way you do. That's completely reasonable. Is it okay if I share what I'd do?"

"Please, yes!"

"Okay. It's powerful that you know what you want, and I agree it's frustrating and crazy-making to try to navigate all these questions one-sided. I would try to mitigate that as much as possible by focusing on what you'd be willing to do to make your relationship work. That will prepare you for the conversation. Do that knowing you may not have to act on any of it, and it's all a grain of salt until you discuss it with Sam. I also have a concern." Hazel raised her head to Rosie. "I understand you were both swept away by your amazing performances at work, which is a great sign of mutual respect, but why did he call? He called instead of sexting, which has been your normal means of communication, and instead of a video call. It strikes me as a little weird. Maybe he isn't comfortable with you knowing about his appearance."

Hazel squeezed the pillow again, watching her fingernails dig into the fabric. "I don't know, I never thought of it like that."

Rosie rubbed her thumb across her lip. "I guess you'll find that part out next week. Unless... Is he on social media?"

Hazel shook her fists at the sky. "Trust me, I've looked. It's something of an ongoing joke. He says he's just not into it."

"Hmm. Aside from that part, my take on all this is positive. I mentioned the mutual respect thing already, but also, you both seemed to enjoy yourself even without visual stimulation. He even phone-snuggled you after the phone sex, something I'm not sure has ever happened before in the history of phones, and he told you not to worry. So maybe don't."

Hazel laughed at Rosie's assessment. "We're making

phone-snuggling history! Here's the thing… the not worrying part makes me worry the most. What does he think I shouldn't worry about? The presentation, our job security, the future of our relationship? It could be anything! And I'm too scared to ask. There's way too much riding on the line with this presentation next week."

Rosie frowned and raised an eyebrow. "So what are you going to do until then?"

Hazel shrugged. "Act normal, I guess? Really, the original plan to talk to him after everything has to stand. If waiting doesn't kill me."

"I wish I could tell you what the best answer is. My only advice is to do what you said you're ready for. Crush those roadblocks, but you have to do it with Sam and not alone."

Fortunately, Sam appeared to have come to the same conclusion about acting normal. The weekend was filled with texts ranging from shared frustrations at the price of milk to their most despised words (Sam claimed 'oozed' was the worst, and Hazel insisted on 'slough'). Hazel was relieved to find there was plenty of continued playfulness as well.

SPierce

I'm going to tell you about your perfect date. 5:31pm

Hazel

Bold of you. Let's see how close you get. 5:31pm

SPierce

> Easy. It's all about adventure. We'd start the day by doing some activity like kayaking or hiking. 5:31pm

SPierce

> Next, we'd get a warm drink inside a bookstore and pick out the latest read. Some relaxing after that, might start reading actually. If it's nice, we'd stay outside in a hammock or a picnic blanket, if not we'd snuggle up on the couch. 5:32pm

SPierce

> Then we'd go out for dinner to somewhere with food or drink we haven't tried before. We'd order different things to share and maximize the new tastes. I'd want a beer, but you'd like the wine more so we'd get a bottle of wine. We're getting some tasty beer next time. 5:32pm

THAT HE HAD USED "WE" was not lost on Hazel; it was a great source of comfort to her. The one downside of both of them acting normal was the fear that he may only think of them as friends with benefits had grown.

Hazel

> I'm a little disappointed. 5:34pm

SPierce

> Oh? 5:34pm

Hazel

> At myself for not being able to find anything
> to pick on. 5:34pm

SPierce

> Hah! :) 5:34pm

THE CARE TEAM meetings next week were not scheduled
in their usual time slots. There was no need for them to
continue meeting as frequently to develop Phase 2, and
now they were focused on meeting for handoffs with
Phases 3 and 4. Working with a new group of people
meant meeting availability was different, and she had
found the first week to be a bit all over the place out of
necessity. Despite the schedule feeling disjointed, the Phase
3 meetings were particularly interesting to Hazel. The
Training department was taking Phase 3 to develop and
give the All Employee CARE Training set to deploy mid-
next year.

Jasmond was staying on the project but transitioning
from stakeholder to leader. He had assembled a team from
Training who would assist him in development. Ariel was
amongst the team along with Keisha, Taylor, and Howell,
all of whom Hazel knew to various degrees. She felt that
the handoff meetings with them were promising but tried
not to read too much into them. At the first meeting, Ariel

greeted Hazel and shared she had heard about her incredible work in Phase 2 and couldn't wait to see the outcome.

During their second meeting, Jasmond went fishing regarding Hazel's interest in staying on with the Phase 3 team. "What would everyone think about having someone else from Phase 2 stay on with us? Only if she were interested, of course."

There was nodding and thumbs up given toward the camera, and Hazel flushed. "I bet she would be really excited if that happened." Jasmond couldn't guarantee anything but said he would investigate.

When everyone else had exited the SyncUp, and it was her and Sam remaining, he winked at her. "Look at that! Training is lusting after you! Just like we planned." He chuckled.

"It is pretty amazing he's going to ask. Even if I'm working with them in a Comms capacity, I think the exposure is a huge plus… and I'm low-key almost done with the How-To and some accompanying training material."

"And you've been holding out on me!" Sam accused.

"It's not done yet, and I've only been able to tackle tiny bits at a time, but it's adding up. You can see it. I'll email you what I have so far."

Sam was satisfied. "Good, thank you. One other thing before we break if you have time?"

"Shoot."

"I was asked to help set up and break down the summit. Instead of arriving Monday with everyone else, I'll get there Saturday afternoon. Unfortunately, everyone will abandon me Wednesday except for the few others staying late. I'll get to fly back home Thursday morning."

Hazel pursed her lips, suppressing her mirth. "Your reward for good work is more work, you know."

Sam agreed, "Yeahhhh, I don't really mind. I wanted you to know, though."

HAZEL ENTERED Tamra's SyncUp with a salute that earned her an eye roll. "Reporting for duty!"

She let Tamra know about all the plans for the summit and emailed her the How-To and training material along with Sam. "I'm flying out Sunday evening because there weren't any direct flights available, and the layovers are killing the timeline. Getting from the mountains of North Carolina to Sacramento is harder than I expected."

Tamra pouted. "I wish I could go! I've heard so many great things about your work on this project and the fact you're presenting on center stage?!"

"Wait, you aren't going?" Hazel had assumed Tamra would be there.

"I was supposed to go but requested an exception to stay home. My wife is sick." Seeing Hazel's face, she quickly continued, "Nothing too serious, but she does have the flu. I'm fine so far, but I can't justify traveling when I might be a carrier. Can you imagine going and getting your whole company sick, literally?"

"I hope you stay well and that she feels better soon." Tamra nodded her thanks. "I think the last thing from me is Jasmond said he might be reaching out to you. In an offhand way, he mentioned that he might see if I can stay on and work with his Training team in Phase 3."

"Aha, now you're encroaching on my agenda items! He already has reached out, and I wanted to talk to you about it."

Hazel's eyes widened. "That was fast."

"Yeah, he doesn't waste any time. So it sounded like he wants you to take care of their communication needs but also took time to sing your praises about the Teaser Trailers. I think he wants to make a similar approach for the All

Employee Training. This is a huge deal for you, but I still want to ask, are you interested?”

Hazel blinked. “Uh, put me down as a hell yes.”

Tamra made a checking motion. “Done and done.”

SATURDAY WAS BORING. Hazel tried everything she could think of to brighten it up. She walked down to her favorite local cafe with her newest book club read, *Romancing Antiquities.* A book about a witch who owned an Antique Shop and put enchantments on her favorite items that would cause the purchasers to “realize their truth in love.” Hazel wasn’t far enough in to know exactly what that meant, but she was wary of what could be a heavily multi-perspective book. Not always her favorite style, but she’d read it anyway.

Sitting next to the window and reading her book had been a decent distraction, except it got old quickly. Rosie and Nick were coming over for dinner and to help her pack, but they weren’t arriving until the evening; that was an impossible 7 hours away!

She opened her phone, but nothing had changed.

SPierce

Getting onto the plane now. 8:48am

Hazel

Safe travels! 8:48am

Being unable to text from a flight is a ridiculous ineptitude of technology.

Hazel brought out a puzzle and turned on *30 Rock* for some familiar background noise. Even these comforting activities didn't relieve her boredom or underlying self-loathing. Was this who she was now? A woman with nothing to entertain her except constant upkeep with her crush?

Uncomfortable with these thoughts, she packed a lunch and went on a long meandering bike ride, letting whatever whim she encountered decide her direction. Making room to feel pulled in a direction pushed everything else out of her mind. She enjoyed steep downhills like a child, squealing and sticking her legs out. To her surprise, she discovered new neighborhoods, even ending up stopping to eat her lunch in a tiny preserved area she had never seen before.

Confidence rediscovered and cheeks blazing with cold exposure, she began the ride back home. She made a game of trying to remember the turns she took so she could travel back the same way in reverse. Only the evergreens retained their leaves now. Even those late-coloring broad-leaf varieties had dropped their load. Hazel loved the colorful fall in the mountains but also the sound of crunching leaves under her bike tires.

At 5PM, Hazel heard her door open and the shuffling sound of dropping coats. "I'm in the kitchen!" She uncorked a bottle of wine and poured three glasses.

Rosie ran into the room, Nick chasing her, making pinching motions at her. Between laughs, Nick raised a bag, "We brought the salad stuff." Rosie had already retrieved a knife and was standing on the opposite side of the cutting board. She gestured for the bag, and Nick delivered it to her by flinging it onto the counter.

Hazel smirked at their hijinks, still looking down, focusing on chopping the tempeh. "Nick, if you want to get the pot started, go ahead and throw the oil and onions in."

He set down his wine and turned on the heat. Stirring onions, he glanced at Hazel. "So how are *things*?"

Hazel shot a look of mock exasperation at Rosie, who shrugged and replied, "What? You know I tell him everything." Hazel glared at her but laughed, "Yeah, I do know." She mashed the tempeh with a fork to crumble it and soaked it in a brown sauce. "I'm good. There's definitely a feeling of culmination. Sam is already at the site. I fly out tomorrow. Our project will be nearly completed by Tuesday evening, and I get to see him and hopefully figure things out."

Nick had stopped stirring. "That part is kind of a lot, no?"

Rosie flicked her fingers at him. "Back to stirring, sir. I won't have burnt onions in my chili."

He shot back, "The beer will deglaze them."

Rosie said, "Hah! I'm getting more and more excited for this recipe all the time."

Hazel answered, "It's a lot. But I'm so ready. It will be a relief to be on the same page no matter what that is at this point. What about you, ready for Thanksgiving with the llamas?"

Nick turned back to the pot and started stirring with a comical speed. "I'm just kidding. Of course I'm ready! It'll be a good time no matter what they've got going on. Can't bring us down."

Rosie said darkly, "That's the spirit." and drank from her glass.

After dinner, Hazel shared the contents of her suitcase,

which received oohs and aahs until Rosie asked how she was doing her hair. The scrutiny of wearing it "down like normal" led the party into her bathroom, where Rosie rifled through every drawer, searching for accessories. She settled on a white beaded elastic hair clip and then insisted on demonstrating how Hazel should use it. Rosie swept up Hazel's hair, making it look effortless and regal in 3 minutes flat. Hazel stared at the result in the mirror. "I… How'd you do that so easily?"

Rosie shrugged. "It is easy."

Hazel shook her head. "Not for me. I love it, though, and I will try." She tucked the clip into a side pocket of her suitcase.

CHAPTER 17
TRAVEL WELL

"You may love working from home (I hope you do!) but remember that occasional travel may be necessary depending on your department and position. If you need to travel, familiarize yourself with the expense policy, and enjoy your time."

HAZEL STARED around at her fellow passengers, jealous of their ability to sleep on a plane. This was one skill she had never been able to master. Her flight had been delayed, so now it was the witching hour somewhere above Missouri or Kansas. She was grateful that, thanks to Sam, she had some offline work to keep her busy. On his flight he reviewed the How-To documentation and Onboarding Training she had worked up and left feedback notes throughout them.

To be fair, not all the notes were feedback. Hazel had found two so far that had been asides. The first was for an unfortunate typo where she had used the word bare instead of bear. Sam had said, "Unexpectedly exciting content ;)." The second was a reply to her section on finding a change of scenery, "I'll never forget the first time I saw your bedroom wall art." Hazel found the rest of his feedback to be precise and inspiring and was implementing most of his suggested changes.

The sun had barely started its ascent, causing the sky to lighten from black to gray as she reached the end of the Training document. She saw a substantially longer comment than the rest at the bottom. "I know it's why you want to move to Training, but what you've built here is a story. It's your success story. I can imagine you giving this training. You'd be telling your personal tale naturally and humorously, which is so powerful. At the same time, the presentation on screen would light up at the right moments. You should try to sell it like that. Record yourself delivering it." She would have never imagined recording herself delivering the training but knew as soon as she read it that it was the right move. She marked her Calendar with a reminder to experiment with recording after the summit and closed her laptop.

EVERYTHING WAS fine until she began to walk up the stairs to the Hilton's entrance. It was 10am on the West Coast, and maybe it was because Hazel was exhausted, but each step she took toward those doors met her with crushing waves of notion. She thought *Sam is in there. I'm going to be on stage in front of everyone. I'm rolling out the most major initiative being presented. I'm going to see Sam for the first time. Where will he be? Where is he now? Do I look okay? Everything might change. My whole life might change.* She felt she was walking through invisible yet tangible barriers weighing against her.

She half expected Sam to be waiting for her at the entrance, but when she pulled her suitcase over the threshold, there was no one around except the desk clerk. She checked in and received her room key, and started toward her room. It wasn't until she unlocked the door and toured the small space that she remembered she was pretty early. The summit activities for day one would not begin until 4pm. She looked at the schedule in her Calendar. Yes, today was only an introduction and a dinner. She still felt heavy, and now her stomach was writhing with anticipation. Hazel made the easy decision to shower the airports off of her and try to sleep.

As a wonderful surprise, she found she was able to rest. She woke up at 2pm feeling slightly more refreshed but still leaden with suspense. Her phone buzzed on the nightstand. She reached over to find she had missed several messages from Sam.

SPierce

> How's flying? 10:39am

SPierce

> I thought you'd be here by now, everything okay? 12:01pm

SPierce

> Your flight landed, are we playing hide and seek? My room is 1005 if you want to come by, or I can meet you anywhere if you want. 2:03pm

Hazel

OMG I'm so sorry, I meant to message you when I got here and I don't know how I didn't. No excuse, I'm fine and I'm here, just took a nap 2:03pm

Hazel

Oh, we're on the same floor I think, I'm 1062 2:03pm

SPierce

No worries, I know traveling is so tiring. And yeah, I think FutureApp has floors 9, 10, and 11 all for us. Maybe others too. There are a lot of people milling around now 2:04pm

Hazel

It was dead when I got here, I was shocked until I remembered we didn't start until 4. 2:04pm

HAZEL INHALED SLOWLY, filling her lungs to full capacity. She held her breath while she typed. This was it. She felt more ready to meet Sam than she had ever been for anything and was terrified at the prospect.

Let me get ready and I'll come meet you.
2:04pm

SPierce

Sounds great :) 2:04pm

She selected the most casual outfit she had packed. Tailored black slacks, a thin black belt, and a burgundy light-knit turtleneck that she tucked into the front. She fussed at her hair which had not yet recovered from the hours of flying and different water from the shower, and quickly applied some makeup. All the while wondering if she would throw up, for the wriggling in her stomach had reached new heights.

Hazel

On the way! 2:14pm

SPierce

Me too! 2:14pm

Oh no, she was going to meet him in the hall somewhere? Her nerves pitched even higher at the unpredictability. She opened the door and started following the signs to lower-numbered rooms.

Hazel could tell Sam was right about more of their colleagues having arrived. She passed many people coming in and out of their rooms, happily hailing at those they recognized. However, these other movements were only distractions as she continued the path toward Sam's room. She focused on steadying her breath and willing herself not to vomit. Her eyes were peeled for Sam's dark hair. His perfect teeth. His dimpled cheek. She felt the same foreboding she had entering the hotel, as if resistance met her at each step, and her mind raced.

THEN THERE HE WAS. Everything seemed to freeze, including Hazel, as she stopped dead in her tracks. All the weight. All the nausea. All the trepidation. It all evaporated into nothingness, and she felt herself float. She resumed walking toward him; she had no choice in the matter because he was magnetic. No, they were magnetic, and she could feel him being drawn to her, too.

They were standing in front of each other in the 10th-floor hallway of the Sacramento Hilton. Sam's eyes were hard, determined. Hazel awkwardly reached out for a handshake, and he grinned and shook his head no before sweeping her into an embrace. Time froze again, and Hazel would have stayed there forever. He smelled of salt and fir, and as she breathed him in, she could feel their difference in height. Sam was tall, lean, and muscular. Her senses were flooded. Taking in everything about Sam and recognizing the feeling of safety, warmth, acceptance, and relief that rushed through her.

Sam pulled away slowly, his voice croaky. "I can't believe you're here."

Hazel was dizzy. Giddy. She breathed, "Me either."

Sam motioned for her to follow, and she walked toward his room. She felt a strong pull to hold his hand but resisted as they weaved through still more people.

When they entered his room, the first thing Hazel noticed was that he had unpacked. "You hung your clothes up?"

"Yeah, I wouldn't normally but presenting, you know, trying to prevent wrinkles here." Sam leaned into a seated position on the corner of the bed. "How was the traveling?"

Hazel sat in the armchair across from him. "Normal stuff. Both flights were delayed, but nothing too terrible. Oh! And your feedback on the Remote Training was everything! Thank you so much! I edited in the air."

Sam's face was kind. "There wasn't much to suggest, a few small things. I was happy to have something to look at on the flight, too."

Hazel asked, "How's it been on the setup crew?"

He rolled his eyes and chuckled. "Feels like busywork if I'm being honest, plenty to do, but most of the morning was printing and making breakout room boxes with Samantha."

"I didn't realize she was helping set up too."

"There were eight of us. I think I was the only non-local. Usually, the people that live right around the area are the crew who comes early and stay late."

A book on the nightstand caught Hazel's eyes. She picked it up and gestured, "What is this?!"

Sam clicked his tongue. "I think you know it? I'm a little behind you, though."

"You're reading *Stocking Full of Love*?!" Hazel was aghast. "Since when are you into romance novels?"

He winced slightly. "I have a confession…. I read with your book club."

Hazel guffawed. "You what?!"

"I've been reading the books you mention. You made it sound so fun, and I thought I'd try one and just… didn't stop."

"But then I've been spoiling you! You always ask for updates, and I love it because I can talk without worrying about referencing something not everyone has read yet." Hazel was falling into his expression. "You let me spoil you because you knew that."

He nodded in admission. "Yes, and honestly, I didn't want you to think I was creepy for reading what you were reading. I was afraid that could have a creep factor."

It slipped out before she could stop it, "Or a cute factor." She remembered seeing familiar-looking books on his bookshelf. "Now you owe me a backlog of book reviews."

Speaking with Sam in person was disarmingly comfortable. It felt just as natural as being with Rosie, and they quickly got lost in discussion. All of the questions she longed to ask him were pushed away by the flow of conversation and the distraction his appearance provided. She had been right about his broad shoulders. When he leaned back on the bed, the buttons of his shirt and the fabric around his thighs strained just so. Hazel couldn't help but imagine what his strong body would look like, would feel like, beneath those clothes. She was finding it hard not to reach out and playfully touch him as they spoke. As she struggled not to give him a shove in the shoulder for disparaging the Beast in *Belle's Beast*, she saw the digital clock on the nightstand shine 3:52pm. She launched from the chair, and Sam followed. They were standing so very near now she could smell him again. Sam asked, "What is it?"

Hazel gestured toward the clock, "We're going to be late!"

Sam grabbed the room key from the pillow, and they rushed into the hall.

They arrived at the auditorium right on time and edged through the door as quietly as possible. Dana was walking out to the podium. Most of the seats were already taken, but Sam pointed to the right, his height giving him a better view. He grabbed Hazel's hand so she would follow but dropped it as fast.

Hazel could feel the heat from Sam's arm against her own. She tried to pay attention to Dana, but transitioning from her and Sam to a room filled with their colleagues brought her questions for him to the forefront of her mind. She wondered how to broach the conversation and when it would be wise to do so. The sound of applause brought her attention back to the stage. Dana had exited, and another Chief Officer was explaining the format for the next three days. The rest of this evening would include dinner and socialization. Tomorrow was the main event where everyone was required to attend the State of the Business Address and CARE Leadership Training. They would break for lunch and return to workshops located in smaller conference rooms. Everyone was encouraged to attend the three workshops they found most intriguing or beneficial to their line of business. There would be a mixer tomorrow night to end the day. The third day began with a short Closing Address and continental breakfast before people departed.

At the end of the meeting, everyone was dismissed and asked to move into the dining hall for dinner. A great scraping of chairs and feet erupted around them. Sam leaned over and whispered to Hazel, "Go to dinner with me?" His breath on her neck sent goosebumps down her body. She agreed, and they joined the throngs of people queueing to find a seat at a dinner table.

The dining hall was more formal than Hazel had imagined, filled with large round tables, each adorned with a long white tablecloth and a floral centerpiece. Looking around the room, Hazel only recognized a few faces. Most of the attendees were higher up the corporate ladder than her peers. She tried to spot Frank to no avail but saw Lou and started leading the way over to him. On the way, she noticed that Sam seemed to know many attendees. He waved to people and gave side hugs to some as they passed.

They pulled chairs at a table Lou had guarded for them and joined four other people, none of whom Hazel was familiar with. She turned to Lou. "I'm not interested in hearing about anyone's flight except for you. I can't believe you flew halfway around the world to be here!"

He leaned close to her and said, "Never again" under his breath with a snicker. Then sat up straight to continue. "It wasn't so bad. I'm just wholly knackered. Not sure how to recover from it. I keep wiping my face with towelettes to stay awake."

Overhearing this, a jaunty-looking man with straw-colored hair across the table said, "Jet lag, huh? It's the worst. You should shine a flashlight behind your knees. Works for me every time."

Sam replied in greeting, "Hey, Peter! Long time no see! And Meredith, wow, good to see you!" He made introductions between Hazel, Lou, Peter, and Meredith. There were two other women seated with them who joined in introducing themselves. One with short black hair named Stacy and another with brown curling locks and dark eyes named Maxine.

The polite conversation continued through the evening,

the group talking about what department they worked in and where they lived. Lou was the furthest traveler and took the spotlight, telling them about living in Cork and the cultural differences he experienced while working with his US colleagues. While everyone was captivated by Lou explaining the pub scene, Sam reached over and held Hazel's hand beneath the tablecloth. Her heart erupted into wings. Their hands were dancing over each other, exploring, fingers gently folding in and out. She felt the calluses on his fingers, a stark contrast from the rest of his smooth skin. Another interesting feature was at the bottom of his hand beneath his pinky, which she couldn't quite place.

When everyone had eaten and plates were cleared away, people began circulating, looking to find friends they hadn't yet seen. As Hazel and Sam stood, their hands fell from each other. Sam was approached by two other coworkers before they could step away. Hazel said, "I'm going to look for Frank," and set off.

After circulating the room twice without finding him, she followed a trickle of people headed for the bar. Frank didn't seem to be there either. Getting worried, she decided to head back to her room. Hazel didn't have Frank's phone number, but maybe she could log into her computer and send him a message.

The room was dark even after she turned on the floor lamp. She sat in the small halo of dim light it provided and unpacked her laptop. To her surprise, Frank was marked as Online in the Chatter App.

Hazel Rogers

Dude, where are you? I've been looking for you everywhere. 6:29pm

.   .   .

Ellipses emerged so that Hazel knew he was typing back to her, though there was a long gap before he sent anything. She expected to receive a long paragraph, but it was only three words when he replied.

Frank Simms

Sick, Room 913 6:38pm

Hazel swept out the door and scurried down the stairs to the ninth floor. When she arrived at room 913, she knocked, but there was no answer. She jiggled the handle and called, "Frank, it's me. Open up!" She waited several minutes, listening to the room beyond. Finally, she heard a toilet flush and what could have been a groan. She knocked again, louder this time. She felt the door give slightly without opening.

"Hazel. I can't open the door." Frank sounded miserable. "You shouldn't even be this close."

"What's happened? How can I help?"

"I caught something on the plane, I think. My stomach is fucked. I can't keep anything down."

"Let me bring you some water and crackers. Do you want any Pepto?"

Frank's breathing was audible, and she could tell he was pacing his breath. "No meds… Water sounds good."

Hazel hesitated, hating to ask, "Are you going to be okay for tomorrow?" There was a commotion on the other side of the door and a splashing sound. Hazel called out, "I'm going to get the water. I'll be back soon!"

She racked her brain, considering anything she could do to help but didn't come up with much. She hated this for Frank. At the front desk, she asked for water bottles, crackers, and additional towels. The clerk read between the lines and loaded two bags of the supplies for her. "I hope your friend feels better soon!"

Me too, Hazel thought as she walked back toward the elevator.

Back at Frank's room, she set the bags in front of the door and knocked. This time the door opened a crack. Frank had been sitting on the floor on the other side, covered in the comforter he had removed from the bed. "Go down the hall, and I'll take them in. Thanks, Hazel."

"I'll go down the hall, but I'm coming back to visit with you for a minute. I'll stay on this side of the door." Hazel moved away and watched Frank reach through the door and pull in the bags. When the door was closed again, she returned and sat on the other side.

"Okay, I'm here. If you need anything, I can go get it, or if you want to chat. Even if not, I'll stay here for a while."

He breathed, "You're the best."

They sat silently for a while, then Frank asked how the day had been so far.

Hazel's mind rushed toward meeting Sam, his embrace, their book banter, holding hands, but she knew he meant the summit events. "As you'd probably expect. There was an opening introduction. Dana and some other dude spoke to us about what to expect and how the next few days would work. Then we went to dinner. That was cool. It was like a real dinner; we made orders at the table and everything. Lots of people here, but I don't know many of them. Sam seems to know everyone."

Despite Frank's state, he lilted his voice. "Oho, how is Sam?"

Hazel cut back, "You really are the worst gossip, you know?"

"It's not gossip if I don't tell anyone! I need to *hear* the drama, not spread it."

She pondered what to say. Hazel didn't mind sharing things with Frank, but the timing seemed so tenuous. Things were going… well. Maybe really well. Maybe perfectly. But she didn't know, and it could easily fall apart. "I'll say so far, things are great."

Frank sniffed. "So… Is he handsome in real life?"

Hazel laughed. "He is a beautiful human being."

There was another quiet stretch until Frank said, "If I'm not better by tomorrow, I need you to present the Emoji Pilot."

Hazel stilled. "No, Frank, you're going to be better. This is your baby. Plus, I can't do that. I'm totally unprepared."

"You're the only person here who *could* do it. It's you or nobody."

She blew out her breath, puffing her cheeks. "You'll be better by tomorrow."

"I emailed you the presentation and all the info, in case. I'm going to try to sleep. Thanks for hanging out with me and everything."

"Get great rest, Frank. I'll see you later."

SHE WALKED BACK to the bar, thinking about Frank's presentation. She could probably present it decently if she had to, not near as well as Frank would do, but at least it would still be represented. But how could she answer questions anyone had? She didn't have the background information or the experience of being entrenched in his project.

The hotel bar was at total capacity, with FutureApp

leadership standing in small groups holding cocktails. The number of people in such a small place made Hazel rethink her destination. She pulled her phone out to message Sam instead but then she heard her name being called. She turned back toward the bar to see Sam excusing himself as he passed through the crowd. He exited the room with a 'phew' and said, "I've been looking for you!"

Hazel explained about Frank being sick as they strolled through the lobby and along the first-floor hallways. When she told him about Frank's request for her to present in his stead and her hesitation about being able to answer questions, he said, "It sounds like you might save the day. And don't stress about the questions; defer them. I always do deferrals if I don't know! You could simply take them and send them to Frank or have the audience email you or Frank directly. Lots of options."

"True. I always forget to do that."

Sam grinned, dimpling his cheek. "Because you like to know everything."

"Oh snap! And you don't?!" She punched him in the arm and noted the firmness there.

"Ouch! You're getting violent on me, Hazelberry?"

"Only when you deserve it."

He restrained a smirk. "Fair enough. I do also prefer to know everything. I just remember you saying that your trailers were in progress when 2/3rds of them were perfectly completed."

"I'm… remaining open to feedback!" Hazel protested.

Sam's eyes fell on a door ahead of them. "Want to see something cool?" They approached the door, and Sam swiped a room key along the lock, which turned green and admitted them.

The room felt large and small at once, but it was pitch

black. Hazel waited for her eyes to adjust and asked, "Where are we?"

She heard him take a few steps to the left. "You'll see." He flipped on a light switch that revealed them in a workspace. Hazel saw several props, some stage lighting fixtures, a cart of janitorial supplies, and three stairs leading up to a platform.

"We're backstage. Is this the main stage, where we'll present tomorrow?"

Sam bit his lip and widened his eyes in excitement. "It is! I got a key to it during the setup. I don't think anyone else will come in this late. Let's look around."

They ascended the stairs and walked onto the stage. Hazel saw the podium and stood at it, imagining what it would be like tomorrow. Brightly lit, seats full of people, a projection behind her. Sam put a hand on the small of her back, sending a rush along her spine. "You're going to do great tomorrow." Hazel spun around to face Sam. "Dance with me?"

She stepped forward to meet him, and he grabbed her hand in his and placed the other at her back. They spun around on the dark stage in silence. Hazel felt electric being so close to him. Without thinking, she laid her head on his chest and heard his heart's steady thump. He played with her hair. This was what home felt like, and Hazel wanted to ask him all her questions. He was right that she wanted to know everything. However, her fear was too powerful, so instead, she took his hand and fingered the small scar below his pinky. "What's this here?"

They continued to sway. Sam hummed, and she felt it vibrate in his chest. "You know what that is. You just don't know that you know."

Hazel reared her head back to look at him, a questioning gleam in her eye. "You have riddles tonight… Let's see… Narwhal encounter gone wrong? You were probably doing a race in Norway."

Sam laughed and shook his head. She could feel the scruff of his beard against her hair. "No, I'm afraid not. This is from a night a few years ago. I was having some Chinese food with a coworker and watching The Office. The thing you have to understand is I loved this woman, but she was engaged to another man. She had been having a tough time recently but was recovering. She was so strong. Then she told me her fiancé had left her. I was an immediate mess. I was selfishly filled with hope and deeply angry at this man I had never met for hurting her after all she had been through. I banged my fist onto a filing cabinet but hit the corner of it."

Hazel didn't know when, but they had stopped dancing. She was looking up at him, heart racing. "I remember the banging sound. I remember you jumping up." Sam's eyes searched her. He brushed a strand of hair behind her ear. "You loved me?"

He leaned toward her. They were so close she could see the bands in his eyes. "I have loved you nearly from the moment we met."

Hazel succumbed to their draw and kissed him. No kiss had ever compared. She felt as if she was warmed from within. They knew how they fit together intrinsically. The tilt of their heads and the parting of their lips were the most natural movements to have ever existed. She stroked his jaw, feeling his facial hair in her hand, and deepened their kiss. His tongue swept into her mouth. A flash of light flooded across Hazel's closed eyelids.

They drew slightly apart, the air between them crackling. She pinched his chest. "Why didn't you tell me?!"

"First, you were with Alex, and it was all so surprising anyway. I told myself it wasn't real. Then when Alex left, you had recently gone through so much turmoil. It would have been unkind to add any emotional neediness or complication."

"But after that?"

"I… I was so scared. I thought you would think I was crazy; I thought so myself sometimes. Then on CARE, it seemed like maybe you had feelings for me too. I was still hesitant, but I couldn't keep away. I can't stop thinking about you."

Hazel looked down, nodding. "I know. You're like an addiction. I think about you all the time, too. The night we celebrated after the dry run, I thought I loved you then."

Sam's eyes sparkled in the low light. "You love me, too?"

"I love you." Hazel's chest filled with emotion. She felt it travel through her whole body. Tears welled in her eyes. "But… I'm scared. I worry about you being several ranks above me, and we're both in Comms, and you're in Oregon."

Sam gently lifted her chin. "There is nothing. Nothing that will keep us apart. We'll figure this out."

They snuck upstairs to Hazel's room without encountering anyone. Most of their colleagues were still at the bar, and Hazel wondered how they would feel the next day. Steadying herself after her soaring emotions had revealed Hazel's exhaustion, and she still needed to review Frank's presentation. She sat on the bed and opened Frank's email. Sam sat behind her and massaged her shoulders. He recommended, "Why don't you present it to me for practice?"

She flipped through the slides and speaking notes to refresh herself, trying to recall as much of his dry run as possible and what he had emphasized. "I'm ready." She turned the computer so they could both see the screen and started from the beginning. When she had finished, she threw her hands up. "It's horrible. I sound like I'm reading a script."

Sam rubbed her leg. "You are reading a script, and given the circumstances, that is just fine."

"I hate the idea of sounding unprepared." She exhaled, "Let me try it again." Hazel practiced the presentation until her vision blurred. She couldn't remember falling asleep but woke up to find herself tucked in and her computer closed in its case. A note fluttered in the air from the fan, "See you tomorrow, Hazelberry <3" Hazel smiled and drifted back to sleep.

CHAPTER 18

MAKE GOALS THAT SCARE YOU A LITTLE

"Development goals are something any professional should make, and they should make you uncomfortable while being attainable."

WHEN HAZEL WOKE AGAIN, it was to a knock on her door. It was only a few minutes before her alarm was set to sound. Bleary-eyed, she crossed the room and peered through the peephole to find Sam outside, hands full. She opened the door, and he strode in, setting the two coffees and the paper bag on the table. He made to kiss her, but she put her hand in front of her mouth. "Morning breath! I wasn't awake yet!" Sam protested that he didn't care, but she ran to the bathroom and brushed her teeth while he unpacked the bag.

She came back around the corner and stared at Sam. He was sitting in one of the two upholstered chairs around the small circular table, coffee in hand. He could have been on a modeling assignment. He was wearing a blue slim-fitting coat jacket over a white button-up shirt with the collar undone. His hair was casually pushed back, but one stubborn piece was falling forward over his brow, and he was smiling at her with those bright teeth. "So, last night was real… I didn't dream it?"

"Not unless we both had the same incredible dream." He picked up her coffee to offer it to her. "It's easy to remember your coffee order since it's the same as mine."

She walked over to him and leaned in for a kiss before taking the paper cup. "Donuts?! These look great, and they aren't jelly!"

"Yep! There's a little local place down the street from here. I picked them up on the run back. Coffee from the hotel."

"Of course, you packed running shoes for the summit." Hazel teased.

"I've got to get a good run in before a big presentation. Doesn't matter where it's happening. It helps clear my mind."

Hazel nodded through a bite of donut. When she swallowed, she said, "I walk to clear my mind before big events. Totally get it." She opened her laptop to clear email, and her heart sank when she saw one from Frank. She read aloud, "I'm wrecked. Don't come by; I can't bear talking about it. I know you will do great, and I thank you so much. Frank." She looked over at Sam. "I was really hoping he'd be recovered enough. He worked so hard for this. Too hard! Probably part of why he got sick."

She quickly dressed, pulling up the skirt Rosie had celebrated and the satiny green boatneck top. Leaning toward the bathroom mirror, she applied her makeup with care and even successfully put her hair up in the pearl hair clip. When Hazel turned to exit the bathroom, she found Sam leaning against the room door, watching her.

Hazel twirled around. "Do I look okay? Like I'll be presenting to FutureApp leadership?"

Sam was awestruck. He cleared his throat, his voice still coming out as a low rumble, "You look…." His lip curled up with pure mischief, "professional… If we had time…." He glanced at the clock, then pouted, "I'll show you how you look later."

Hazel glided to him, and they shared a deep kiss. She could feel his erection pressing against her, and her curiosity and craving raged. But they didn't have time.

THEY WALKED TOGETHER to the large conference hall. Hazel made to enter the hall, but Sam called to her, "We should come this way." He gestured to the door leading backstage. "Everyone presenting will wait back here, so we don't have to get up and come all the way around with the audience watching."

Hazel peered through the crowd. "We need to get Lou… There he is." She worked her way over and tapped him on the shoulder, telling him to follow her.

The backstage door was ajar, held slightly so by a wedge. Hazel, Sam, and Lou entered to find a small group already present. There was Dana, the man who had presented yesterday (who Hazel learned was the CFO), FutureApp's Head of Customer Experience, and a woman wearing a headset who seemed to be organizing the event. Dana greeted them warmly, pulling each of them into a two-handed handshake and making introductions.

Steve, the woman in the headset, stepped into the circle of people, saying, "We're at 8 minutes to go." She then explained the button on the podium which would progress the slides that were projected behind them and asked if they had any last questions. Nobody did. However, looking around at the faces, Hazel thought everyone seemed as nervous as she felt except Dana and Sam. She wished she could somehow siphon off some of the relaxed confidence they were exuding and inject it into her and Lou.

At two minutes to go, Steve insisted they line up in appearance order. They had to wrap around the small space. Steve counted them down, and Dana stepped onto the stage, waving at the crowd. The line became a timer for Hazel, ticking down the minutes until it was her turn to walk out and kick off the CARE training. She was at once confident she knew the material and that her timing was ingrained and queasy at the idea of looking out over the sea of people from the stage.

When Philip, the Head of Customer Experience, went out on stage, only Hazel, Sam, Lou, and Steve remained in the backstage area. Hazel was too busy looking for cues indicating Philip may be wrapping up his portion of the State of the Business presentation to really hear what he was saying. Sam was immediately behind Hazel, still in their order of appearance. As Steve was counting her down, Sam gently squeezed her shoulders and whispered in her ear, "I love you, you're going to do great, and then we're going to celebrate… alone." The word alone was a primal purr, sending shivers through Hazel.

Steve said, "…one," and nudged Hazel to move her onto the stage. She stepped out into the light and walked to the podium. She was conscious that her steps seemed loud enough to echo. She turned to face the crowd at the podium. The heat from the stage lighting was intense, but the light also made it impossible for her to see the attendees. Something in Hazel's brain clicked into place. This was precisely the same as presenting remotely. Being unable to see the crowd was emboldening; all those lights melted her anxiety.

Hazel started, "Hello, FutureApp leaders! I'm Hazel Rogers, a member of Phase 2 of the CARE development team. I am beyond thrilled to be with you today to kick off your leadership training for CARE. However, I will say following our fearless leaders from the State of the Business seems a little bit unfair." There was an appreciative chuckle from the room. "Let us begin with something I know you're all familiar with. There's been quite a buzz leading up to this." She pushed the button on the podium to begin the presentation and saw the projector start. Hazel's instincts took over, and as she spoke her script, she also moved around the stage, gesturing at the imagery shining there. She felt powerful. When her introduction was over, she glanced backstage and saw Sam with his fists raised triumphantly in the air. She exited the stage on the other side and was met by another person in a headset who kindly led her out the door. Hazel let out a celebratory jump, then sped to the conference room entry and snuck into the back of the room to watch Sam and Lou.

THE ADVANTAGE of having presented to such a large forum first was that Hazel was much less nervous about giving the Emoji Pilot workshop. Hazel, Sam, and Lou had briefly celebrated before heading their separate ways. Lou was going with most of the crowd to retrieve lunch. Sam was attempting to do so also, but Hazel noticed that he was making slow headway as many people intercepted him. Hazel didn't have time for lunch. She had practiced Frank's presentation last night but did not know how the rooms were set up for presenting or even the room's location for Frank's workshop. She fetched her computer from her room, opened the email Frank had sent, and then went back downstairs to find the room.

The room was like a small classroom; five long tables stretched its length, and a whiteboard and projector were at the front. Hazel set up the computer so she could project the slides and practice the presentation a few times in the room.

She wondered if Frank had told anyone she would be presenting in his stead. The answer came in the form of Holly, Frank's manager, bustling into the room looking harried. She saw Hazel, and relief settled her face. "Oh, thank god. I just got Frank's email. I was looking for you at lunch, but I see you've found everything already."

Hazel agreed. "I didn't know how long it would take me to prepare, so I wanted to start immediately after CARE."

"You did a great job in there," Holly said it to herself more than to Hazel. It struck Hazel that she might be convincing herself everything would be okay with the workshop. Holly looked around the room and then back to Hazel. "Is there anything I can do to help? Frank seemed convinced that you would be fine."

Hazel walked her through her plan for the presentation and activities and then asked her preference for handling questions she may be unable to answer. By the end, Holly seemed reassured and settled into a seat at the far end of the first table.

The sound of a crowd of people traveled toward the open room door. Hazel's nervousness was renewed when many people she recognized from Training began to stream through the door. She had not considered who would choose to attend the Emoji Pilot workshop. Now that she thought of it, it made sense for Training to have a presence in every workshop. When every seat was occupied, she greeted the room. However, more people streamed through the entry. They looked around the room and back at Hazel for direction. "I guess we're going to be standing room only. If everyone could line up along the back wall, that might work."

She waited for everyone to get into position and began

again. "Welcome everyone to the Emoji Workshop. Today we'll be reviewing the results of a lot of research, history, and our internal pilot, as well as covering the next steps. Before we begin, I have to apologize that you're stuck with me presenting. Frank Simms led this pilot and project with passion and dedication, but he is ill today and couldn't make it to present. Full credit for what I'll cover goes to Frank."

Hazel started the slide deck. She did everything possible to replicate Frank's passionate delivery, playing his dry run like a movie in her mind. It was not a perfect presentation. Hazel was acutely aware that she progressed slides too soon on several occasions. She took talking points out of order when discussing business use precedence and stumbled over the instructions for the activity. All said, though, things went well. The attendees followed her and participated in the activity where they passed notes to each other first without emoji faces, then with them to demonstrate how emojis convey tone. Hazel opened the floor to questions at the end, explaining that she would direct them all to Frank, who would follow up in an email to every attendee. As the workshop was letting out, people stopped and thanked Hazel, telling her she did a great job and expressing their excitement about emojis.

Two exciting events down, and Hazel was craving stillness. She had to remind herself the day was not over. She needed to attend other workshops. She couldn't remember what she had registered for, so she took out her computer to check her registration receipts. Goal Setting for the Future and Beyond Engagement were her following workshops. She remembered Sam was committed to others, but maybe she would see him in the hall.

Eyes peeled for his tall, dark head, she saw him walking in the same direction she was but significantly ahead of her. He slipped into his workshop room without turning around to see her. After Goal Setting for the Future, Hazel made a right out of the room, knowing she would run into Sam. He spotted her immediately and called, "Hazel, a word, please?" She jogged the last few steps to him. He said with a touch of projection, "I wanted to talk to you quickly about the feedback we received this morning." She followed him into an empty room.

As Sam closed the door, Hazel asked, "What feedback did we get?"

He turned to face her, his face ravenous. "Not why we're here." He approached her with a rumbled growl of desire and backed her up against the wall. He kissed her deeply, hands aside her cheeks, then roaming down her body. He cupped her breasts, slid down her back, and grabbed her rear. He hoisted her up, and she wrapped her legs around him. "I can't stop thinking about your ass in this skirt."

For the second time that day, she felt the length of him pressing hard against her. She ran her hands through his hair as their kiss resumed. Their bodies ground against each other. Hazel's heart was pounding. She reached down to grasp the outline of his cock.

The door opened. Sam dropped Hazel, and she straightened her skirt down. They both struggled to regulate their breathing. Samantha entered the room. She looked them up and down, suspicion etched in her stance, then smiled coolly. "I was looking for you, Sam. Iterative Performance Management is getting started."

Sam was flushed but replied, "I was just telling Hazel about the feedback from this morning."

Samantha paused, said, "It looks that way." and walked from the room.

Sam turned to Hazel, "We'll talk more later."

Hazel ironically felt Beyond Engagement during her final workshop, but not in the direction the name implied.

She vacillated between lusting for more of Sam's body against her and being haunted by Samantha's smile.

WHEN THE FINAL workshop round was dismissed, there was not a mass stream of FutureApp employees as there had been in transition times before. The movement was more disorganized as some people chose to head to dinner, and others went upstairs or out until the mixer. Hazel walked out to the lobby area, searching for Sam. She saw him emerge from another hallway and lock eyes with her at the same time as a male voice called her name in the other direction. She turned to see Jasmond beckoning to her. With an apologetic look back to Sam, she walked toward Jasmond. He clapped her on the shoulder. "We have a lot to talk about. Join me for dinner?"

He led her to a partially occupied table in the dining hall. She recognized some of the faces there from the Emoji Pilot Workshop. Jasmond pulled out a chair for her and indicated she should sit. He wasted no time with chitchat or introduction. "I heard back from Tamra, and I'm so excited you'll be staying on with the crew and me in Phase 3. Honestly, I'm even more jazzed about having you now. Do you know why that is?"

Hazel wasn't sure how to reply. She hummed at him inquisitively, "Mmm, I guess not?"

"Not only did your CARE training go off without a single hitch this morning, but I heard you presented the Emoji workshop spectacularly on short notice." He raised his hand to the people she recognized from the session.

She smiled and shook her head. "Thank you so much. The workshop could have used more polish, but I tried my best to do Frank's work justice."

Jasmond turned to his Training colleagues. "See how humble she is?" There was an appreciative chuckle before he turned back to her. "Your ideas, the quality of your work, your ethic and flexibility. You're getting noticed by my friends and me in Training but even beyond us. I was wondering about your career interest. I remember interviewing you not so long ago. Are you still interested in Training, or are you thinking bigger now that you're a hot shot?" He grinned at her.

Hazel blushed under the weight of such direct and public compliments. "Thank you again. I didn't expect to receive such praise!" She put her hand over her heart. "I'm absolutely still interested in Training; it's where I belong, I know it." People around the table were nodding their heads in agreement. "I hope it's okay to bring this up a little early, but I've been working on a How-To article, *How-To Work Remotely*. I've also made a Training deck to cover it in Onboarding. Obviously, it would need to be vetted, and I don't know if you'd even be interested in it. Still, I'm always thinking about what I can do to work alongside you, and it made sense...." She trailed off, registering that the whole table was listening to her.

"Exactly what I advised you to do!" Jasmond beamed. "I'd love to review it."

Hazel got to know the rest of the people at the table over their meal. She found the Training team, at least those in attendance, to be delightful and quirky. They bonded over reading and their hobbies. Bianca was even familiar with the *Clan of Fog and Destiny* series. She made Hazel promise they would discuss their theories for the next book "when there aren't so many non-Fae-loving people around." She then looked around the table in disgust. Notable, too, was that a surprising number of them were into bowling, and they all played instruments. Hazel made a note to ask Sam about his stance on bowling. Maybe they could try it together someday.

The conversation at dinner flowed so well that Jasmond

was forced to break it up. He glanced down at his watch and announced they would need to leave for the mixer or suffer the fate of watered-down drinks.

Hazel left the dining hall, chest full of excitement about Jasmond's conversation with her and getting along so well with the other Training representatives. She found Sam leaning against the wall next to the conference room. He was still wearing his outfit from the morning but had another button undone on his white shirt. The newness of everything thrilled through her as she secretly observed him. His tallness. His confidence. God, he was handsome. She relived the feel of his hands, their confessions to each other in the dark emptiness of the stage. They hadn't discussed specifics, but she guessed they were together now. He had said they would figure it out, but everything after had been a rush of FutureApp business.

Sam spotted her and waved as he walked over to meet her. "I wanted to be with you when you saw...." He gestured towards the room.

The mixer was in the same main conference room they had presented this morning. Except now it was transformed. The seating was gone, there seemed to be a DJ outfit on stage (though it wasn't playing anything yet), and the room was lit primarily by string lights suspended from the ceiling. As they joined the line for drinks, Hazel noticed a table of finger food and desserts across the room. The only seating was a smattering of small, high, round tables, each with two barstool-style chairs on either side of the room. "I can't imagine all the work done between lunch and now to accomplish this. The transformation is beautiful. There's a certain romance to string lights."

Sam studied the lights, swaying slightly. "There's a certain romance to *you*." He used his peripheral vision to watch her. When she lit up with a smile, so did he. "So, tell me about everything with Jasmond." They moved through the line, Hazel regaling him with how dinner went. Sam listened attentively and grabbed their drinks as they reached the end of the queue. "First, this seems so promising. You know hiring season is coming up. I can't be 100% sure, but it sounds like they were vetting you to me. Second, you've never mentioned *A Clan of Fog and Destiny!* How'd I miss that?"

Hazel spotted an unoccupied area and led Sam to it. "Taking those backward. *A Clan of Fog and Destiny* isn't a book club read, though it is required reading." She punctuated the requirement with her hand movement. "And I do feel hopeful, even despite myself. I shouldn't read into anything, but it felt like some vetting to me too! Can you imagine we wouldn't be in the same department anymore and…"

A man Hazel didn't recognize swept in to join her and Sam. "Loved the CARE preso this morning!" Sam chatted with him for a few minutes until he drifted to another group of people.

Hazel hid her shock when another woman came up to them immediately after. "Sam, you were great. I always learn so much from your presentations. And you're Hazel, right?"

Hazel stood on her toes when she left to whisper to Sam, "Why are all these people coming to talk with us? Do you know them?"

Sam shrugged. "That's the nature of a mixer. We should probably be mixing too."

Hazel frowned and lowered her brows. "I thought it was called a mixer because of the drinks."

"Don't fret. After we make a round, maybe we sneak outta here? I believe I made you a promise earlier." Those model teeth flashed even under the low light.

Hazel let Sam lead the way through the crowd. Everyone was warm and welcoming, but chatting with new people was still exhausting. She was distracted by the loudness of the room and annoyed at how difficult it was to hear conversations. As they spun from their most recent circle of colleagues, Hazel spotted Frank. She tugged on Sam's sleeve and pointed over to him. "I'm going to check on Frank. I'll catch you in a few." Sam nodded his agreement and was absorbed into a new group.

"Frank! I'm so happy to see you! Are you feeling better? You look so much better!"

Frank reached his arms around Hazel and brought her in for a hug. "I'm much better, and listen, I owe you so much. I've gotten messages on messages about how great the workshop was."

"It was well put together and received by the group, too." Hazel gestured for him to follow her closer to the door. "It's quieter over here." She explained when they came to a stop. "Did you get to eat anything yet?"

Frank was singing the praises of the finger food spread when Hazel felt a comforting pressure on the small of her back. She perked to her full height and looked up at Sam. Frank stopped mid-sentence looking from Hazel to Sam, and said, "I, uh, will just be going over this way. Thanks again, Hazel." He pointed randomly and strode off.

CHAPTER 19

EXERCISE

"It is well documented that desk jobs are not the healthiest occupations for our bodies. Now pair that with unlimited snacks available from your very own kitchen. Keeping active and maintaining a healthy diet should be items on all remote worker's radars."

As they exited the mixer, music started to blare from the DJ booth. They turned around to see their FutureApp colleagues with their hands and drinks in the air, boisterous cheers sounding over the song. It was amusing to Hazel, seeing the high-ranking professionals in her company act as they would in a nightclub. She locked her gaze on Sam. He said, "Perfect timing," and they rushed to the elevator.

The moment they were alone on the elevator, all the tension from the day locked in between them. Hazel's gaze was stern, and Sam met her with the same intensity. They were at once upon each other. Hazel untucked his shirt and slid her hands beneath it, up his abs, and around his back. She felt his muscles flex beneath her fingers as he worked his hands down to the crease of her ass. He dipped his hands beneath her top and unclasped her bra in one smooth motion. Hazel gasped. "How'd you do that? Aren't you supposed to be out of practice?"

Sam growled. "It's like riding a bike."

The elevator dinged, announcing their arrival on the 10th floor. They didn't bother to adjust their clothing but hastily moved toward Hazel's room. In her rush, she struggled with the keycard to the door and had to scan it three times before their admittance. Hazel sat on the bed and faced Sam, who stood at the door. He bit his lip. "The things I'm going to do to you."

Hazel leaped from the bed and pinned him against the door while taking off his jacket. He pulled Hazel's blouse over her head and threw it aside. She could see his cock pressing against the fabric of his pants. "I want you in my mouth."

He exhaled shakily. "Yes. You're so fucking hot."

He unbuttoned his pants and used a leg to fling them off. Hazel pulled down his boxer briefs, unveiling the most beautiful dick she'd ever seen. She stammered, "I, I don't know if I can fit you all the way in my mouth." Sam smirked. Hazel grasped him, first working his length with her hand. She cradled his balls in her other hand, gently cupping and pulling alternately while she stroked. She commanded him to the bed, and he moved with her to sit at the edge.

Hazel dropped to her knees and flicked her tongue around the head of his member, causing him to sigh. She smiled at his reaction and took him into her mouth. It was a tight fit. She wasn't sure if she would be able to go as deep as she longed to; not only was Sam blessed with length but girth. She used her hand at the base and experimented, pushing herself to take more and more of him with each stroke. She swirled her tongue around his shaft.

Sam leaned back with a groan, and Hazel found her

hand was now in the way of her mouth. She looked up at him, causing him to writhe with excitement. She moved her hand to massage his perineum, allowing her to continue gliding down to his base. She felt his cock twitch in her mouth, and she quickened her pace. She was finding this new rhythm when she felt him tug her hair. "Stop, stop. I don't want to come yet." The sudden pull of hair caught her off guard, and she gagged slightly while pulling away.

"I don't want you to come yet either. I need you in me." Her face fell. "I don't have a condom."

"I got some from the front desk this morning." Sam got up and retrieved a small square from his back pants pocket. Hazel sat on the edge of the bed while he pulled it on. His body was a greek statue, ideal to Hazel. Sam was muscular but lean; she could see the tone in his legs and glutes. His back and shoulders. He leaned forward over her, and his throat bobbed. He kissed her passionately while Hazel wriggled out of her skirt and panties. Sam sat up and observed her body, running his hands gently along her shoulder, over her breasts, down the curve of her hip. "I see your stars," he said as he caressed the line tattoo on her hip.

"I see your hearts," Hazel stretched her neck to kiss beneath his clavicle.

He pounced on top of Hazel, and she arched against his chest. Sam reached down and swirled gently around her clit. He licked his lip. "You're so wet."

Hazel's chest felt like it would explode with desire. "You've had me soaking every time we were close today." He dipped his fingers into her, using his thumb to continue the motion around her clit. Hazel ground herself on his hand. "I want you inside of me. Please, I can't take it. I need to feel you."

He removed his hand and leaned over her ear. He

purred. "What the lady wants, she will have. From now on." He edged his cock into her slowly. Going in slightly, pulling out, then pushing forth a little more, learning their fit. The pressure of him drove Hazel's mind to blank. She felt perfectly full, but she needed more. She used her feet on the bed for leverage and pushed further against him. Sam swiveled his hips in a circular motion as he slowly dipped in and out of her. His face was projecting his pure pleasure, and with each low moan he made, Hazel could feel the rumble through her body.

Their rhythm quickened. Sam dipped his head and sucked at Hazel's nipple. He pulled back, watched as it hardened, and whispered, "Good girl."

Hazel's breath hitched. She wanted more, all of Sam. She wanted to feel him everywhere. She felt feral. She pushed at his shoulder. "Roll over."

Sam swept his arm behind Hazel and rolled them both over so she was on top. Hazel grabbed the headboard and rode Sam hard and fast, rocking herself back and forward without thought or hesitation. She laid down on him to feel his whole body work against her. The pressure in her was rising. She nipped at his ear lobe and rasped, "I'm going to come."

She lifted herself back up to grasp the headboard. Sam grabbed either side of her hips and growled, both of them grinding in unison. The room erupted with stars as Hazel shook with release. Sam's head reared back, and he roared his finish before Hazel collapsed on top of him.

She rolled over on her side, hooking a leg around his, and ran her fingers through the small dark patch of chest hair between his pecs. Sam closed his eyes briefly before rolling onto his side to face Hazel. "That was…"

"Something out of a romance novel?" She offered.

A smile crept onto his lips. "Exactly. It was almost perfect."

Hazel scrunched her face. "Almost?"

"I didn't get to taste you." His face was wicked. Hazel hit him with a pillow. "Hey!" Sam grabbed another pillow to block her attack.

She said between pillowy blows, "I. Guess. That's. Something. To. Look. Forward. To." She stuck out her tongue at him. Sam reached his long arms around her and pulled her into his chest.

THEY MOVED to the bathroom to clean up. Calmed and fulfilled, heart beating at a normal pace for the first time that day, Hazel embraced the reality of what had happened. She exclaimed, "I can't believe this!"

Sam turned toward her, "That I've just made love to the most beautiful woman in the world? Me either!" He moved behind her and started soaping her body.

"No. It's… Hard to explain. It's like I've been dreaming about being with you- not only sexually, but being together. It's been for such a long time, and now it's real…. Is it real?"

Sam raised up from washing her feet and met her eyes with his. He dropped the soapy washcloth and took her hands into his. "It's real. And you have no idea how long I've imagined life with you. This feels like a dream to me too, but Hazel, it's real." He squeezed her hands and kissed her.

"What are we going to do about working together?"

Sam nodded and chewed the side of his mouth as if the question was on his mind too. "I see a few options." He started gently positioning her to rinse the soap from her body. "I do think you're going to be moving to Training soon, but we can't count on it, and I don't know about you, but I don't think I can keep us a secret after this."

Hazel arched a brow. "I can't imagine doing that, no."

"Then one of us can ask for a transfer. We can seek an exception with HR. Or I can resign."

She playfully pinched his shoulder. "Don't resign! I could leave, too!"

"I would never ask you to resign, plus you're in a position for growth with your career right now. I'm not. It would be easier for me to find a new position." Hazel's face was mutinous, but he went on. "I've thought a lot about this. I don't *want* to resign, but if one of us had to, it should be me, and honestly, it's a low cost to be together. I'd do it happily if it's the only option."

Hazel's lips were pursed. "It won't come to that, then. Whenever we disclose, we'll ask for the exception first, and if they can't grant one, I'll move anywhere they want."

Sam seemed unsure. He hesitated, then said, "Or I'd move. Either of us could. I want to be as accommodating as possible." He added, "What do you think about disclosing after Thanksgiving? That would give everyone a chance to finish this summit week; next week, we're all shut down for the holiday, and then first thing when we're all back?" He waited for her to reply, but Hazel was peering far into space. "You okay?"

She shifted her focus back to Sam. "Yeah, that sounds great, after Thanksgiving. It was only yesterday we saw each other in person for the first time. And tomorrow, we're going to be apart again. It feels like we've spent a year together in a single day. It's hard to imagine you being so far."

Sam's eyes were dark and shining solemn. "I know." He smiled. "We'll figure that out too."

Their snuggled under the covers, lightly brushing their fingertips along each other, talking and laughing. Hazel wished the night could last forever, and to Time's credit, it did seem to drag on slightly.

When Hazel awoke, she turned to see Sam sleeping beside her. She smirked, thinking this may be the longest he had ever slept in. She checked the clock with a sigh. There wasn't much time left before they needed to be downstairs, then she would be catching her flight, traveling further and further away from Sam. She turned off the alarm and enjoyed lying next to him.

When she saw the clock shine 7:30am, she knew it was time for them to start moving. A devious idea skated through her mind. She turned onto her side, facing away from Sam, and scooched herself back against him so they were spooning. She wiggled her hips slightly, and Sam's arm wrapped around her, pulling her closer to him. He smelled her hair, then exhaled, hoarsely whispering, "This is how you wake me up?"

She rolled out from his side. "We honestly don't have time. I just couldn't resist!" Hazel got up and opened her suitcase, intending to dress and pack. Sam stood up, too, and silently went into the bathroom. He swished his mouth with the small complimentary bottle of mouthwash, reemerged, and said, "We have time for one thing." Hazel narrowed her eyes in question. "I've been waiting a long, long time for this." Sam moved across the room swiftly, picked Hazel up, so she was straddling him, and laid her back on the bed. "May I?" She opened her legs for him in answer, and his face lit with hunger.

Sam began with a long, slow swipe of his tongue up her middle. He twirled it around her clit when he reached the top, and Hazel gasped. He ran the bottom of his tongue back down her and continued in lazy circles. His responses to every move and sound Hazel made were attuned to her body. Sam rested his head in her lap, looking up at Hazel. "You taste of plum. Your pussy is perfect." He dived back down, quickening his tempo. He slipped his hands under Hazel, cupping her ass, and lifted her slightly. He sucked her clitoris and hummed. The low vibrations of his humming were like lightning. Hazel could feel them down to her toes. She arched her back, moaning. Sam reclaimed his hands, gently letting Hazel down. He inserted a finger into her, exploring her anatomy. She playfully squeezed at him, and he uttered an O of surprise. Sam inserted two fingers, thrusting gently at first, still worshiping her with his mouth.

Hazel was warm and physically flushed through her cheeks and chest. She returned the thrusting of his hand with grinding of her own. Sam growled, sending vibrations through her again. She grabbed his hair and pulled. "I love it when you do that." He trilled back at her. Hazel's breathing was coming fast. He picked up his pace again, sucking her clit and humming deeply, penetrating her. Hazel shuddered, a howl slipping past her lips, then fell back onto the bed, giggling. "My whole body is tingling."

Sam sat on the bed next to her. "That's what you get for waking me up with those luscious hips."

Hazel inhaled deeply, and she reached out to brush his thigh. "I'll keep that in mind." They both chuckled.

SAM LEFT for his room to get changed and ready for the day. Hazel lay on the bed for as long as she could, soaking in the remnants of pleasure firing through her. When she could no longer ignore the pressure of the clock, she rose, dressed, and threw clothes pell-mell into her suitcase. The morning was strained for time. They would have a quick bite, the closing address, and Hazel would need to Uber to the airport immediately if she wanted to make her flight.

She turned on her computer to check email before

packing it up to leave, but was distracted by several Chatter notifications from Tamra.

Tamra King

> Hazel? 7:15am

Tamra King

> Is everything okay at the summit? 7:15am

Tamra King

> HR asked for a meeting with me later, about you. 7:20am

SHE CLOSED the lid on her laptop and jumped from the bed. Adrenaline pumped through her. She had to find Sam.

Hazel jammed the elevator button impatiently, earning sidelong glances from those around her. Her brain was speeding. She knew this was about her relationship with Sam. There was no other reason. Nothing else made sense for her manager to be reached out to by HR regarding Hazel. The image of Samantha smiling swam in and out of her mind's eye. But she couldn't figure out how or what it all meant. She sped into the lobby and found the continental breakfast, but Sam wasn't there.

The crowd was beginning to move into the conference room. She was running out of time. She stepped into the crowded room but didn't see Sam there either, so she turned around and fought against the traffic back out the door. Hardly anyone else was here, and Hazel was beginning to panic. Sam was probably chatting with someone. He was frequently pulled into conversation, but where could he be?

She spun around to observe the conference room again and saw Dana peeking her head from behind the stage curtain. Hazel stood dazed for a second but made her decision and ran out the door heading for the backstage area. The door was locked, and she didn't have a key to it, so she banged it loudly, praying someone would let her in.

Dana whipped open the door, face distressed. "Hazel?"

"Dana, I have to talk to you. Please, it's important." Dana stepped back and gestured for Hazel to enter the small room. Hazel walked through and looked around. "Nobody else is here with you?"

"No, it's only me this morning, a simple closing statement doesn't need much, but Hazel, I do have to go out there," she checked her watch, "right now. Can you wait here? Is this something we can discuss in a few minutes?" Hazel took a deep breath and nodded. Dana walked up the stairs and out of sight onto the stage.

Hazel leaned against the cool wall and waited for Dana to return. Waves of panic and nerves rose in her chest; she would talk herself down only to have them swell again. She was determined, though. If this meant she needed to resign or take a demotion, it didn't matter. She needed to get in front of this. Dana had said to come to her with anything… Hazel hoped she had meant it.

SHE EMERGED from the backstage area 40 minutes later. Aware that she had been sworn to absolute secrecy by her CEO, that nothing was yet resolved, and that she was likely to miss her flight if she didn't leave immediately.

CHAPTER 20

COMMUNICATION IS A PRIORITY

"Prioritize clear communication and verify understanding by recapping expectations and being open to questions. Communication is the key to achieving goals."

HAZEL RAN TO HER ROOM. She grabbed her phone off the nightstand and opened the Uber App while hastily throwing her remaining items into her suitcase. Thankfully, there was a driver immediately available. She zipped her luggage and started back toward the lobby, phone in hand, replying to Sam's messages.

SPierce

I know we said we'd meet downstairs for breakfast but I'm coming back to your room. We can go down together. 7:35am

SPierce

> You're fast lol, guess I missed you. Okay
> coming downstairs. 7:40am

SPierce

> Where are you? The Closing Address is
> starting 8:01am

SPierce

> Kinda starting to worry, message me when
> you get this 8:20am

HAZEL THOUGHT about what to say as she moved. She was restricted even from discussing the matter openly with Sam, at least for now. Still, she felt she had to reply with something.

Hazel

> Hey I'm fine. I am disclosed so I cannot
> discuss. 8:56am

THAT WOULD HAVE to work for now. As she entered the lobby, she was alerted that her Uber driver was waiting for her. Hazel made it through the front door when she heard Sam call her name. He was standing off the side of the door in front of a potted evergreen. Samantha was directly in front of him. "Hazel! I've been looking for you everywhere!"

Samantha turned and sneered at Hazel. She mouthed something indistinguishable.

Hazel watched Sam but kept moving toward her car. She handed her suitcase to the driver. Her chest ached. She said, "Sam. I can't talk right now." She held his gaze for as long as she could and hoped she communicated everything to him with her eyes.

Doubt was closing in on Hazel as she closed the door to the car. Samantha had renewed talking with Sam, but Sam was watching the car as it drove away.

SPierce

She did something didn't she? She was acting so weird just now. Don't worry Hazelberry, we already had a plan, we'll be fine. I'll take care of whatever. 9:11am

IT WAS the most challenging act not to tell Sam everything that had already happened. She felt guilty keeping things from him that involved their livelihood and job security. Hazel also worried he would misinterpret her silence or do something crazy himself. The past few days' events were internally unpacking themselves as the turn signal clicked from the driver's seat.

Tears snaked down Hazel's cheeks. She wrote back four words, "Please understand. I'm disclosed." and turned off her phone.

Hazel experienced roiling emotions on her way back home. She was furious at Samantha and worried about everything- her job, Sam's job, if Dana would be able to help or not, when she would find out, what would happen if she couldn't, if she and Sam would endure or if they had both been in a fantasy state. During her layover in the Atlanta airport, she dared to turn on her phone, but Sam had stopped messaging. All the emotion was yanked out of her and replaced by a sense of hollowness.

She felt the sensation of nothingness for hours as she waited to board the flight, flew to Crestwood, and ordered another car home. This was her life, she thought, as she looked around her home, but the color was gone. Hazel unpacked dispassionately. She went to the kitchen to scrounge for food, knowing she should eat despite her lack of hunger.

Her Mom's journal sat next to the empty fruit bowl on the counter, and she felt something. A slight easing in her chest as she picked up the book and flipped its pages, familiar handwriting flashing before her eyes.

May 29th, 2017

Car and I were in the car earlier today, and I saw a bumper sticker I hope I always remember. A bumper sticker, of all things! But it gave me such perspective!

I often hear people recite the phrase, "Everything that can go wrong will." Murphy's Law. They say it and throw up their hands in acceptance of defeat.

This bumper sticker said, "Everything that can go right will." I'm embarrassed to say it made me tear up. How would things be different if people thought that way? If we looked for things to go right instead of wrong, I am certain we would see them go right.

It's beautiful and so simple. I will try to leave space for things to go right in my life. I may even find that bumper sticker and put it on my car. If anything is worth proselytizing and marring my car, it's this.

Her Mom had loathed bumper stickers. She laughed at the memory and found the sound surprising. What would it look like if everything went right in her current situation? Did she dare to envision her hopes and risk seeing them not happen? Didn't she already know the answer in the depths of her? It was inspecting the dream that would be difficult. She felt it was already there.

Hazel grabbed her phone. It was very early, after midnight for Sam, but she messaged him anyway.

Hazel

> I'm an idiot for not realizing this (very in my head)… but obviously we can still talk about everything else. Right? How was clean up? 4:22am

SHE DIDN'T EXACTLY FEEL BETTER. Hazel was still consumed with worry. Their careers were a huge deal, and having their relationship reported when they knew it was an HR violation was a terminable offense for both of them. She did feel again, however, and that was an improvement.

Hazel imagined explaining everything to Rosie. She tried to feel her friend's comforting hand on her shoulder and hear her no-nonsense reply. Rosie would empathize with her and understand the strain Hazel was under. She would tell her that she had already done everything possible for now and to try not to dwell on all the outcomes because there was no controlling them. She would wait with Hazel until whatever was going to happen did come to pass. She drifted to sleep with Rosie's voice in her ear.

The sensation of falling made Hazel jolt awake. She caught her breath and realized she was safe in bed but had no sense of what time it might be. Her arm shot out for her phone. 10am. Sam would be up by now, but there were no messages from him. She cursed traveling across time-zones and, feeling miserable, rolled out of bed.

There wasn't enough energy in the world. Hazel brushed her teeth but didn't bother with her hair or clothes before starting the kettle in the kitchen.

Technically, she was already late to work, but Hazel was afraid to log in. Anything could be waiting for her there. Tamra may be waiting in the wings for her to log in and fire her. She saw images of emails from Dana flash before her eyes that read, "nothing I can do," and, "so sorry, but we're letting you both go." And she did try; she really tried to imagine good things as well, but the weight of fear and guilt were not helped by Sam's continued silence.

He had asked her to please talk to him. Was her traveling enough time for him to change his mind about every-thing? Was the reality setting in for him regarding the costs of their being together? She attempted to soothe these unwelcome questions as well. Reminding herself that they had become so close, she knew all the names of his friends and family. Even though being together was new, their friendship was not, and Sam had never let her down before.

HAZEL SAT AT HER DESK, computer closed, coffee mug wrapped in both hands. It was threatening snow outside, and the view out the window was gray. She opened the laptop lid and logged in, and nothing happened.

Tamra didn't reach out. She had only the regular emails in her inbox; meeting recaps and IT newsletters. Chatter wasn't pressing her with notifications, but there were none from Sam either. Everything was normal. Her shoulders dropped slightly, and she went about her tasks.

Hours passed, and she found working to be an outlet

for her nerves, apart from a wave of nausea at every email and Chatter sound. She decided to practice after remembering Jasmond's request to send him the How-To Work Remotely outlines and Sam's suggestion to record herself delivering the training. Hazel inspected her background, rearranging a few things that would be in view. She adjusted her lighting and opened a SyncUp. The webcam kicked on and reminded her how the day had begun. Her hair was tangled and sticking out at odd angles on the left side, and she had dark circles beneath her eyes, betraying her lack of sleep. She was still in a white shirt with a stretched-out neck and stains, which had caused its demotion to sleepwear. Hazel leaned in to look at herself in the camera. "Oof."

She walked back to her bedroom and started pawing through her wardrobe. The doorbell rang. Hazel ignored it; it was probably a solicitor or some package delivery. She continued rummaging through her clothes. How could she have so many shirts and not want to wear any of them? The doorbell rang again, and she stopped pushing clothes aside. It rang a third time. She sighed, annoyed. "Okay, okay."

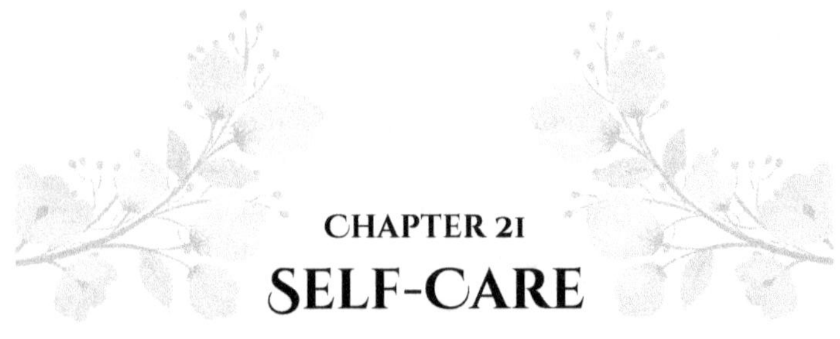

CHAPTER 21
SELF-CARE

"Remote work isn't for everyone. I hope this How-To has been beneficial, but I know even with all my best practices, some people will need a different environment. The advice I would give anyone is to do what works for you. Self-Care is more important than any job."

HAZEL STOMPED to the front door, disheveled and ready to dismiss whoever was on her stoop. She cracked it open without really looking. "Thanks, but I'm not interested in… in…."

Sam stood before her. He wore the same clothes she had last seen him in at the Hilton entrance, though they were now distinctly wrinkled. He seemed equally tired as she was. He cleared his throat, but his voice still came out gravelly, as if he hadn't spoken for a long time, "I was hoping you'd be interested in having Thanksgiving with me?" She realized he was holding several grocery bags, his suitcase behind him.

Hazel swallowed. "Who will make the sides for Don and Summer?"

"They'll figure it out." He shifted the groceries.

Hazel opened the door for Sam to enter. She grabbed his suitcase and brought it in behind him. "The kitchen is to the right. Did you shop?"

Sam walked into the kitchen and laid down the heavy bags. He started unpacking them. Butternut, wild rice, kale, cranberries, corn, sweet potatoes, cheeses, and spices lined the counter. It felt unreal seeing him here, in her kitchen, unpacking groceries. "You bought all the things for a pescatarian Thanksgiving."

He met her eye. "I know it's a week away, but I thought these things would hold pretty well."

Then a dam broke in Hazel, and a waterfall of questions and regrets rushed from her. "How'd you get here? What did you do? Why didn't you message me? What about the 5k? I'm so sorry for not replying quicker. I should have missed my flight. I should have found you."

Sam patiently waited for her to finish. He leaned on the counter over the squash. "I left almost immediately after you left. As soon as I could. I was supposed to stay to help clean up, but I was upset. I had suspicions about what was happening after I couldn't find you, and Samantha cornered me. I couldn't be around Samantha anymore, so I made an excuse and caught a flight home early. As soon as I landed, I realized I had caught a flight to the wrong home, so I booked a flight here. I didn't reply to you because I was in the air, then when I landed here, I saw your message, but I felt crazy for being here. It seemed easier to figure out where you live and explain in person."

Hazel felt warm, like his words were massaging the tension from her. She ran a hand through her hair, fingers catching in the still-uncombed knotty section. "How did you find my house?"

"Rosie. I made an Instagram account and found her profile. I messaged her to please call me, and thank goodness she did. I explained that I needed to see you, that I wasn't entirely sure what had happened, but that I had come here to find out and fix it. She gave me your address."

Hazel laughed. "I am… so glad you're here, but I am also going to have to talk with her about information security."

Sam pointed at her with both hands and chuckled. "It was very forward of me. I'm sorry if this was a huge overstep." Hazel shook her head, and he continued. "Other than that, I haven't done anything. I still am not completely sure what's going on… and Crestwood has a 5k on Thanksgiving. If I'm here, we could both do it together. Actually, I have a gift for you." He came around the counter to his suitcase. "I was going to give it to you before you left." He pulled out a shoe box and placed it next to Hazel.

Hazel raised the box lid and folded back the tissue paper. "Are these…" She lifted a shoe. "Are these shoes with Thanksgiving turkeys on them?!"

Sam made a cheesy open-mouthed smile and nodded quickly. "I have a matching pair."

Hazel spun toward Sam and embraced him in a mighty hug. He returned the squeeze, and they melded into each other. Hazel whispered, "It wasn't too forward."

Sam replied, "You have nothing to apologize for."

Hazel led Sam to the couch. "I want to tell you everything. The truth is I don't have the entire story either, and what I do know I can't talk about."

Sam contemplated. "Mmm… What if I guess?"

Hazel looked to the ceiling, thinking. "I still can't break my promise about everything, but we can try."

"Samantha turned us in to HR, and you found out about it somehow before me, probably after I went back to my room before the Closing Address. I was worried when I couldn't find you. I wondered if you had regrets or second thoughts and checked out early, but that didn't feel right. Eventually, I decided to wait for you outside, and that's when Samantha cornered me. She asked me on a date. When I refused, she asked if I was looking for you and commented on how I shouldn't worry about you anymore. Which is when I started putting the events together. If that's right, how did she report us, though?"

Hazel slowly nodded, considering if she was okay to confirm anything. "I think I can say you're correct. I don't know how or when she reported us either. You left to change, and Tamra messaged me about HR requesting a meeting with her regarding me. I knew it had to be about us, and I was almost positive it was Samantha because remember her smile when she walked in on us between workshops? It was all I could think of."

Sam listened attentively, nodding along. "I'm guessing we're at the part where you can't tell me anymore?"

Hazel's email alert swooshed to indicate an incoming message. "I'll be right back; any contacts I'm on high alert for." She stepped into the office and wiggled her mouse to wake her computer. An email from Dana was in her inbox, subject line [HR Investigation 730928C] Supporting Evidence. Her heart quickened as she opened it.

The email was addressed to HR, not to Hazel. She looked at the recipients and realized she had been BCC'd.

Hi Sandra,

Regarding HR Investigation 730928C, I have attached the information for the relationship disclosure for Sam Pierce and Hazel Rogers.

I apologize for not being able to locate their official disclosure form. However, I recall the conversation and have supporting evidence that it occurred in my personal notes (attached and pasted into the body of this message below) on April 6th, 2019.

Our policy discouraging interdepartmental relationships was put in place in August 2019. As Hazel and Sam's disclosure predates that policy, it is my recommendation to close this investigation with No Fault Found.

Excerpt from my notes (also attached):

APRIL 6TH, 2019

- *Began prep for Board Meeting on 4/22*
- *All meetings as expected, watch Regional Quality regarding relationship between behavioral adoption and CSAT*
- *Intervened Sam Pierce after personal event. Amicable fellow, lovesick over H. Rogers. Monitor for resumed behavior*

Regards,

Dana Jessup
CEO FutureApp

HAZEL READ IT TWICE. She wondered if this meant everything was over when the thread was updated. Sandra had replied.

Thanks Dana,

HR Investigation 730928C is closed with No Fault Found.

Hazel felt her phone buzz in her hand. She didn't realize she was grasping onto it so firmly. An unknown number messaged her. "All set."

"Sam! Come here!" Sam poked his head around the office door and then strode in. "Look at this!" Hazel pushed her chair back to roll out of his way.

Sam read the email aloud, giggling as he approached the end of the second email. Hazel pointed at the text message from the unknown number. "You've got to be kidding! DANA!" He jumped in the air tucking his feet high. He pulled Hazel's hand and twirled her office chair around. Hazel felt the same unbridled joy for life as she had in her favorite childhood memories. Energy thrummed from them as they danced around the house.

"So you can tell me now!" Sam said, "Where'd you go?"

Hazel's fingers caught in her hair again. She sang, "I've got to take care of this. Come with me!" She brushed her hair and explained. "I was looking for you everywhere. After Tamra's message, I wasn't sure what would happen. If anything could happen at the summit, if it would be later, or if decisions had already been made. There were a lot of high-stakes scenarios. So I ran down to warn you. We were supposed to meet at breakfast, but you weren't there. I looked in the conference room but didn't see you there either. We were minutes away from the Closing Address, and I saw Dana peek out from backstage, and I don't know… I felt a little unhinged about going to the CEO, but I didn't see many other options. I ran to the backstage door, and she let me in. I had to wait backstage while she gave the address. It was the longest 20 minutes of my life. Then, when I explained, she pulled out her phone and called HR to confirm what was happening. She told me there was a complaint about our relationship, but obviously not who reported it. Then she said she believed she could help but wouldn't tell me how. She swore me to secrecy because, in her words, 'I'm going to get creative.' She told me her idea might not work, and she wanted to be realistic. If it didn't, there wasn't anything else she could do outside normal channels."

Sam sat on the edge of the bed. "Wow! We missed each other because I came back to your room instead of down to breakfast, then we must have just missed each other when you went backstage. I...."

They both heard Hazel's computer. It wasn't a usual practice at FutureApp, but someone was calling her directly through SyncUp, and a loud ringing sounded through the house. She ran back to the office, sliding her chair back into position across the room.

Hazel answered Tamra's call and was greeted with an apology. "Hey, sorry to call you like that. This can wait if you're on break or busy. I thought you'd want to know about it right away. I just met with HR."

"Thanks for calling! I want to know everything."

"I figured. So it looks like there was a misunderstanding. I'll go ahead and let you know; you have nothing to worry about. The incident is already closed."

Hazel chewed her lip. "That's a relief... Can I know more about it? It's been an emotional rollercoaster since you mentioned the meeting."

Tamra looked up to the right. "Since it was about you, I think I can tell you. I'd definitely be covering it if the investigation was still ongoing. Frankly, I'm also curious to hear from you." She seemed to decide. "Someone reported you for being in an inappropriate relationship with Sam. That would be a concern since you're both in Communications and you were both working on CARE. Remember, he even chose you for the CARE project, which looked like favoritism."

Hazel kept her face as neutral as possible. "What evidence did they bring forward? Or was there any?"

"That's where the meeting got weird. I was with our HR Partner, Kimberly, and someone else, I won't say their name, and we were all talking through the investigation. Kimberly led the conversation and had her fill in the blanks to get me caught up. When she asked about what led her to believe you were in an inappropriate relationship, first, it was things she had overheard. I felt like, okay, this could be her reading into things or misinterpreting. There wasn't much to stand on. But then she had pictures that were hard to refute, which leads to my question. You and Sam?!"

Hazel's jaw dropped. "Wait, what pictures?"

"She had a picture of a phone. I'm guessing Sam's phone, and you had texted him, and it showed it on the lock screen. He has you programmed as 'Hazelberry.' That was still not very solid, in my opinion, but the other picture was clearly of you two kissing on a stage."

Hazel's eyes popped. She remembered a flash of light while they were on stage in the empty auditorium but had interpreted it as seeing stars. "I… What? We were alone in there! We thought we were."

Tamra hummed. "It *was* obvious the room was dark and empty. Anyway, she had just shared the photo when Kimberly paused the meeting. She returned in a few minutes and said the investigation was closed. You and Sam had disclosed years ago, and they had it on file. The other person was pissed. She said it wasn't possible. Kimberly even had to ask her to be professional. But Hazel, why didn't you tell me?"

"I um…" Hazel was not prepared for the question. She

searched for a reason. "We have a rule that we don't discuss our relationship at work. It's cleaner to compartmentalize. Though, I guess now everything is out." She shrugged.

Tamra was put out. "Well, I wish you had. Honestly, you two should not have been working on CARE together, and he should have never asked for you to join." Tamra looked down at her keyboard. "Look, this didn't come up, and the investigation is closed, but you absolutely can't do that again."

Hazel nodded emphatically. "I accept that. I totally understand. Hearing it out loud… we should have been aware of the optics. It will never happen again."

Tamra's demeanor changed like a switch. "Thank you. So, how do you do the long-distance thing?"

Hazel saw movement at the door. Sam was standing there, body framed with gray light streaming around him and a look of concern. Hazel chuckled, "The distance has been our biggest challenge. We recently started talking about moving in together. Nothing set in stone yet, but we'll figure something out." Sam's face was sheer amusement. Hazel saw his cheek dimple out of the corner of her eye.

THE MEETING CONCLUDED and a sense of euphoria mixed with utter exhaustion coursed through Hazel as she stared at the screen. She turned her head toward Sam, disbelief etched on her face. "We did it. Everything worked out."

Sam's grin evolved into a shining smile, and a softness settled in his eyes. He reached his hand toward Hazel, and she rose from her chair to take it. She let out an oh of surprise as he twirled her into his arms. They started a slow sway. Sam whispered, "I guess now it's just the question of moving in, eh?"

Hazel replied, "Sorry about that. I didn't know what else to say to Tamra."

"I hope you aren't sorry. We don't have to rush into anything, but I would be honored to share a home with you someday. We'll have so many warm blankets."

Hazel added, "We'll have to install a shoe rack." She pushed her hand against his shoulder to stop their dance. "I want to start… everything with you. Our life… but can we take a nap first?"

Sam laughed and answered by picking her up and carrying her to bed.

EPILOGUE

Hazel Rogers

What's your day look like? 8:49am

Sam Pierce

I've got a meeting at 10 then a block of meetings from 2-5, including the preso on Quality Standards Grading Changes. You? 8:50am

Hazel Rogers

Onboarding class starts in 10 minutes, we lunch at 12:30, then end of day is at 4:30. I'll be out by 5. That'll be the rough schedule the next month. 8:50am

Hazel looked up at the knocking sound at the office door.

"If you're starting in 10 minutes, it was high time I delivered your coffee." Sam swept in gracefully, placing the coffee cup beside her keyboard and kissing her head. He exclaimed, "Your first Onboarding group as a Trainer starts in 9 minutes!"

Hazel suppressed a smile. "I know!"

"You're going to do great. If you need anything, I'm a Chatter away."

She reached for his hand and gave it a gentle squeeze. "Thank you. I'll be fine, there's going to be a learning curve, but I'm so excited to be on it."

Sam's eyes crinkled, and a devious look crossed his face. "Your curves are always the most exciting." He swept his hands down her sides.

Hazel swatted him away and dramatically cried, "Harassment in my workplace!" They both covered their mouths and looked from side to side as if having witnessed something salacious. "Remember, we're on for dinner with Rosie and Nick tonight."

"Oh, no chance of forgetting. The Cards Against Humanity grudge match rages on!" Sam shook his fist in the air for emphasis. "Okay, headed to the office." Sam stepped toward the door.

Hazel scooted her chair back. "Aren't you missing something?" They usually started the work day with a peck.

Sam was back to her in a single stride, leaning over so they were face to face. Hazel bathed in the deep brown and golden bands of Sam's eyes for a second. He tilted her head back, ran his hand through her hair, and kissed her deeply.

AFTERWORD

Dearest Reader,

Thank you for reading my book! I hope you enjoyed it as much as I enjoyed writing it (a real love-love situation).

If you're curious about Sam's perspective when meeting Hazel, I've written a bonus chapter just for you.

Check out Sam at the Summit here- bit.ly/RemotelyBonus or scan below.

Happy Reading!

ACKNOWLEDGMENTS

The experience of writing *Remotely Love* is something I'll never forget. It's my first novel, and I adored everything about writing it.

Thank you to Tim Thorn, my forever partner. You listened to me excitedly explain how the story was developing every night and encouraged me along the journey.

Heather Balcerek, Steve Cahill, and Tim Thorn were the best beta readers I could have ever hoped for. Your feedback helped shape this work into something I'm proud of. The sections you particularly enjoyed gave me confidence when I needed it. I can't thank you enough.

My friend, Alyssa Westler, is a wellspring of support. You believed in me and this story before I even began writing it when it was a baby idea. Thank you for always seeing the success ahead.

To my many unnamed work-from-home friends around the world, you know who you are. The experiences we shared working and creating together are the finest I could dream of. I hope the remote shenanigans in this book made you smile.

About the Author

Lori writes in various genres, including romance, children's books, and anthologies.

She draws inspiration from her life, including working remotely at major corporations since 2012, trying to convince her children that they're lycanthropes on long summer afternoons, and her love of music and food.

Lori lives in Florida with her husband, Tim, and their three kiddos. She enjoys playing clarinet in the community band and preparing scrumptious vegetarian meals.

tiktok.com/@glorylace

instagram.com/glorylace

About the Illustrator

Heather Balcerek is a passionate creative and lover of books. While her design experience has been born out of necessity in her past roles, she eagerly learns new programs and tricks of the trade whenever she can. Whether she is drawing Zentangles or noodling around on ProCreate or designing in Canva, Heather puts all her love and energy into each piece. Aside from visual creativity, she also hosts the Connect the Dots podcast, which focuses on career development.

Heather lives in Clearwater, FL with her husband. Together they run the food and travel blog, It's a Salty Life.

Connect with Heather
  @msheatherbdot
  @connectthedots podcast
  podpage.com/connect-the-dots/
  @saltylifefft
  itsasaltylife.com

www.ingramcontent.com/pod-product-compliance
Lightning Source LLC
Chambersburg PA
CBHW060910210726